Meet the crew of the Earth Ship Black Hole:

Larry Baker—pilot, conceived in a test tube by master scientists of earth. His creators gave him genius, agility, strength . . . everything but the ability to feel emotion.

Napoleon—co-pilot, purchased from the feline planet, Mandarin. A five-foot intelligent cat used for genetic experiments.

Harlan Trigor—a nine-foot soldier, seething with revenge for being branded a traitor and exiled from his home world.

Titu Trigor—Harlan's sister, kidnapped by aliens and converted into a pleasure slave for the powerful—a pawn in this intergalactic conspiracy.

And, finally, the Black Hole, more a friend than a ship, held together with spit and baling wire and managed by a neurotic computer.

Can Larry Baker bring this crew of galactic misfits through space battles and across the universe before time runs out!

Also By RICHARD S. MEYERS

THE ILLUSTRATED SOAP OPERA COMPANION
TV SUPERSTARS
MOVIES ON MOVIES

DOOM STAR

Richard S. Meyers

CARLYLE • NEW YORK

DEDICATION:

To Steven Schonberger
Who has a part in everything I do

ACKNOWLEDGMENTS:

Thank You—

Al Sirois
Kevin O'Donnell Jr.
Rick Sternbach
Jeff Rovin
Howard Zimmerman
Kerry O'Quinn
Norman Jacobs
Ed Naha
Dave Hutchison
Howard Cruse
Ted Enik
Laura O'Brien
Ward Damio
Roy Kuhlman
Melissa Nichols
The Duke of Wellington

EARTH

ONE

Larry Baker's back was turned when the piece of space debris sat up. He knew something was wrong, however, from the screeching howl of Napoleon and the way Mess started booming, "Permission to fire, permission to fire, permission to fire!"

Even if he had been deaf and unable to hear the reactions of his co-pilot and on-board computer, he still would have known something was amiss from the way half a dozen balls of flashing red light burst on across the control board, signifying everything from a broken scope to a missing engine.

But Larry was not deaf, so not only did he hear his associates' exclamations, he heard the roar of warning alarms as well. In one second, the bridge of the Earth Ship Black Hole was turned from a majestic mansion floating back into earth orbit, into eardrum hell.

Larry tried to close his ears, managing only through a great effort of will to prevent his hands slapping over the sides of his head, directing them instead to the control board. Another concentrated effort was necessary to keep his eyes from screwing shut, only he couldn't prevent their watering. So while his hands flew from one alarm neutralization to another, he felt his ducts open wide, letting the tears flow out without clouding his vision.

As he reached for the switch farthest to the right, cutting off the "escape hatch ajar" alarm, he noticed that Napoleon had backed under her own control area, spitting and arching her back. As suddenly as it had begun the bridge was quiet except for the hissing of the co-pilot and Mess continuing to intone stentoriously, "Permission to fire, permission to fire, permission to fire!"

"No!" cried Larry, his voice higher than he would have liked it in cases like these. "Damper down. Recheck orbit re-entry coordinates!" If he could keep the damn machine busy, he could find out what all the panic was about.

"Coordinates rechecked and locked in," Mess said hurriedly. "Permission to fire, please."

Larry thought he noted a new edge of panic in the machine's voice. He spun around to face the trouble. Sitting up in front of him was nine by five feet of rocky space debris where there used to be nine by five feet of *lying* space debris.

Larry was stunned into inactivity. He half stood, half sat in his chair, hands gripping the edge of his control board to remain almost up.

"What, what, what," he managed to stutter.

"It sat up," Mess shouted, almost as hysterical as it ever managed to get. "While we were entering orbit. Permission to fire, oh, hurry, quick!"

"But that's impossible! Rock can't bend. What do your imputs say?"

"To the Earth Father with my imputs! Permission to fire!"

"No, you stupid thing! One blast from you and we'll all be asteroids! Damper down. There's nothing to shoot, it must be a new element of something. It's simply reacting to the atmosphere inside here, that's all." Larry was pleased with his reasoning. After all, that's why he had brought the hunk of space junk into the bridge area in the first place. For further study once they had regained earth orbit.

In all the Black Hole's years of scavenging they had never come across a piece like it. Although it was small as asteroids go, Mess had judged it extremely rich in rare material. And although it looked exactly the right size for an ancient satellite or part of a second-stage rocket, it was bumpy and rutted like a rock. But not like any rock they had ever seen. All the bumps and ruts were smooth. Even where one might expect a certain grade to end in a point, it felt rounded to the touch, like a living optical illusion.

"I don't like the looks of it," Mess had said.

"You don't like the looks of anything," Larry had retorted. "Bring it in."

And they all had watched as Mess maneuvered above it, reached down with one of its hugoes and scooped it into the bottom hatch. They were all so intrigued with it, though, that Larry had the machine set it down in the back of the bridge area for further examination after reentry orbit.

But now it was after reentry orbit and the piece of space something had sat up. Five feet were still parallel to the floor while four feet were bent up at a right angle. Earth light, coming from the front viewport, reflected off the top foot-and-a-half, which suddenly looked like a dome more than anything else.

Larry rose slowly, completely to his feet. "Yeah, it's just a molecular reaction," he repeated. "Surprising, but probably not dangerous."

His crew members seemed to want to accept his reasoning, too. Napoleon edged out from under her co-pilot's board and rubbed her back across the one bolted leg of her chair, in the same movement rising to her hind legs and swishing her tail. Mess stopped talking, but its doubts still seemed to hang in the air.

"You see?" said Larry soothingly. "Nothing to worry about . . ."

And that is when the whole rock stood up. One moment it was still sitting passively, the next second nine feet of hard substance was at ninety degrees to the floor. Larry couldn't keep his arms from crossing in front of his face, his brain's first thought being that the huge thing was going to topple forward onto him. Napoleon threw her body backwards, twisting around in mid-air to land on all fours and scurry back under her control board, her hair standing on end. Mess took a moment to redirect its interior weaponry, then started in again, "Permission to fire, permission to fire, permission to fire!"

Larry pulled his arms down and stared at the monolith before him. His mouth wanted to rip open to let his vocal chords do their stuff and his knees wanted to bend, but Larry regained control. He stared hard.

The space debris seemed solid but twice it had moved, once changing shape. Even now, though it seemed to have an uneven surface, it stood completely level, no rocking or tipping. He imagined that Mess could fire and the thing wouldn't even topple, let alone sustain damage. What did it do, reorganize its molecules? And if it did, what would it change into next time?

Larry had a sudden urge to let Mess blast it, just to see what would happen, but he knew that Mess would do such a thorough job he wouldn't have anything left to see with. Nor would any living matter in the general area. Mess would as soon kill itself to avoid injury.

"Permission to fire, by the Earth Father, permission to fire!" Mess shouted.

Larry found his voice. "No! For the last time, damper down, you paranoid pile of spare parts."

"Then let me call Earth Control," the voice begged.

That got a rise out of Napoleon. "Noooo," she howled. "Any trouble here we handle ourselves." Mess' suggestion had drawn her up to her hind legs. "What do we do, Larry?" She stood to the right of the standing hulk.

Larry slowly raised his arm out and moved over to the left. "Go get the beamers. If it seems to try anything else, we'll bathe it."

The debris remained silent, rooted to the floor. Napoleon began to pad over to the beamer compartment.

"You're not going to let me shoot, are you?" asked Mess.

"What do you think?" replied Larry.

"I don't think," said Mess. "I make logical conclusions based on my core information ingrained on my circuits by Dr. Palsy-Drake at the date of my conception."

Larry moved over to the left, dampening the urge to raise his eyes. "The Earth Father you do. Now quiet, you stupid system of self-service."

Mess continued oblivious. "I also respond based on new information either spoken or programmed, and based on your spoken information I conclude you're not going to let me fire."

Larry now felt he was far enough away from the thing that if it did change or fall, it would not take him with it. "Correct," he said, allowing a sigh to escape after the word was spoken.

Napoleon had reached the compartment and retrieved her own padded beamer with the extra large trigger guard to fit her foreclaw, and Larry's beamer rifle with the four lens barrel, and was even now returning to cover the thing from her side.

"Well if you're going to shoot it, why can't I?" Mess complained.

Larry moved over to Napoleon and got his weapon. "We are not going to shoot it if we can help it," he said quickly. "You, on the other hand, would blast it, us, and the ship to kingdom come if we let you."

"I have no Kingdom Come in my memory banks," said Mess.

"No one likes a smart computer," said Larry.

"Then what good are we?" replied Mess.

Napoleon remained tense, all her sinewy attention locked on the space debris, but Larry felt himself relaxing, not knowing whether Mess had instigated this banter for that very purpose or if he was simply reacting to Mess' unreprogramable psyche. That is, the core information impregnated on the computer's circuits by Dr. Palsy-Drake, the infamous gentlemen who was the last scientist executed by the Lasser-Welles act of 204 AND—After Natural Disaster—for trying to program feeling and inductive reasoning into a machine.

Somewhere along the line the good doctor decided that a computer's main concern was for itself since man was too stupid. Therefore Mess' first rule of thumb was self-preservation. Unfortunately Mess was created by Palsy-Drake shortly before the latter's nervous breakdown and execution, so the unaltered circuits decided that total and sure-fire safety lay in the destruction of anything moving nearby before it could possibly become a threat.

After killing three engineers and one scientist, the authorities managed to disconnect Palsy-Drake's machine, break it down to its elements, and store them away. And there they sat until Larry had collected most of them to build the Black Hole's on-board computer.

For a time, the newly christened M.E.S.S.—Multi-unit Electronic System for Space travel—contented itself with navigating and computing while blowing out of the sky anything within three parsecs of the ship, whether it be vegetable, mineral, or living matter. Larry managed to temper this antisocial behavior somewhat by programming in a damper that allowed Mess the ability for destruction only after a verbal acknowledgement was given by either Larry or Napoleon.

It was a risky business, to be sure, given the fact that both living beings could be asleep or unconscious when danger struck, but it was less risky than leaving Mess on its own recognizance. Further modifications were necessary as time went on, but living with the difficulty was worth it in exchange for a computer not directly tied in with the United World Government's machines.

Besides the privacy it ensured, the machines were also unaware of the extracurricular activities the Black Hole indulged in, like this particular scavenger run. Even in the relatively small area around the moon, it was possible to pick up various metal materials valuable to the United World scientists below. Raw material was greatly loved on Earth and Larry was in the position to exchange the space junk for monetary rewards, bypassing the U.W. Government that usually handled all such transactions.

So, this time, on a quick supply run from the Denver Plateau to the Alphonsus-Moon Lab, they managed to find the nine-foot rock plus the usual assortment of trash.

"You want to know what you're good for?" Larry took up the conversation. "I'll tell you what you're good for . . ."

A hum filled the room. Larry stopped his words in midsentence. Napoleon's hair stood on end again and her tail lashed back and forth. She brought her beamer up. Larry managed to keep his hands from gripping his own weapon too tightly.

"Mess, is that you?" he inquired.

A pause filled the room, accompanying the hum.

"No," the answer finally came. "Permission to fire, please, please, please."

"Uh. Better check the ship's circuits for a problem, then." Napoleon had begun to crouch, her tail straight up, her weapon aimed high at the middle of the space debris. Her intention was clear. If it moved again, she would slice it in half.

"All circuits functioning properly. Permission to fire."

The top foot-and-a-half of the debris began to turn to the left.

Larry shouted, "No!" as Napoleon pulled the trigger. An orange band of light streaked from the end of the barrel, widening perceptibly as it crossed the room. It did not seem fast, but Larry had just enough time to fall forward before the beam hit the debris, broke into two halves, and shrieked off *around* it. The rays sliced into two walls opposite and dissipated, leaving wide gaping grins in the metal and an antiseptic stench.

"Permission to fire, permission to fire, permission to fire!" Mess cried.

Larry raised his head, turned, and looked at the opening in the wall directly behind him. He thanked his luck that he was neither standing in front of a viewport nor standing, period. He turned back to his shaken co-pilot and a screaming computer.

"No! For the last time, permission denied! Report damages!"

"Look for yourself!" Mess screamed back. "I'm getting out of here!"

Larry leaped to his feet as a noise like air entering a vacuum filled the room. Suddenly a section of the main computer console, which occupied most of the center of the room, slid back, and a triangular-shaped box flew out with two balls of multi-colored sensors on the front, three levitators on the back, several flashing systems along the top, and an agitated aerial slashing back and forth. It circled the room crazily once, then sped out the rear hatch.

"Get back here, you computerized coward!" Larry shouted after it. "Damages, reentry orbit, time of alignment! You tinplated ton of tubes!" He took a quick glimpse at the still-turning top of the hunk of space junk, then ran over to where Napoleon stood snarling.

"Keep it covered," he said, scratching her neck roughly. "I've got to override the electronics of the escape pods before Mess can jettison himself." Napoleon shook off his hand and nodded curtly.

Larry stabbed a button and clicked off a line of switches to the right of the co-pilot's console, then returned his attention to the space debris. The top part had risen two inches during the previous action. Napoleon understood it before he did.

"By Cheshire," she said. "There's someone in there. It's unscrewing itself."

Larry ran over to where his beamer lay and lifted it to fit snugly under his arm. He turned the barrel quickly to the paralyze position and aimed it at the turning top, which had risen another inch. Then, just as suddenly as it had started, the turning stopped.

The room was silent once again. Larry and Napoleon rechecked the aim of their weapons and waited.

The top foot-and-a-half rose quickly and fell backwards.

Napoleon managed to remain perfectly still but Larry could not keep his legs from propelling him backwards. He lost his balance and fell, his gun skittering across the floor. Extremely upset with himself, he leaped to his feet and the first thing he saw was a human face crisscrossed with throbbing blue-green veins popping out of the top of the space debris. The creature's mouth opened and a small voice at Larry's waist said, "Greetings. What language to you speak?"

Harlan Trigor was a space bullet. After climbing out of his nine-foot suit and pulling off his exoskeleton, he explained in unaccented English exactly what that was. A self-contained armament and limited space vehicle created for the purpose of one-on-one battles in the upper atmosphere of the planet Destiny.

It was simple enough for him to say. It was extremely hard for Larry and Napoleon to understand. Napoleon had kept her beamer on him during his laborious disembarking, a defense that seemed to give him amusement.

"What's so funny?" she asked of the seeming man, who

was peeling off the throbbing blue-green body suit from just above his brows.

"Besides a cat who uses contractions in perfect speech, your weapon," he replied. "It is fairly useless," he continued, pulling off the exoskeleton's hood to expose a rugged face haloed by a rich black beard.

"I'm not a cat," said Napoleon. "I'm a feline female from the planet Mandarin. Who are you?"

Trigor repeated his preliminary explanation then went on to elaborate. "A piece of jade in the black velvet of space, Destiny is a mythical garden world, long ago populated by a superior race of man, and long an inviting target for warring races and space pirates. I was born for the sole purpose of being a soldier, a space bullet created to avoid damage to the lush planet surface itself.

"The weaponry in my suit is so complicated, abundant, and advanced that I have the ability to neutralize and destroy any known spacecraft in seconds."

Napoleon scowled at this theatrical dissertation as Trigor took off the last of the skin-tight outerwear, leaving his short, wide body encased in a skin-tight black shirt and hose. He touched the exoskeleton with his toe, the pulsing blue-green having changed to a heap of unmoving grey.

"This suit enables me to withstand the terrible pressures of space and battle. And I must say, I'm very good at what I do."

Larry had moved over to his pilot's chair and sat down. The ship slowly circled the Earth in orbit.

"What you say seems to be true, since the translator," Larry lifted the thin bar, grated at both ends, up from his belt, "knew what lanquage you were originally speaking."

"It was an ancient vocabulary created for the early space travelers," Harlan explained. "Once other inhabited planets were discovered, we needed a universal language."

"You know English very well," said Napoleon.

"My ancestors came from Earth," Harlan repeated. "Did yours?"

Larry looked quickly over to his shipmate with worry touching his brow, but her only reaction was a pause and a slight squinting of her eyes.

"No. I learned the tongue the hard way."

Larry changed the subject quickly. "You say you're from Destiny. We have no evidence that such a planet exists. The legend goes that it is vastly powerful and hateful toward the rest of the universe. If you are from there and so strong, why didn't you just blast us when we picked you up and continue on your way?"

"The legends have grown melodramatic with time," Trigor said simply. "Your ship was unlike any I had ever seen. I was curious."

Larry could understand why. The Earth Ship Black Hole had been created and built by Baker personally in the hard years of his youth, in orbit, in space. It was a patchwork quilt of materials he had found in the garbage storage areas and the Providence Space Center junk piles. He had done it for therapy, to get away, for experience, for the education, and he had used it as an escape from the Galactic Pool.

No other excess of humanity had his own space vehicle in use. Larry had managed to avoid a life of drudge work by becoming the ultimate "go-fer," an educated messenger transferring precious materials from one lab to the next. The idea soothed his a-place-for-everything-everything-in-its-place masters. So for the last ten years, since he was seventeen, Larry had piloted the Black Hole for fun and profit, on call to the U.W. Government.

Trigor interrupted Larry's thoughts. "I would be pleased if you could show me around," said the dark-haired man, looking slightly ludicrous in his tights.

Napoleon flashed Larry a feline frown, but he could see little harm in it. It was obvious that the man was unarmed unless he carried rockets under his fingernails and it would give Larry time to think this uncomfortable situation out. What was the man doing here? What did he want? Might as well give him the grand tour, Larry finally figured. If nothing else they could retrieve Mess.

As the trio moved out of the pilot area into storage, one half of Larry's thought processes were concerned with pointing out the solar mirrors, the sensor scopes, the observation bubble, the various locks, cameras, and hugoes, while the other half was considering the situation.

By the time they came upon Mess' manifestation, the triangular box blinking madly in one of the six escape pods, trying to get the jettison mechanism to respond to its electronic command, Larry had it boiled down somewhat.

What he had here was a refugee from the most talked about and dreamed of planet in the galaxy. A man, a soldier, who, somehow, for some reason, wound up in Earth orbit, rational and communicating.

Larry tried to figure out what to do about it while he showed their visitor the main hatch and engine area at the other end of the ship. Napoleon trailed behind looking bored but holding her beamer as tightly as ever by her side. Trigor nodded, smiled, murmured, and generally showed innocent appreciation.

"Tell me," he finally asked. "Does your ship have any weapons?"

Larry shot a glance over his shoulder where Napoleon's face hardened. He took a subtle approach. "Oh, the usual. Why?"

"It just seemed strange to me that an Earth craft would have no weapons."

"We have weapons, we have weapons," said Mess' manifestation, hovering in.

"Why should you be interested in weapons if your suit is so powerful?" Napoleon cut in.

"It just seemed unusual to me . . ." Trigor began.

"What do you want to know for?" the feline demanded.

"All right," said Larry over the din. "All right, let's go back to the bridge. We have to do some talking."

"Right," Napoleon echoed, pushing her beamer into Trigor's back. "Just keep a safe distance away from that suit of yours."

Larry entered the area first, Mess' manifestation speeding by his head and moving straight for its console. Just before it would have smashed, a door slid open and the triangular box with the whipping antenna disappeared inside.

Trigor entered, guided to the left of his nine-foot enclosure and exoskeleton by Napoleon's prodding gun. Larry sat in his pilot's chair and pulled his beamer across his lap. He waited a moment to make sure that the possible threat was made clear. Napoleon brought the man to within ten feet of him and stopped. If he tried anything now, either attack or retreat, one of them could cut him down without damage to each other or the ship. And if he wanted to try using Napoleon as a shield after disarming her, he was welcome to. His arms would be so much confettied meat.

"Now I'm not much for clear thinking," said Larry. "But it doesn't take a genius to see something's wrong here. A soldier from the most-loved and sought-after planet in the galaxy just doesn't get up and leave for a vacation. At least not in uniform," Larry motioned toward the suit, "and not all the way to Earth. Which is how many light years?"

"Approximately or exactly?" asked Mess.

"The Earth is exactly . . ." Trigor began.

"Let's say a lot," said Larry. Trigor nodded.

"Don't you want to know?" asked Mess.

"We've reached a satisfactory conclusion," said Larry.

"If you knew the answer why did you ask?" said the computer.

"I didn't ask you directly. It was a rhetorical question," Larry shouted at the computer console.

"Well, I wish you would let me know that in advance," huffed Mess. "I wouldn't waste my time. We really should set up a system for this. How difficult would it be to say, 'Mess, this is a rhetorical question, there is no need for . . .' "

"Damper down, you egocentric excess of electrodes!" Larry screamed.

Silence hung in the air so Larry returned his attention to Trigor who looked as if he were imprisoned with the hyena creatures of the Zoo World.

"Now we've had an interesting chat and given you a sight-seeing trip," Larry continued. "But now it is time for some straight answers. What are you doing here? What do you want?"

Trigor spread his arms expansively at which Napoleon moved back growling. "I was merely curious as to . . ."

"Don't repeat your old story," Napoleon snarled. "That lame tale wouldn't fool a booger."

Trigot stiffened when the last word was mentioned and

turned toward Napoleon. She became extremely still, her face washed of all emotion.

"You, you have Mantases here as well?" he asked.

Napoleon's beamer remained level with the man's chest as Larry spoke. "Yes, but not as many as many other planets. Then again, we have less land area than many other planets."

Larry had leaned in to speak and was honestly taken aback by Trigor when he turned to face him. In less than a few seconds the soldier had changed completely. His strong face was now crumbled in wrinkles of despair. His mouth hung down as if his insides were being eaten out. His brows rose to a point, bending his eyes up toward each other. The lines on his forehead made a succession of peaks. His chest caved in, his shoulders hunched, and his knees buckled.

"Then all is lost!" he cried and dropped to the floor with a resounding thunk.

Larry pulled himself up in shock as Napoleon moved nimbly back, her weapon still aimed at the prone Trigor, wary of a trick. Larry stared in wonder at the man cringing on the floor.

"Something is definitely wrong here," he said, stepping around the fallen man. He went and stood by Napoleon, still looking over his shoulder at Trigor. "What do you think this is all about?"

"I don't know," the feline said simply. "I really don't care. You figure it out. But whatever happens, I want to be ready for it." Her weapon remained steady and centered on the prone man's back.

Larry nodded and scratched her back three times, then moved onto the back of the bridge. There he leaned up against a wall, put his hands together and his index fingers under his front teeth, and tried to think it out.

Astrophysical and engineering theorems kept interfering as his mind pondered the situation. If "a" is an alien crying on the floor of his ship while "b" is the Earth lab waiting for the Alphonsus-Moon supplies and "c" are the administrative Mantases, then what is "x"? Larry was soon content he could not make head or tail of it. He really wanted to but he couldn't. He cursed his masters. Why couldn't they let him think?

He stood and moved back to his pilot's chair. "I'm afraid I am going to have to ask you for an explanation," he told Trigor politely.

The Destiny soldier raised his head and Larry saw plainly the tears cascading down into the black beard, beading up. The man rose to one elbow and wiped his arm across his face. "I will not apologize," he said.

Larry shrugged, looking up at Napoleon, whose face showed nothing but boredom.

"I don't know what the trouble is but maybe . . ." Larry began then let it trail off. What else could he say? That he'd try to help? What could he do? One ragged spaceship made from the junk of other spaceships, a feline co-pilot, and two beamers was hardly an impressive start.

"It's all right. It's all right," said Trigor, waving his right hand and rubbing his left across his eyes. "It is my training, you know. I'm making a fool of myself."

Larry did not know at all but couldn't help agreeing. "Talk about it," he suggested for want of something better. "Make me understand."

Trigor stood, some of the military bearing returning to his stance. He finished brushing the tears away and looked at Larry's face, which the pilot had tried to make impassive.

"No," Harlan said finally. "No. You could be of no help." Larry nodded helplessly. "I must be on my way," Trigor finished.

"Fine," cut in Mess. "Go out through the hatch, take a left, then a right, then another left. I'll take care of the pressure. You can't miss it."

"Be quiet, Mess," said Larry, getting up. "Now wait Trigor, you can't just go and . . ." The space bullet turned toward Larry threateningly. The pilot moved back, "Well, maybe you can."

Harlan stepped over to his exoskeleton, keeping his head facing Larry. "I can assure you that even without my suit I could rip you into pieces. Do not attempt to stop me."

"I'm not surprised," said Larry. "But that's hardly the point . . ."

"I must insist you allow me to leave without incident," re-iterated Trigor.

"Can I blast him *now?*" asked Mess.

Napoleon spat, a sharp hiss. The two men and machine stopped talking and looked around to see where the feline had gotten to. She was curled around the seat of her chair, her beamer still held level with Trigor's chest.

"Larry gave you a choice," she said. "I'm not so soft-headed. You are not putting on the suit, you are not leaving this ship. You are going to explain fully or I'm going to slice you in half."

Larry stepped quickly back, out of the range of fire. Trigor stared at her, his face beginning to crumble again.

"And don't cry or fall over again," she said. "It's disgusting."

Trigor saw that she was serious. As with an actual cat ready to spring, one can feel its energy rising to a crescendo scant seconds before. Trigor sobbed and tried to clear his brain. His hands rose to grip his skull and he sat heavily on the floor. He looked between Larry and Napoleon in their chairs and stared out the middle viewport.

He saw the rim of the blue world, Earth, and the sparkling blackness of space beyond. He knew even within his view were several habitable planets. Planets with creatures discernable to the human eye and within the understanding of the human brain. Creatures with problems as seemingly insurmountable as his own. He stared and tried to pinpoint when his life had become so complicated. He opened his mouth and spoke to the stars.

"Long before the Holocaust and the Natural Disaster, Earth was an exciting place, full of life and hope. Scientific discoveries were being made constantly. Huge advances in medicine, transportation, and communication seemed almost commonplace. But the fallout of these achievements was bitter and widespread. The experiments for these advances were paid for by businesses who were more interested in profit than humanity. The rich countries prospered while the backward states stayed in the dark, disease ridden and ignored. Interference cost too much.

"If a new energy sourse was needed it was harnessed, such as solar heat and the Danvy-Mann Generator. If new food sources were necessary, they were created, like the Greenfield Labs' Vege-Matter and Foodstufs. If faster transportation was mandatory, ways were implemented, as in the tour tunnels and transport bands. If more living space was called for, bigger and larger space colonies were built and inhabited. So said our teachers.

"America and Euro-China prospered while everyone else watched and wanted. Charity was plentiful. All one had to do was sign over the country in question, teach the inhabitants a new language, donate all the wealth of intelligence to the good of the nation, and go along with whatever the new government decreed. Then, if one rated, one enjoyed. But if one didn't rate, one would be supplied with one's every need in return for labor. But no questions, please. Any nation great enough to send its best to foreign worlds knew better.

"Soon, by necessity, most animosities were broken down into America and Euro-China. Each spent as much as necessary to keep up with each other. Ships were launched farther and farther into the galaxy; many were never heard from again. My ancestors were on one such ship. Generations were born and died on that great ship. The O'Neil warp drive was invented on that ship. The ship finally found a home on our Destiny, named by Kevin O'Neil, from where his triumphant descendant, the last of the O'Neils, Craig W., returned to Earth to share his family's legacy only to discover wholesale destruction.

"Huge patches of the third world from Sol were totally uninhabitable from the wrath of nuclear weapons. Teeming space habitats circled the world, broken and burnt. The more considerate warring factions had bombarded other areas with neutronic devices, disintegrating humans but leaving the environment untouched. Other enemies had unleashed clouds of deadly bacteria that were still roving the surface, their effectiveness lasting for centuries.

"Craig W. found the survivors on the bands of mountains and deserts in America. Most were military men and scientists, the only ones who had had enough warning and knowhow to protect themselves from a war only they knew was coming. What O'Neil heard from them destroyed his soul. They had not changed. Rather than learning from the mistakes, they plotted to get around them, using them to accrue power. Insanity, radiation sickness, loneliness could have contributed to their state. It mattered little.

"Women were at a premium and were treated accordingly. Not as princesses, but as prized prisoners. They created new beings and satisfied lusts and that is all. Even after death, certain parts of them were studied and used to make the reproduction process more exact. Crag W. sent a transmission back to Destiny saying he was returning. He was afraid of what the Earth survivors would do with his warp drive. He never returned.

"Many years later we received a transmission from an Earth ship outfitted with a variation of O'Neil's engine. It was landing on our planet to offer us the same opportunity it had presented the other habitable planets in the galaxy. The Earth Ship Opportunity landed and greeted my forepeople with a simple business transaction.

"In return for certain natural elements to be chosen after a thorough study of Destiny was made by their on-board experts, Earth would supply laborers for any purpose. Human, but not human. Living but not living. Workers of flesh and blood and bone but with minds set to any one purpose the buyer, the *buyer*, wanted. Earth was again a slave planet. Their experiments with female parts had worked only too well.

"Our forepeople discovered that these techniques were perfected during the Great Natural Disaster. The politicians and scientists had gone underground again when nature paid them back for tampering with the planet for all those years, taking with them all the useable females in the deplenished world, kidnapped in lightning raids made possible by a variation of the O'Neil engine.

"During the floods, the earthquakes, and the tornadoes, the scientists worked creating life and their continued well-being, using the human materials with as little feeling as they had had for their lab animals centuries before. 'It was for the ongoing good of their world,' was the reasoning. 'Otherwise they would die out' was the rationalization. If only they had.

"After nature's raging calmed, the scientists and military set up shop above ground. They created a fleet of space cruisers to bring their message to their old friends in the stars. We are alive and have slaves for sale. Laborers for sale. Whatever you need, the Earth labs could supply them. Need that forest cut down? We'll create men who are all arms with hands specifically suited to axes. Need miners for that dangerous cave? We'll whip up a breed with exaggerated nasal control and incredible stamina. Need soldiers, need butlers, need companions?

"With an offer such as this, very few humans or human descendants could resist. The powerful on the inhabited planets gave their orders. Earth filled them and prospered. With the help of the O'Neil drive every planet in every part of the galaxy was serviced.

"We killed the members of the crew on the Earth Ship Opportunity and destroyed the vehicle. We did not even bother to transmit a message, leaving their superiors to conclude that the dangers of space had done them in. But after six other earth ships disappeared in our sector of space, the message was clear. We would have nothing to do with Earth or Earth people. And they were too few to incur our wrath, so our planet became the stuff of legend to you. Destiny, never reached. Only dreamed of."

Trigor's head sank. His feet were crossed and his hands lay upward on his knees. He sat in the pilot area that was suddenly huge and bathed in the blue light of the Earth below. Napoleon moved over and rubbed herself against Larry's legs, settling down around the base of his chair. She closed her catlike eyes and her normally serene face showed great pain.

Larry sat straight and tense, trying to feel her pain. He shared it but he could not feel it. His face was slick with moisture, his eye ducts open, but no tears came. His head rose until he was staring out the top of the viewport, which climbed from the floor to the ceiling.

Stars stretched out into infinity, blinking their wonder at him. He saw that one bunch made what looked like a sword-wielding gladiator, another like a gem-breathing dragon. He watched the motionless tableau drift by, wondering why feeling would not come to him.

Trigor's voice continued. "We have survived many generations untouched by other worlds since that time. Our females were rulers, our men warriors. We all cherished and protected our world, living with the land, but creating technological might to protect it. Destiny offered up a seemingly endless supply of raw materials. But we knew it was finite; Earth's disasters were not lost on us. We developed systems that wasted nothing, the only opulence reserved for our ruler, our Queen. But this is where my sad story begins."

"You mean there's more?" blurted out Mess.

"Damper down or I'll disconnect you," said Larry evenly.

Trigor rose from the floor and went over to where his exoskeleton lay. He reached down and lifted the grey mass, holding it before him. He spoke as if alone, floating in a bubble of space. "We had been alone, unique in the Universe until the arrival of the Mantases. They had much to offer a thriving world in their ability to communicate, evaluate, and solve complicated problems. They offered their services. We accepted them. No one knew then what I know now."

Larry and Napoleon looked at him at the same time.

"What?" they chorused.

TWO

Harlan Trigor was not born a soldier. He was made one. It was not enough that his ancestors had adapted genetically to the harder surroundings of the forest and jungle. It was not enough that his father was a premier space bullet as was his father before him. It was not enough that his sister and mother were among the most beautiful on a beautiful planet. This would not help him survive.

Only he, and he alone, could guarantee his own future. Through strength, stealth, intelligence, and training. Years of training, starting from when he was knee high to his father, training from the time he rose to his hind legs. Training from the time his brown eyes opened to the light.

Strength, which he developed, stealth, which nature provided, intelligence handed down through the generations through genes, and training from every living person and thing. If his world had anything to do with it, he would be nothing short of magnificent.

His childhood games were formulated to develop the talents he would need. A sort of kick-ball, but never using the same limb twice. A player would have to use each appendage to its best advantage. Not only to move the ball, but move it correctly. A forefinger could be used for passes better than a knee. Neck, head, shoulders, forearms, elbows, wrists, palms, all five fingers, upper torso, lower torso, hips, thighs,

28

knees, backs of knees, legs, ankles, feet, toes, soles of feet. Incredible contortions aided by natural double joints.

His education further stressed these limber talents but cerebral exercises were begun as well. Motor coordination of the eyes and almost every muscle in the body. Move the eyes to the right while lifting both third fingers, move the first toe up while turning the head fifteen degrees to the right, bunch the left neck muscles while pressing down the right little toe.

Students were put in hollow tubes, with a flashing screen at one end and a speaker in both ears. Calibrations of light and sound were learned. The ability to know every facet of stimuli and important automatic reactions thereto.

Then physical training of a more violent kind. Offensive and defensive arts of several worlds adapted for two arms, two legs, one head, ten fingers, and ten toes. And along with them the psychology that made it possible. The "center" that enabled a man of any strength to do incredible feats. A mental peace pact with one's own body that created an unacknowledged superiority to the physical ability of others.

The secret of the accumulation of these talents and the mark of a truly extraordinary man is to take the sum total and improve on it. To go on from the highest. This is what Harlan Trigor did.

Already a striking young man with a tightly muscled body, warm dark eyes, and a wavy mane of black hair and beard, he not only garnered the unanimous respect of his fellows but stunned his teachers with the ability to improve on what they had taught him.

His blows were simpler, his judgments more exact, his muscular control more precise, his innate abilities seemingly fathomless.

The final proof came in his defense against the space pirates of the planet Skull. Actually of no set home planet, they give any asteroid they inhabit the name Skull. At one time they considered Destiny a possible Skull planet. Their ships began to accumulate over the central city when a team of space bullets were dispatched, led by Trigor.

It was hardly a battle. He moved into the thickest area of their ships and within seconds dispatched five. His speed, use of weaponry, and aim were surprising even to veterans. Years of experience were united and improved in his one body. His legend began and grew immediately.

Yes, if his world had anything to do with it, he would have continued being magnificent. But another world led to his downfall. They had appeared before he was born, in various cities of Destiny. The backwoods people discovered their existence first. Six-foot creatures with large triangular heads, two antennae, large, cylindrical bodies, two long, two-jointed hind legs, and two long, two-jointed arms with three mandibles hanging underneath.

The human-descended people of Destiny immediately dubbed them Mantases, since they were discovered to be highly intelligent and helpful. The intelligence was discovered only after some deadly misunderstandings, with whole settlements of the creatures being wiped out by the humans' advanced weaponry. Great pockets of Mantases were destroyed because of irrational fear. Trigor was soon to discover the fear was not as irrational as it appeared.

The remaining Mantases were shepherded into their own settlements near the central city. There, once they were studied and educated, they showed a miraculous ability for mathematics and logistics. They came up with excellent solutions for some very difficult problems dealing with semantics. The Second Great Forest Problem was brought to a satisfactory conclusion with their assistance, a solution far more consistent and fair than the first.

Through cooperation a language was created for their use, incorporating their own hissing and clicking tones. Soon that was phased out when the Mantases mastered English. Other adaptation problems were solved through political and architectural means.

Equipment was adapted to suit both the human hand and the mandibles of the Mantases. Toys were created bearing their shape and features for little children to play with. In general, a Queen-approved plan was put into effect, making the Mantases' transfer into the Destiny society as easy as possible. Soon their presence was natural, their assistance appreciated, and their appearance commonplace.

So it was not unusual for Harlan to find a Mantas waiting for him outside his take-off center. Trigor had been promoted to the central take-off center, the best-defended one, since the bullets shot out from this one were first to burst through the atmosphere.

His suit was kept in the center under lock with a key only he had, so no one could try to use or tamper with his custom-formed suit.

"A fine battle, one that you can well be proud of," the creature hissed. Across the Mantas' chest was a wooden medallion with a sparkling stone, the seal of a Queen's aide. This was Ministic, the one Mantas close to the ear of Destiny's ruler. It was a high honor for the Queen to send the insectlike aide to him.

"A higher pride is felt for your presence," Harlan replied, aware of the eyes of his fellows and passersby.

"I would be pleased to join your return home and share your happiness," Ministic said formally.

"Your wish makes the happiness greater," he said, just as formally.

The two set off, the walk at odds with the proper conversation. Fellow bullets would tap Harlan with the bottoms of their fists lightly against his shoulders and chest in approval. Women would nod and smile their approval, offering their future company in the act. Harlan moved easily through the adulation, the aide at his side making his steps all the more impressive and notable.

The city was built to be harmonious with the environment. Wood begat wood, stone begat stone. Vehicles were simple, glasslike compartments fitted with variations of the O'Neil drive. Certain channels connected city to city. Paths connected town to town. There was the highest technology anywhere, using the natural waves of energy in the atmosphere and earth, which were housed in one- and two-story stone buildings.

Even the most opulent of dwellings were treated wood, made as tough and long-lasting as any Earth steel. With the help of the Mantases, cycles of supply and demand were perfected and strictly adhered to by the entire Destiny population. Most enjoyed their lives. Those that did not were controlled.

Harlan moved through the city, admiring it all the more

after each mock or actual space battle. Here was, indeed, something to fight for. He loved the feel of the good earth beneath the soles of his boots. His chest swelled as he breathed in the unpolluted air. The hide shirt and breeches felt good against his skin.

He came to his house where his parents, sister, and all their friends were waiting. Among the crowd were one or two Mantases. His sister, Titu, got to him first. She, too, had black hair, but hers was long with just a hint of a wave at the end. Her eyes, too, were brown, but big and deep and rich. Her skin was not pale or pink but light brown, smooth and creamy. Boys all over the city dreamt of her as their partner.

She wrapped her arms around Harlan's neck and assailed him with a long kiss. He robustly returned her affection with a rousing smack to her behind. He then swung her across his shoulders and bore her into their home, the group following behind, laughing.

He set her down, she howling with laughter herself, at the great oak banquet table where he greeted his mother and father. He kissed his mother's forehead and she hugged him to her. After a few seconds she stepped back, looked him up and down in mock disapproval, and said, "That is no way to treat your sister, young man."

The crowd roared with laughing approval as his father spun him around. He looked at his son, his hands on Harlan's shoulders, then they, too, embraced. Another roar went up from their neighbors and friends, then Harlan made way for Ministic the Mantas. A hush fell over the group as they spied the Royal Seal. She was steel blue, as were all the females of her race, and she stood among the brown hues of the home and its occupants.

"The Queen bears me with her greetings and congratulations," the creature began. Titu moved to her brother's side and placed her hand on his arm. The Trigor parents anticipated what followed. "She also extends an invitation. To be her honored guest for the next moon at a dinner honoring all the brave space soldiers."

The house was once more filled with the joyous roars and

pounding feet of the guests. As the din died down the Mantas spoke again.

"Now you have a celebration of your own, I am certain. I will return to the Queen to tell her of your happiness and approval."

The crowd gave way as Harlan accompanied Ministic to the entrance. As they passed, animated conversations started in their wake. By the time they had reached the outside the house was ablaze with exultation.

The Mantas turned to Harlan. "This is for your knowledge only. We think it best. At this dinner you shall be awarded the Seal of Destiny."

Harlan was stunned into silence. The reply he was framing disintegrated into thin air. He was expecting some sort of honor, but not the highest, most precious award his world could bestow. Even his father had not recieved the Seal.

"I cannot, I know not how, to express my wonder," he stammered.

"Grave situations arise," the Mantas said. "Your appearance makes them lighter. Easier to bear. You deserve what you shall receive."

With that mysterious message the steel-blue insect moved into the night. Harlan stared after her for a moment, trying to organize his thoughts. Then a rush of pride and achievement swept over him until he crowed to the night sky, and leaped back into his home.

The night was a jumble, a rush and tumble of good people and good times. It cascaded by him like a sea of warmth, building a fire's glow in his heart and soul. They ate, they drank, they laughed, and they sang.

We came from a world
All rotted with death;
To a garden, like Eden,
Given life's breath;

Protect it we must,
For the Queen we serve;
In the air above us,
The land to preserve;

Space Bullets all,
Shot into the deep;
We out-dive all others,
The planet to keep.

From the womb we are born,
It is what we must be;
We're divers for glory,
And the sky is our sea.

During the festivities it was hardly noticeable that all the Mantases made their way back and out the door into the night.

By the time the last guest left the sun was rising for the new day. The family had stayed up all night talking with valued friends and Harlan's fellow space bullets. Humming their song, the last of them left.

The parents decided to wait until later to clean up, and went to their bed. Titu went to Harlan and stood before him, the top of her head reaching his brow. She looked him in the eye for a moment, then lightly tapped his hard chest with the bottom of her fist.

It was the most beautiful day of his life. Harlan encircled her and they held each other for minutes. He released her and she stepped back seemingly by mental consent. She stood a moment more then went to the stairs. In the middle of her ascent, she stopped by an open window, and turned back to him. The sun, moving through the leaves of trees outside, made soft golden shadows across her face and along her hair.

Harlan knew from that moment on what angels must look like. She turned and continued up the stairs. He had a powerful urge to race after her and clutch her, bearing her away for protection. Such beauty and grace no man deserved. No pain should ever come to such a one.

Harlan moved slowly to his own room to rest up for the meal with the Queen.

All the preparations had been made. Harlan wore his finest tunic, boots, and breeches, his dark brown sleeves set off by the lush green encircled dot, the mark of a space bullet. His hands, long, hard fingers and smooth, but tough, palms, were encased in gloves.

Ministic had visited earlier in the day with strict instructions. Being the honored one, he must arrive early to the southeast point of the Mile Long Castle where he would be welcomed. Ministic promised to meet and take care of him personally.

The day had been long and Harlan was unable to fall completely asleep. He flittered at semiconsciousness until he could wait no longer. He dressed and decided to walk to the castle to work off a little of his tension.

By the time he reached the southeast point darkness had almost returned to Destiny. He raised his fist and pounded on the door. In a few seconds it opened and Ministic stood before him, her insect body shrouded in garments of rose. The sight was not ludicrous to Harlan in the slightest. Having been used to the Mantases since birth, he was accustomed to their habits and proximity.

"Welcome," came her hiss. "Come, we must prepare you further."

Harlan had been in the castle only once for his official induction into the space bullets and that was in the mile-long throne room, which occupied the center of the palace. This new visit held only renewed wonder for him.

He was led through stone corridors with wooden floors, illuminated by ceilings that shone. Then they came out into a large room with tall, open windows. Dotting the floor were clear bubbles the size of the Destiny glass vehicles. But instead of seats and an O'Neil drive inside, there were recreations of nature in amazing forms—three-dimensional representations of the forests of Destiny, the jungles, the space around the planet and its moons, and even one of the Earth with pieces of rotting space habitats keeping pace with the moon. Then, to his further surprise, he saw rain start to fall in the forest bubble.

"Our room of natural wonders," said Ministic. "Here we can see how many things are actually alike."

Harlan did not understand nor did he completely notice that he was the only human in the room. The rest was occupied by blue, black, and grey Mantases. Even as the Queen's aide led him away that fact did not completely register.

The two moved into a corridor of great opulence. The wood of the walls was carved, as were the floors, except for a path down the center and to all the rooms. The ceiling was not uniformly illuminated—rather, half-globes of light were interspersed with more wood carvings. The work was exacting and must have taken ages to create.

Harlan was speechless, in awe. Even a magnificent Destiny male was still very much a yokel when it came to obvious personal wealth. His mouth did not hang open but he was hard-pressed not to stare all around, stumbling down the hallway.

Ministic stopped before a doorway to the right and motioned. "You will wait here until called. There is illumination if you wish it, and a drink. Please help yourself. It will be long before you eat."

Harlan moved to the door and stepped in; Ministic closed it behind him. The room was fairly large, but no longer than a normal living room. To the left of the entrance and against the wall was a large, soft-looking bed. To the right of that was a table with a button that controlled the illumination.

The light coming into the room now was from the window where one full moon shone. In that light Harlan also saw a wooden chair carved beautifully into interwoven shapes, like locking sinewy branches, and a broad, strong table, on which sat a round, treated-stone mug filled with a purplish liquid.

Harlan moved over and lifted the cup. He breathed in deeply, smelling the sweet aroma of the wine. His stomach tightened, gurgling. He realized he was much too nervous to drink. It would do little good to start spitting up during the dinner. Drink still in hand, Harlan moved over to the window, trying to calm down.

He looked out, taking in the family of trees embracing just outside. Beyond that was the central city, alight with yellow warmth and brown yewn security. All around that were the stone factories and security settlements, guarding and working in the forests and jungles beyond.

Harlan realized that he would gladly risk his life in any way for this virginal world. He also realized that he was still holding the drink in his hand and someone was coming. He did not want to insult Ministic by not partaking of the castle's hospitality but he certainly did not want to drink, so he hastily poured the liquid out the window. In the many long days that followed he often wished he had drunk it.

The door opened and Ministic entered. "We will come for you shortly," she said, then, eying the cup, asked, "Are you finished?"

"Yes, thank you," he replied, handing her the cup. She put it in the crook of her left arm then moved slowly back.

"Shortly," he heard her say as the door closed once more. Harlan moved over to the bed and sat down. The nervousness started clawing at the bottom of his stomach again. *Perhaps if I lay down*, he thought, *that would quell my tension*. He slid over and settled down onto his back. That decision saved his life.

The light was not on so no one could see that he was conscious. And when the pirate entered, Harlan's lack of movement did not deter him. That was exactly what he expected. That the drugged drink had done its fast work. What he did not expect happened next.

Harlan knew the space pirate was in the room. He also knew he had a disruptor in his hand, a pencil-thin, pointed blade that uses energy waves to hemorrhage internal organs. If the man was to plunge it into Trigor's body, within seconds of switching it on, his interior would be so much mush with hardly a drop of blood missplaced.

Harlan also knew he could not raise an alarm or allow the pirate to do so. Who knew how many associates he had with him? In one second the space pirate was moving up toward him, the next moment Harlan's foot lashed out and the disruptor was sticking in the table. The top of Harlan's other foot was curled around the pirate's neck and the original kicking foot was buried deep in the pirate's face.

The man died with a small crushing sound, like air was pushed out both his ears. Hardly two seconds had passed. Harlan lowered the pirate to the floor with his legs. He released the head that flopped down like a deflated rubber ball, and wiped off the bottom of his boot on the tunic.

He quickly retrieved the disruptor from the table and

stepped over to the door. His eyes were already accustomed to the room's darkness and he listened intently for any sound. Hearing nothing, he hazarded stepping out.

The hallway was empty but the illumination was not as bright as it had been. Could the pirates have taken over the energy source? And why had their landing ships not been spotted? Their entire fleet had supposedly been wiped out the previous day by Harlan himself. What madness was it that they were on Destiny's surface trying to kill him in silence?

Harlan instinctively moved over to a doorway as he heard a sound ahead. He saw a group of black and grey Mantases come around the bend, several of them rubbing antennae. With an inward sigh of relief Harlan came out of the shadows.

"Quickly," he said with his sharp, deep, leader's timbre of voice. "You must protect the Queen. I will notify the space bullets . . ."

That was as far as he got. A grey Mantas to his left suddenly rose into the air, its wings sliding open and pushing down. It sped directly toward him. Harlan hardly thought. He switched on the disruptor and hurled it into the oncoming bulk. In the same motion he was speeding toward the other two creatures.

The flying Mantas crashed to the wooden floor as Trigor leaped into the air, planting both feet into the chest of the black one on the right. It was hurled backwards landing heavily on its head as Harlan landed on his feet, spun to the right, coming up below the left hand Mantas' chopping mandibles and smashing his forearm against the creature's eyes with a force that dropped it like a sack of stones.

He retreated quickly then, trying to gather some sort of coherent thought together as he leaped over the cringing Mantas with the disruptor in its adominal area.

He stopped momentarily by the doorway to the room where the pirate's corpse lay. There had been no doubt. These three Mantases were intent on doing him harm. A space bullet could recognize physical threats from any known living thing in an instant. But still, the "why" eluded him. The first thing he could think of was to get to and protect the Queen. But as the half a dozen other Mantases came streaming around the corner, the only thing he could think of was escape.

He knew from their movement that they were here for a purpose. They swarmed at him. With a jump he was over the bed, another step and he was on the window sill, then with a mighty leap he was in the air, soaring through the night toward the tangle of trees thirty feet beyond. He heard something thunk in the window behind him, then all his senses were centered on the the branches beyond. Even as his appendages prepared for impact his mind was picking the strongest and most strategically placed wooden limb.

He felt the rush of night air across his body, the flash of star and moonlight, the jumbled haze of color, wood, ground, stone, and fire, then his feet smacked a wide branch. There was a crunch of loose bark, and his body hurled forward. He dove through a small frame made of several trees, then grabbed another round branch that gave slightly when he swung beneath it.

Almost at the bottom of his swing another branch smacked into his lower belly, but rather than let this stop him and do great inner damage, his body moved around it, curling like a gymnast, allowing him to spin, his legs moving up and over, the top of his figure following. Suddenly he was rising, his body arching, his arms held out, like an upward swan dive. He brought his legs forward and dropped down twenty feet, hitting the twig- and leaf-packed earth. He rolled into a ball, somersaulted, and was on his feet running through the brief forest, toward the central city beyond.

Now any assailants would have to pursue him on foot. No grey flying Mantas or float-belted pirate could navigate the tangle of trees. And no stinger could be fired without raising some sort of alarm. Although the blood pounded in his ears he could not tell if anything else was unusual. The castle seemed quiet behind him and he could note no fighting in the city beyond. He could hardly believe he was the only target.

No time for that now—two Mantases were moving in from both sides. They were trying to keep pace with each other but Harlan knew the one on the right would reach him a few seconds before the other. That would be all the time he needed. He moved even faster toward them. Their arms were up and their triangular-shaped mandibles faced him. The three hurtling figures moved at each other.

Just before the Mantas' forearm mandible seemed destined to be part of Harlan's face, his ankles locked, his knees bent, and he hurled himself sideways through the air. His feet dove into the Mantas' body. Using the falling creature as a backstop he pulled the top half of his body forward, his head becoming the tip of a missile that smashed into the other approaching creature. The second assailant collapsed and, checking the area before him, the still-moving Trigor spread his arms, dipped, somersaulted once more and spun to finish off the attackers in a crouch.

At that second a mandible chunked into a tree behind his right ear. If Harlan had risen to his full height the sharp appendage would have sunk deep into his neck. A *third* Mantas had waited to ambush him. His reaction was immediate and explosive. Practically before the sound of the attack reached his ears his left elbow shot back and settled into the center of the steel-blue Mantas' face. It was a female but it was not Ministic. The creature dropped onto its back, its legs kicking from shock.

By then Harlan was moving forward again. The Mantas who he had butted was trying to rise. Trigor came down on the center of his back with both feet, almost succeeding in getting through to the ground beneath. Then one foot lashed out sideways to catch the other Mantas in the face. It, too, dropped heavily back to the ground. That's when Harlan noticed the stench.

He turned to see the mandible still stuck in the tree with thick liquid beginning to ooze out of it. The fallen blue Mantas' right forearm had only two mandibles and a space where the third should have been. Harlan realized that they were organic weapons, detachable, and that the thick liquid was probably a variety of poison or paralytic.

Sudden dread began to overwhelm him. They meant to kill him. And if they had kept this biological fact secret what else did the residents of Destiny not know about them?

He knew he stood no chance of reaching the Queen alone.

She could be anywhere in the castle while the other space bullets at the dinner would be without weapons. He needed to reach his take-off center or his home. The home was closer and even before he had decided completely, he was moving.

He sped through the woods with an incredible animal grace making split-second decisions and adapting his ankles and feet in order to make each step land flat on the uneven forest surface, and his route as straight and swift as possible.

As soon as he broke through the forest into the town he knew he had made a mistake. Things were too quiet, too many houses dark for that time of night. He slowed to stand in the shadow of a neighbor's wall and listened intently. He heard sounds of celebration from the castle. Of course, the people had gone up to cheer the space bullets. The Queen had declared it a holiday. His only choice now was to get to the take-off center.

Harlan looked up and saw the second-story window open. He gripped the treated wood wall and pulled up. For several seconds he found thin purchases, small bumps and curves in the wall to make his way, then, breathing heavily, his fingers seized the sill and he pulled himself in.

The house was dark. He waited several seconds to hear if there were any sounds of movement or breathing. There were none. He moved forward to the opposite window. What he saw there chilled him in the warm Destiny night. There was a dim moving light on the second floor of his house. And in the back yard were shadows of Mantases and men.

Harlan found his hands gripping the window sill. His knuckles were bright white. He lifted his palms, not noticing the nine indentations in the surface of the wood. He moved to the back of the room and stepped out the window there. He jumped easily to a branch of a tree growing behind the neighbor's house, landing so lightly and moving so quickly that the tree hardly had time to shiver. His face set in a horrible grimness, he began to make his way among the trees to his house.

The Earthman moved slowly from foot to foot. He breathed into his cupped hands even though it was not cold. Ministic had little use for nervous posturing. She simply kept track of the passing moments, making sure they kept within their strict time schedule. The Earthman stopped rocking and rubbed his hands on his pants.

"What if this guy gets back here?" he asked. He was short, even for a human, and had wavy grey hair. He wore a dark jacket over a brown shirt.

The Mantas did not deign to answer, checking instead the waiting orbit shuttle piloted by a space pirate and crewed by the Earthman's assistants. It was a compact vehicle, dark in color and unmarked. It was capable of almost silent flight at almost any altitude. It was but one of the Earthman's private fleet.

The Mantas turned back to the Trigor home and looked up. The girl would have to be nearly prepared, she thought. If Ministic had looked up a second earlier she would have seen Harlan jump from a tree into the open window. Instead she saw his shadow recede into the room and did not recognize it for what it was. A noise made her look down. The back door had opened and the Earthman's assistants came out with the girl.

Her brown eyes were covered by a padded strap that was tied tightly behind her head using three cords. Her mouth was stuffed with her own clothing and sealed with a wide strip of cloth, treated with a substance that binds to flesh. If she tried to move her lips too quickly her skin would tear. Her graceful arms were bound from the elbows to her fingertips with bandages. Another strap wound around her upper arms and beneath her breasts, pinning her arms against her back. Another rope stretched a little more than a foot from just above her left knee to just below her right knee. She could move but she could not run. Her feet were bare and she was naked.

The Earthman smiled, hard-pressed to contain his excitement. This female was a prize among prizes. Her long black hair cascaded across her torso, spilling across her breasts as she was led to him by his assistants, one at each shoulder.

They stopped her before him. He looked her up and down wishing he could see her frightened eyes and the condition of her teeth. The teeth were so important. They gave a clue as to the female's interior condition, and, if perfect, saved him money replacing them. Instead, he tossed back a bunch of her hair, uncovering her molded torso, staring with appreciation. Ministic did nothing, since she had already calculated this into their time schedule.

The Earthman placed both hands on her breasts. Titu reared back trying to pull away from the soft, pulpy hands. The assistants held her in place. The Earthman pushed harder, then squeezed. A small gargled mewing was all the night heard.

Finally he turned to the Mantas and nodded, smiling. They had a deal.

Harlan moved with the utmost skill, which meant his way was totally silent. To a normal man his presence would not be felt even if one were to look directly at him. At all times his body was in shadow as if he carried the darkness with him. He heard movement below the stairs, he heard movement in the back of the house, he heard movement even from outside the castle. But he heard nothing here or anywhere from his family's rooms.

He moved into his sister's room. Empty, save for a bed unmade, the dressing half on the floor. He moved slowly over to the doorway, like an animal, sniffing the air for danger. He formulated his plan. He expected his family had gone to the castle to partake in the festivities and that this group of villains were guarding the area in hope of snaring him. He would check the rest of the floor then get over to the take-off center.

Harlan slid into his parent's room. He was hard-pressed to keep from howling in rage.

The assistants moved up the stairway. They would let Bishop-Fortune have his fun with her now. Their time would be forthcoming they were sure. But first they had to finish cleaning up. They moved into the room, opening their plastic bags.

On the floor were two people, a man and a woman. Both seemed to loll against the wood beneath them as if their skin could barely hold their insides. The skin that could be glimpsed was unnaturally rounded and smooth with nary a crease. The faces were slack, limp, longer than expected, the eyes big, jellylike balls.

The two assistants bent down to stuff the bodies in the bag. One lifted the man's hand, which he thought felt like a jello sausage. It was his last thought before his head became mush. The other assistant thought he saw a dark shape drop from a rafter but he could not see the foot that rammed his jawbone into his brain.

Harlan bounded to the back window. Looking down, his sanity was further torn from its foundations.

Ministic was looking at him beside a man bending over his helpless sister. At the same instant dozens of stingers were fired from the dark shape of the space vehicle beyond.

As Harlan was driven back into the room by chips of flying wood and the deadly buzzing of the spinning projectiles, the honorable Bishop-Fortune dragged Titu Trigor toward the open door of his ship. She heard the cry of her brother and she tried to call back but pain tore at her mouth and the sopping padding choked her. Her arms were numb and un-moving. Her legs sought some sort of purchase but the rope binding them snapped taut, preventing her from gaining any kind of leverage.

She heard shouts, the man who fondled her was instruct-ing his men to move outside. She heard Ministic tell them that Harlan must be destroyed for the plan to take effect. Then she was roughly thrown on a soft couch, her arms beneath her. A sudden whirring noice and a hiss of sealed air. Calm, spoken instructions.

"Belt in. We're taking off."

A heavy weight crashed onto her. The air was knocked out of her body. She tried to squirm from beneath it, unable to breath. When she could finally suck air in through her mois-ture-filled nostrils, she realized a male body pinned her to the couch. Thus was she robbed from her world.

Harlan's mind had given up trying to comprehend. There were no plans being formulated. His parents had been mur-dered, his sister shamefully assaulted and kidnapped, and the Queen's aide was trying to kill him. He did not understand why and he did not care. The beauty of the planet had no more meaning. It might well have been the surface of the sun. His body now simply reacted, being controlled by the years of training.

He gathered up the disruptors from the bodies of the dead assistants, jumped over his dead parents, and ran out the door. From the top of the stairs he heard feet running toward the front door. He switched on a disruptor and sent it spinning down the stairs. It sank with a humming thunk into the wood of the front wall. As the door below sprung open the stinger-armed pirates entered and collapsed on top of the assistants.

The next disruptor flew from Harlan's hand into the floor. The remaining pirates pushed on only to drop into the cellar, the wrenched-apart wood spinning all around them.

Harlan catapulted from the stairs over to the cracked entrance. He rolled outside, collecting a stinger from an outstretched hand in the process. As he rose he sent a needle through the neck of a pirate rushing for cover. He took not one backward glance at his home, now a sagging, rotted structure, but sped toward the take-off center. His parents were forgotten, Ministic was forgotten. His only hope now was to get into his space bullet and stop the ship bearing off his sister.

The Queen's Mantas came out from behind the tree where she had taken shelter.

"Finish cleaning up," she instructed the remaining survivors. "Make sure the bodies will never be found. I must return to the castle quickly."

The pirates needed no elucidation. They would do as they were bid and get off the heavily defended planet quickly. Once back in the relative safety of space they would hurl the Trigors into outer space where they would disintegrate.

Harlan gained entrance to the take-off center with the key he always had with him. He moved down the sloping hallway to his compartment. He was not even thinking of raising an alarm. Not being in direct communication with the castle he would have to wait for his companions' return to explain.

He could not wait. He knew that the unmarked ship bearing Titu already had a dangerous head start. He would have to use drastic measures.

Harlan went quickly to the technical lab and mounted a force crane on his shoulders. The device fit over one's head and had armrests that ended in hand grips with two metal forks pointing at a diagonal of thirty degrees. Place any object between the two points and energy waves would allow one to lift that object. Harlan lifted an O'Neil warp drive. It, too, was shaped as his suit was, curved, bumpy, and rock-like. This exterior was only the housing made to fit onto the upper back of the space bullet. He moved through the hallway back to his compartment.

The take-off center was lit at all times and the machinery was automatic, ready for use at any time. Each separate piece of equipment had a built-in power supply so even in the event of the central energy source being destroyed the space bullets could go into action. Harlan placed the O'Neil warp drive on his suit where it sealed itself automatically.

Although he did not have to exert any pressure either lifting or sealing, his body was covered in sweat, as if he had spent all day working.

He released the force crane with an effort, his body tight and hands slick with moisture. Now he had to get his exoskeleton and settle into the suit. More precious time would go by, but he reminded himself that with the warp drive he could catch up with them. Harlan began the necessary preparations.

Ministic slipped out of her O'Neil vehicle at the front of the castle. She looked to see if her rose draping was sufficiently marked by wood chips, and the inner liquid of her fellows. She instructed her Mantas driver to go. She did not speak or touch antennae, however. She did not even turn toward him. He just nodded and went.

Ministic entered the castle, moving quickly toward the throne room. As she grew nearer she heard the sounds of celebration. All the city's residents must have been brought into the mile-long room to join in the reveling. Several guards noticed the Mantas' condition but did not react because she did not show that she needed assistance.

She reached the main door and waited until the cheering inside had quieted down. Knowing the Queen's area was just inside the door, she flung it open yelling, "Traitors! The Trigors have attempted to steal your life and your rule!"

Harlan was ready. His eyes did not see, but his brain knew everything. His limbs did not feel but his body was solid and safe. He was inside his suit. Warm, at peace, supremely powerful.

He floated across the floor until he was centered by the take-off chamber. After switching it to "operative," he would move into position, lock the chamber, and shoot out into orbit. When his whole team was present their take-off looked like a gatling gun, all its chambers firing at once.

His suit-encased arms set off a tiny beam of force. The chamber became operative. His mind raced, trying to eliminate the emotion he felt in order to decide on the best plan of action possible. He would either have to neutralize the pirate ship without destroying it or follow it to its destination.

Sensors had already indicated that it was almost out of orbital range. Some more force jets pushed the directional aiming equipment to the proper calibration. With a turn of his thumb he was in the chamber. With a miniscule flick of a muscle his suit was primed for take-off. With a blink of an eye his suit was moving up at an incredible speed. Multiplying his speed by the second, Harlan blasted out of the take-off center.

Information burned into his senses at a rate that he had long since learned to comprehend but he never would get used to. Automatic movements of obscure muscles checked and re-checked his equipment. It was a "go," a "green light," a successful take-off in a long line of successful take-offs. He experienced the wave of power that accompanied the knowledge that he was conquering space. His sister was *not* helpless. He had to, he must, he would save her. He initiated the warp drive.

A lightning bolt of red arced into his brain for a second, then it was gone, telling him that his suit had been damaged.

More signals crowded his consciousness. He had been hit with fire power when hardly out of the atmosphere. No ships were in orbit or lying in wait. The fire had come from below. Only Destiny had the ability to circumvent a space bullet's powers. His planet had fired upon him just as the warp drive was taking effect.

Harlan Trigor, space bullet, spun into space at warp speed. In the wrong direction.

THREE

The stars stared on impassively as Harlan neared the end of his story. He remained on his haunches, arms upside down on his crossed legs.

"I sped for countless light years. After I managed to regain my senses I found I could not shut down the warp drive. I could not correct my course. The navigational equipment was damaged as well. I traveled faster than light speed in the wrong direction for six months."

"Six months!" Napoleon cried. "Six months in that thing?" She pointed at the suit. The idea of an hour in an environment as small as that made her tail curl. Here was a strange bird indeed.

"After, the warp drive broke completely, and I drifted for six months more."

Napoleon fell to her forepaws and shook.

"A year," Larry said in wonder. "A year in that thing." He stared at the rocklike hulk in confusion. To him, used to the Black Hole, the company of Mess and Napoleon, and the vastness of space visible through the ports, a year inside the space bullet seemed like being buried alive.

"You do not understand," said Harlan. "Inside I am at peace, at one with the universe. Sensory imput never ceases, is always changing. All aspects of my brain and body are stimulated and treated. All aspects, I can see myself doing anything, being anything. I am fed, cleansed, and exercised.

49

My psychology has been adapted. I am motionless but always moving. Neither my mind nor my muscles atrophies."

Begin human, Larry still couldn't understand it but the reality sat before him. Trigor was tortured, betrayed, and lost, but he did not seem crazy.

"What was the Mantas' purpose?" he said when Harlan remained silent. "Why did they kill your parents and not your sister? Why not kill you?"

"I have thought on this long and hard," Trigor said quietly. "I had much time to think. My family had done nothing to them, so revenge was not the motive. The Mantases seemed uninterested in human lust and held much wealth, so greed and envy could not be the cause.

"The only thing I could think of was that they needed a . . . what is the word, a person to take the blame for another's actions."

"A patsy, fall-guy, prey, sacrifice, dupe, come-on, easy mark, tool, cat's paw, sucker, gudgeon," said Mess.

"What's that about cat's paw?" interjected Napoleon.

"Do you want the antonyms?" inquired Mess.

"I want you to damper down," Larry directed at the omnipresent computer. "Fall guy for what?" he returned to the off worlder.

"Nothing short of a takeover," Harlan replied. "Destiny is a lush jewel, a shelter, a home, the ultimate prize. Many races would do almost anything to possess it. The Mantases have shared this with us for years with treachery in their hearts."

"Mantases don't have hearts," said Mess. "They have brains, but only the thought of treachery could fit . . ."

"Damper down!" shouted Larry. "So why kill your family? Why not the Queen?"

"I am not sure, but I feel that by eliminating us, they could blame subsequent occurrences on my family, so that the populace would not revolt."

"You mean they meant to kill the Queen and say your family did it, then set up a puppet rule to placate the citizens?" asked Napoleon.

"Isn't that what I just said?" replied Trigor.

"Well, it is obvious they haven't succeeded," interjected Larry.

"It has been a year," said Trigor, head hanging down. "How can you be sure?"

"Well the Mantases are all over the place, or at least on every inhabited planet I know of. If they had taken over Destiny it would be wide open to galactic traders by now."

Harlan seemed to ponder Baker's statement for a minute. "The creatures have always seemed to think out everything before they acted . . ."

"Your escape has gummed up the works!" said Napoleon. Harlan's head remained low, his tone remained glum.

"Still I am helpless. My suit needs repair, my warp drive is probably useless, my sister is lost to me, my planet is doomed."

There was no great grief in his monotone, just empty failure. This apathy made Trigor's declaration all the more chilling. Larry sat with Napoleon again curled at his feet. His mind tossed Trigor's story back and forth. If "a" is a conspiracy, and "b" was the catalyst, and "c" was the takeover, then a minus b did not equal "c," And if "d" was his sister and "e" was Destiny than "e" minus "d" equals "x." What was "x?" And what about why? Larry's eyes drifted to the Earth floating above. It was a sparkling blue marble but not very inviting. Larry made his decision.

"You can repair your suit here with Mess' help, your warp drive can be replaced, maybe we can find your sister, and as for your planet, well, we'll see what can be done when we get there."

It had taken a while to quiet Mess down and convince him he should do as he was bid, but finally, as the two pilots were preparing to drop down to the surface, the machine had dipped into its spare parts and manifested itself into a four-wheeled, four-armed vehicle. A moving tool box.

It begrudgingly assisted Harlan in what he foresaw as at least a twelve-hour tune-up job, even with the computer cross-checking. And once any damage was found, at least twelve more after that, given that the proper repair materials were available.

Napoleon and Larry moved across the bridge area and replaced their beamers in the weapon compartment, to Mess' disapproving flashes. For the return Napoleon, usually choosing to go without clothes during their time in space, chose a pair of beige shorts and matching beige "v" covering with pockets over the breasts. This allowed her almost total freedom of limb movement.

She would have worn a matching "v" on her hips but she found it best to use that only in the relative privacy of her Earth-bound room. Even so, the beige cloth did little to mar the attractiveness of the feline. It might even have made the yellow-orange furred creature more alluring.

Her serene countenance, with its rich green eyes, gave the impression of some secret and cosmic knowledge. And the "v" top, locking at the front and back of the shorts, followed the contours of the supple body covering, the round, small, fur-covered, humanlike breasts.

Larry, comfortable with his co-pilot any way she dressed, simply slipped on a blue, long-sleeved, U-necked top over his tall, thin, wiry-muscled body. He kept on his pair of grey pants, one of the two he had, tucked into the brown boots. He smiled a wide smile at Napoleon and the two moved to the exit hatch.

They followed the central core until they came to a series of tunnels leading in all directions.

"We had better go separately," said Larry. "In case of trouble."

"No, let's go together," said Napoleon.

"But it would probably be better . . ."

"Let's go together all right?" Napoleon's voice was tight. Larry suddenly realized she was scared. He wondered why he wasn't.

"All right," he answered, moving down a tunnel to his right. Napoleon padded after him getting used to the cloth constricting her legs.

Larry pulled himself through a compartment coming up behind two seats in an opaque ball. Before these two seats was a U-shaped control board, and to the side were two thin doorways. As Napoleon rose behind him through the hatch, Larry sat down and pressed a button. Instantly the ball turned clear and the vastness of space stretched around them.

The first time they did this, back when these new reentry pods were salvaged from a dead ship, Larry cracked his head on the top when he jumped in surprise and Napoleon nearly scratched her way back inside the Black Hole. But by now they were used to it, more or less. Napoleon still hurried to her seat. Larry threw a row of switches and pushed another button. The hatch was secured and they were off.

Floating away from the ship Napoleon looked back. Every time she did this it seemed she spotted something new hanging on the outside of the large, cylindrical hulk of spaceship. From the cone-shaped bridge area to the variety of shacklike compartments jutting out of the central sides, there were balls, squares, antennae, holes, mirrors, fans, and grids all signifying something. A few were very important, a few were all but forgotten.

In back of that was the gridlike housing for the six reentry pods, then the cylindrical engine area with the great wealth of storage space, grids, cat-walks—if she would excuse the expression—metal jungle gyms of excess equipment, boosters, dampers, switchers, and the like. She turned back to look at Larry, hardly believing that the sandy-haired, lanky young man with the bright grey eyes and the body seemingly fashioned from metal bones and coiled muscles had made it work.

If it were not for the years of exertion and punishment etched into his skin, he would appear almost goofy. Instead he looked hungry, but still, somehow, innocent. She tugged at the bottom of her shorts, letting her crotch breathe, then settled back into her chair.

"So where are we going to find a faster-than-light engine?" she asked.

"I don't know," said Larry. "We'll look."

"And how are we going to find his sister?" Napoleon continued, looking down at the world.

"By Trigor's description, it sounded like a human craft took her," Larry replied. "How many Earthens are there capable of trespassing on another world simply to steel some flesh?"

Napoleon sniffed. "And, by Cheshire, how do you expect

us to get to Destiny? Earth has its grip around our throats and Destinians are supposed to kill all Earthens."

Larry looked over at his co-pilot. "No one, in his kindest moments, could honestly call us Earth people. Tell me, Nap, how much longer do you suppose we'll last down there?" His thumb jammed downward. Napoleon did not answer.

The world of black and pin-pointed white changed to overwhelming blue as they came through the clouds. Everywhere was the incredible variety of blue sea—here some choppy grey-blue, a little while later some wavy green-blue, then a bright, sparkling yellow-blue with the sun reflecting off the deep blue sea under the blue sky. Larry introduced a yellow tint to their ball, coating their surroundings in green.

"Thank Cheshire," Napoleon breathed as the ship neared the American coast. They sped by a wide strip of land, then moved out over the sea again. This was the outcome of the Natural Disaster. America had become donut-shaped, crossing into a great chunk of what used to be Canada near its top and sweeping down into a thinner band across what used to be California and Texas, then back up to what used to be Kentucky, Ohio, and New York.

Larry applied the preliminary retro-rockets as they neared the Denver Plateau, wherein lay the Providence Spaceport. The city had the same things as any other American city. A military post, communal dwellings made from uniform construction plans, amusement centers, and laboratories. Lots and lots of laboratories. The Spaceport had all these things as well, only they were far more concentrated.

Even as Larry's final landing coordinates were locked in and they were settling down to the circled cross on the concrete touch-down area, advertisements began to crackle through the radio. High-pitched electronic wooing and beeping preluded an English-speaking voice, low and inviting.

"Hard trip? Relax and visit Providence's best Dreamport, The Lush Siesta, where your every wish will be granted." Then in a more conspiratorial tone, "Your *every* wish." Followed by a lulling musical tune by an all-girl chorus, "Your every wish—our command—at the Lush Siesta."

Larry looked helplessly at Napoleon who looked about to

spit at the radio. As they got up the messages went on regardless.

"Need your valuables handled with personal, individual care? Then just press i.d. 01141 for Spaceport Transfers. The only service with style! If it's *that* important, you need Spaceport Transfers."

"Hungry, thirsty, bursting for love? Your wish is our command! At Dream Universe! See what you want to see, do what you want to do!"

Larry and Napoleon moved out of the pod, grabbing their belts and pulling them on. A man-shaped machine with a small hole in the middle of its chest moved toward them on treads. It slowed as it neared the duo and Larry pulled off a thin device from his belt. It was a metal rod with a flat-ended bulb at one end and a "T" at the other.

Larry stuck the bulb end in the machine's chest and used the "T" to turn it. The machine whirred and clicked recognition. Larry had been acknowledged as an official messenger of the Weinstein-Hubbell Earth Laboratory and his pod would be kept in top shape every hour of the day and night.

Larry and Napoleon moved on toward the L-shaped Spaceport building. As they walked, several robots on treads crossed their path, moving to and fro for a variety of reasons. Some to welcome in-coming ships, some to load and unload cargo, some just to seem busy. They paid as much attention to the human pair as the pair paid back. The doors of the terminal building opened as the two approached and Larry went immediately to a panel in the wall.

He inserted the thin metal device and turned again, then typed out his instructions on a numbered keyboard. The message was acknowledged and Larry rejoined Napoleon knowing that Mess would send down their salvage from this trip directly to the lab. If, for some reason, they could not retrieve the pod, the larger equipment vehicle would be at Weinstein-Hubbell's waiting for the signal to return.

Before exiting the arrival area Larry had to use the bulb device three more times and it was necessary to get Napoleon's alien standing rechecked. Then they waited until the "all-clear" signal was given, signifying that their pod had been checked, searched, and was clean. Then they were put through to the debriefing area.

Up until then all the checks and cross-checks had been done by machine. But as they entered the large room with no windows it was two men who faced them. The same two men who always faced them on landings. Two other men handled them at take-offs. And they all handled them roughly.

"Well, if it isn't our makeshift man and his cat," said the brown-haired one behind the desk. He shuffled some plastic cards.

"Yes, indeed," said the blond-haired man standing beside him. "It is our hardly human and his meow-meow," He stared at Napoleon and barked, "Woof, woof."

Napoleon did not react. She stood beside Larry, motionless, expressionless. The men facing them wore khaki outfits with the letters E.G. in a diamond patch emblazoned on their sleeves. The Earth Government was composed only of the military and many, out of sheer boredom, enjoyed abusing their power. Even the employees of the labs were not safe. But at least they were familiar with the routine and prepared for the sarcasm and humiliation. Knowing this, the landing officials tried harder every time.

"Well, let's get the chores out of the way so we can have some fun," said the sitting man, grinning. He brought up a pair of papers and slapped them on the desk. "However, today, we are going to do it orally. We don't want you two copying from each other." He handed one sheet up to the blond person then said to Larry, "Name?"

"Larry Baker."

"Not Larry Butcher?"

"No."

"Larry Candlestick Maker?"

"No."

"Lar-ry Ba-ker," said brown hair, writing laboriously. "Age?"

"Twenty-seven."

Brown hair wrote that down then looked up at Larry framing the next word practically letter by letter.

"B-o-r-n?"

Larry stared back hard, trying to keep his face impassive. If he let any emotion show, let it be rage, discomfort, or cynicism, the man would really start digging in.

"No," he replied.

"Good!" brown hair shouted to the laughing accompaniment of blond hair. "We finally taught you, eh? You do not have a birthday because you were not born. You have a made-day since you were made. So for you and you only we have created a special form. So from now on you won't have to answer that uncomfortable question. Get ready, here's your brand new landing form! Name?"

"Larry Baker."

"Good. Age?"

"Twenty-seven."

"Very good. Made?"

Blond hair started giggling.

"May seventh . . ." Larry began.

"No, no, no," said brown hair. "On this question you say 'Yes,' no date, just 'yes.' Understand?"

Larry nodded.

"Understand?" the military man repeated ignoring the head movement.

"Yes," said Larry.

"Very, very good. Made?"

"Yes."

"Parents?" said brown hair, going on to the next question.

This was a new one. Usually they spent all their time with the question of his creation. Larry knew that anything he said would be wrong so he answered quickly.

"None."

"I'm sorry," brown hair replied just as quickly. "That will not do. How can anyone have no parents? Our computer wouldn't understand. So you must answer fully, like this, 'I have no parents, only chemicals.' Repeat after me, 'I have no parents . . .'"

"I have no parents . . ."

"Only chemicals."

"Only chemicals."

"I was not born . . . come on, come on."

"I was not born . . ."

"I was made in a lab."

"I was made in a lab."

"I am less a man."

Larry did not echo the sentiment. It was a useless gesture, he knew, and stupid to boot. Any stubbornness made their job more enjoyable to them.

Blond hair chimed in. "You had better answer, fake face. If you weren't to return one day the lab would just whip up another of you."

"I am less a man . . ." brown hair repeated.

"I am less a man," said Larry.

"Good," said brown hair. "Now I want you to fill out your new form that way every time. Don't worry, we've plenty of space on the page for the answer."

It was blond hair's turn. He stood behind the table and directed himself to Napoleon. "Not to worry, peach fuzz, we haven't forgotten you. You need a whole new form, too. You left such a big empty space in the middle and last name section before. Not to mention the parent section, date of birth section, age section, and hair color section. Now here it is, a tiny little section for your name. Name?"

"Napoleon."

"No last name?"

"No."

"No middle initial?"

"No."

"Darlin', darlin', darlin', if you would only take our suggestion, you could have a full name. Earth Ship Napoleon, that has a nice ring to it, don't you think?" Brown hair smilingly concurred. "What do you think?" blondie asked Napoleon.

"I have no choice in the matter," said the feline. "I was named for the ship I was brought in on, as were my eleven sisters. I cannot change it. Nor can I learn my original language. I was taught English and Cheshire was named as my God."

Blondie and brown hair laughed together like it was choice humor.

"My parental origins are unknown," Napoleon finished.

"Don't you at least have a number?" asked blondie between chuckles. "With eleven sisters all named the same thing they must have at least given you numbers to tell you apart. Napoleon 1, Napoleon 2, you know . . ."

"They used us as they saw fit. They did not have to tell us apart." Napoleon's voice was empty of emotion. It helped that it was so long ago.

"I'd love to use you as I see fit," said brown hair, eying her up and down. "Rowr, rowr."

"Sure you don't want a number?" said blondie. "Six is nice."

"No."

"Oh, very well, no need to get testy. You're not like your fake friend, you know. You're precious. There aren't many of you left with full brains. We're supposed to take very good care of you. As a matter of fact we've been instructed to make sure you're all right after every trip. The lab doesn't want you damaged in case they need to do experiments again." Blondie moved slowly up to Napoleon, towering over her. "But remember the lab won't be of any help if you attack a Government official."

With that, blond hair began to search her. Fondling her head, petting her shoulders and back, peeking under her "v" cover, scratching her waist, then getting down on his knees to rub her legs up and down.

"Nice pussy," he cooed. "Nice pussy, pussy."

Larry looked over to check, but she stood motionless and impassive. He did notice, however, that her claws were out.

Blondie finished getting his kicks and moved back. Suddenly brown hair was all deep-toned business.

"Now listen, you two. If you are seriously considering reporting us the worst that will happen is that we'll be reprimanded. There aren't many of us real people around and none of us is going to listen to the complaints of a guinea pig and a test tube baby. We'll see you next trip."

Larry and Napoleon moved out of the room stiffly, side by side, walking down the hallway slowly. They knew both military men were probably watching them so Napoleon fought her urge to clean herself and Larry kept himself from running. As they moved nearer the turn of the L-shaped building, Napoleon whispered, "When do you want to steal that warp drive?"

Larry had accompanied Napoleon to her off-worlder dwelling, a building with rooms like cells, especially reserved for laboratory aliens. It was stark but relatively comfortable, set away from the main city area and staffed by machines.

He then moved back into the nearby tour tunnel and hopped on a transport band to the Weinstein-Hubbell labs. Troops of humans dotted the variety of bands, all kept in order by one or two khaki-clothed military men. Occasionally another lone man would move by or one or two Mantases would make their way along the colorful way dotted with garish advertisements heralding the great satisfaction to be found at various dream factories and other establishments that offered the services of artificial people. No food, no drink, just all variations on Earth's main export: people.

Larry stepped off and stuck his bulb device in another hole by the underground entrance to the labs. A door slid over and the band moved him down. No more adverts, just bright yellow walls with strips of other colors, denoting the levels.

Red for military, blue for administration, green for the labs, and orange for the scientific services. Larry moved off the belt, and repeated his bulb maneuver at this new door. It rose and Larry moved into a maze of offices, all encased in yellow blasted brick. He came to a small door on a large wall. For the third time he used his belt bulb then moved through.

Dr. Weinstein-Hubbell was standing in a huge warehouse hangar, checking off a list he held in his hand and occasionally saying something to the lab-coated Mantas beside him. In front of them was the pile of salvage Larry had picked up during the last run. The doctor was thin, balding, and had bright, slightly crossed, light blue eyes. He pulled those eyes off his list and directed them at Larry as he approached.

"Baker?" he said not waiting for a reply. "Good. Cormundin?" he addressed the Mantas. "You may go." The creature did just that. Weinstein-Hubbell's watery orbs settled on Larry again. "An interesting collection. Several safety plates, fusilage sections, another piece of the Moffat-Blake shuttle craft, several good panel fronts . . . do you know what this is?"

He held up an orangey disk with a small hole in the

middle and with what looked like circular grooves. Larry shook his head.

"No matter," continued the doctor, throwing the disc back on the pile. "We will find out. We received the supplies with no problem. Come down to my office."

Weinstein-Hubbell moved off. The doctor, like many other scientists, had the unnerving habit of talking to himself more than anyone else, introducing any subject that came to mind, and seemingly, he existed in a world of his own.

Larry imagined it was from having created so many people himself. He just could not understand how anything he made from his hands or head could be equal to him, or even superior to him at many things. Weinstein-Hubbell could not pilot a space ship to save his life. His creation, Larry, could not only pilot one but he built one himself. An amazing thing for almost any engineer, but unfortunately Larry had been created to be a biochemical scientist. Earth certainly didn't need another mechanic.

The doctor entered his office with Larry in tow, moved around his desk, and pulled out a thick sheaf of papers, which he plopped down on his blotter.

"Fill this out like a good lad, will you, Baker." he said, disappearing out the door. His voice receded down the hallway as he said, "Use your room, I'll have dinner sent up."

Larry moved around the desk and sat down. He stared at the heap of papers knowing them to be yet another test for biology aptitude. He had taken many different tests over the last few years, approximately at quarterly intervals. The doctor never gave up the hope that Larry's brain would suddenly show the correct leanings toward medical talent.

Larry slowly hefted himself and the test up and moved to his room at the very apex of the labs, in the second story of the above-ground area. A comfortable living quarters, it was filled with scientific texts. There was a table and a chair facing the one window. He sat down and leafed through the papers, thinking.

Gone were the golden days of discovery and learning. For a few short years, as Larry gained awareness, he was full of wonder at the miracle of his creation. Weinstein-Hubbell was his father, and his God. They had these long creator-creation talks, an opportunity even Adam and Eve were denied.

Larry's tailor-made mind was filled with the greatest learning his world had to offer. All manner of development was crammed into a few short years. Larry never forgave the doctor for that. Instead of experiencing something, he learned it. He knew of things, he rarely did them.

Still, the wonders he witnessed, and was part of—the mass creation of life—was amazing. And he was the lucky one. He was chosen to possess a full brain, the only one of his kind to be allowed an uncontrolled mind and education. He was the sole participant in an experiment to see if freedom added to a central ability. The experiment was initially labeled a failure.

Weinstein-Hubbell had since created hordes of biochemical technicians with just a slight alteration of Larry's original formula, but he still could find no reason for Larry's lack of natural capacity. Their talks were fewer and fewer and the tests got longer and longer. The wonder left as fast as his love for a man who built fellow men to alien specifications.

Dusk had settled on the labs and shadows crossed Larry's room. He didn't turn on the light until his door opened and a man brought in a tray with high-protein foodstufs. He set the tray down on the table, picked his way back through the texts, and left. No words, no acknowledgments, no eye contact. That was not what the server was made for. His brain was not big enough to question. His vocal chords had not been developed.

It was like grafting a dog's head onto a human body. He could be trained to exist to serve. That was all he was capable of. If you wanted a bigger ability you would have to re-order through your friendly Earth representative. The one with the E.G. in the diamond-shaped patch.

Larry concentrated a little more on the test. It was harder than usual. Not in terms of the medical questions but in terms of the psychology behind them. Larry had an unhampered brain, developed to human status, so whatever answers he needed could be learned but the ability to *purposely avoid* showing an aptitude was getting increasingly difficult. He had to do well enough to avoid suspicion and poorly enough not to show an unusual ability or the lab scientists would knock his comfortable world topsy-turvy.

Pretty soon his charade would become obvious. They would discover that his latent medical talents had appeared six years ago and that he was covering up. Harlan Trigor had appeared not a moment too soon.

Larry looked out across the empty landscape, a monument to nature's ability, filled with the intrinsic wonders but virtually empty of man's grace, and thought about the dazzling invitation of deep space, of Destiny. There was a chance. Somewhere out there might be some sort of answer. Or at least some sort of decent question.

Larry hunched down over the papers and went to work.

The hot lights flashed across Napoleon's face as she moved through the street. The various signs and speakers blazed out their messages to the business people and tourists alike. Here! Here! Here is where your wildest dreams become reality! Make love! Murder! Rape your brother! Blast your superior!

And it will all be real, the blood will spurt, the flesh will really give and burn, the fingernails will really scratch, because the person is really human. Really made of skin, bone, and muscle, organs, brain, and veins. It is life and death, live and die, give and take. And it's all for you! Buy! Buy!

And the yokels loved it. Here, by the Spaceport, dozens of these establishments made a decent living after paying fees to the Government. And some eliminated that problem by being the Government. Napoleon was on her way to one such establishment.

But even on a street surrounded by Mantases, humans, and semihuman creatures, she got unwanted attention. A feline female was rare in the galaxy and her short-haired, fiery-furred form was interesting to almost every race.

Not back at her dwelling, however. She stayed in the rear of the first floor of a two-story building, filled with mindless lion-men, unsuccessful results of the experiment that killed her sisters. The retarded cats were kept by the Government until a use could be figured out for them.

The Government never wasted anything. Their abilities were tested and registered in the Galactic Pool, and if any alien order called for their talents they would be trained and shipped out forthwith. However, Napoleon could not think of any planet in need of huge, hairy beasts who ate and slept all day, bunched together like a group of newborn kittens. And Napoleon had to live with them. The one other alternative was inconceivable to her.

Her back remained straight and her expression haughty although she wished she could have brought her spitter with her. But to be caught with a working weapon was a serious crime. She suppressed an urge to slink into an alley and continued walking until she came to an opulent-looking dream factory called The Palace of Pleasures.

A huge lion-man approached her as she entered and said, "Can I be of service?" His deep growling words set her hair on end. These were the first truly intelligent words she had ever heard a lion-man speak.

"Grossman-Smith," she managed to mew. "I would see Grossman-Smith."

"Certainly," the male feline roared pleasantly. "And afterwards perhaps you would like to visit with me again?"

Napoleon was inwardly near to hysterics. Years of control kept her outwardly calm, however. "Yes, perhaps," she said, daring a smile. "Perhaps I shall."

"Wonderful! This way please," said the lion-man, moving up the stairs.

Napoleon really didn't see the ornate surroundings, the levels and levels of sculptured glass, the different areas built specifically for several alien types, she only saw the magnificent lion-man. Where had such a one come from? Where did Grossman-Smith find him? Could it be from Mandarin? Her thoughts petered out as the lion-man turned and gestured.

"This way. Grossman-Smith is waiting." Then he disappeared completely.

Napoleon felt herself sinking to her forepaws until she heard laughing from inside the door to which the lion-man had gestured. She felt only dark rage as she entered, seeing Grossman-Smith's form convulsed with levity.

"You should have seen your face!" he hooted, his dark eyes

alight and fake goatee trembling. "It is the first time I have ever seen you shocked."

He stood behind a magnificent white oak desk lined with glass sculptures. Artifacts and tapestries from almost every known inhabited world lined the walls. A chair suited for every alien type was positioned before him and four translators were attached to the desk top, angling off in every direction.

Napoleon saw behind him a panel of electronic equipment with several red lights on. She stared hard at his jovial countenance and saw that his eyes were unamused. He was really pleased that he could embarrass her. It gave him an edge.

Grossman-Smith liked edges. Anything to hold on to and tear apart made him feel at home. He had spent his whole life creating those edges for himself. The one and only edge Napoleon had was the knowledge that behind those black hairpieces were Dr. Masterdon-Barnes, a noted Earth Government official in charge of the fee collection in this sector of the city. But an edge like that was a dangerous one. It could turn on her at any moment. Her uniqueness was her only protection.

She moved forward until she stood directly behind the chairs.

"I do not like being humiliated," she said.

"Few creatures do," he replied, smiling. "That is what makes it so much fun." He slapped his forehead in mock remembrance. "Except for your housemates naturally. Beat them and they'd probably lick your hand. I thought it would be nice if you met a relative with a backbone for a change."

"You knew what effect it would have on me," Napoleon said. "Hardly a friendly gesture. How did you do it?"

"I thought it best to take a little starch out of your stride. You may be an alien feline, but you're still a biped female and adaptable females on this planet should be kept," he said with iron in his voice.

"I am not adaptable as you call it and don't change the subject. What was the method of my embarrassment?"

"Not child-bearing, no, but useable, yes. You could supply all the pleasure with none of the, shall we say, mutated side-effects," the iron was consumed by fire.

"We have had this discussion before. I have not returned

to beg residence. But I would like to ask again how you achieved the effect."

"As a gentleman, I shall reply," said Grossman-Smith, bowing slightly at the waist, the flame of his oratory subsided. "A three-dimensional image, naturally. An invention perfected in my lab and one that I couldn't resist testing when I heard of your impending visit. Please, sit down, my girl."

"I am not a girl, no matter how much you would like to think so," Napoleon replied hotly.

"You dress like one," said Grossman-Smith, eying her, "You act like one and physically you can react like one. I see little gain in discussing titles. Sit down anyway, your feline highness."

Grossman-Smith sat down himself, touching his facial hair to make sure it had not loosened. Napoleon circled the chairs and sat in a plump one made of wood and covered with red pillows. She decided not to deny his hospitality since their bantering would only go so far before he lost his patience.

"If not to plead for my luxurious sanctuary, what have you come for?" he asked. "Surely not the pleasure of my company."

"Surely not," she replied smoothly. "I am interested in your associates."

It was her turn to be pleased. Although she had never seen him get taken by surprise, this was the closest he got. His movements stopped and he hung in time and space for a moment, then pulled his own chair in and leaned over his desk.

"Whatever are you interested in my companions in pleasure for? Surely if you have turned down my own protection, you certainly could not be interested in theirs."

"I have said nothing of protection. I have not even framed the nature of my interest yet."

"What else could it be?" Grossman-Smith continued, his arms on the desk. "Information is not my trade. The only thing you could hope to achieve is upping the price of bidding by setting my offer against theirs. I warn you, I could tolerate your freedom when no one else knew what a treasure you were, but now I will possess you or no one will!"

Even though his reaction was part of her plan, the intensity of it worried Napoleon.

"I tell you the question of my possession is not involved," she blurted.

"Who is it?" he raged on, regardless. "Taylor-Barnes? A life of drudgery I can assure you. One freak after another with little reward. Perry-Hirsh? His illusions are not half mine. Nor are his dividends."

"I have no interest in Spaceport small-fry," said Napoleon. "My situation concerns more powerful . . ."

Grossman-Smith rose out of his chair, discovery lighting his face, his finger pointing at the seated feline. "Bishop-Fortune," he spoke slowly. "Bishop-Fortune has discovered you. With the pick of all space he has to spot you. I would think that he would be satisfied with the raven-haired witch, but . . ."

"This witch," Napoleon asked quickly. "Is it a girl?"

"Yes, yes," he replied, preoccupied. "Of course it is a girl. A very beautiful girl whom he had acquired as a courtesan. But it makes sense that he would want another exotic creature for his factory."

"This Bishop-Fortune, where is he?" Napoleon knew it was the wrong question as it popped out into the air.

Grossman-Smith snapped out of his reverie quickly. "What is this, woman? Have you been toying with me? Trying to raise your worth in my eyes?" By the last question he was around the desk and yelling.

Napoleon rose quickly. "The question of worth was introduced by you, as was the competition for a body not for sale. I have no interest in your establishment, your business, or your wants. I only wanted information. I will not require it if the price is myself."

"Do you know how many cat-women I create for my patrons daily? Do you know how many times I myself have enjoyed your company? Do you know the price people would gladly pay to share the favors of a living Mandarin female?" Grossman-Smith stood before her, shouting.

"*I* am the power on this planet! I control destinies! If there were but one more of you on this world I could do what I wanted with you, with or without your cooperation. By the Earth Father, I *will* have you! I will have you now!"

He seized her shoulders and pushed back, falling upon her.

Larry turned the last page, fighting the urge to check over everything immediately. He knew that even signs of great care were a giveaway. For him, if it wasn't right the first time, going back would only complicate matters. Now if he had done a good job, the doctor would check it over, nod, then start formulating a new test.

But if he had missed too much, or stopped concentrating in the wrong place, or answered too many times, Weinstein-Hubbell would watch him like a hawk; he would be observed day and night, a battery of scientists would be assigned to check and recheck his every mood. Further tests, just waiting for his first sign of aptitude, would be dropped on him like so much mental gravel. And that just would not do if his plan were to work.

Larry had learned not to trust his instincts in these matters. Even if he felt the test went well, it meant nothing. Stealth counted, not sincerity. And now that he had, at last, an opportunity to escape completely, not just for one trip at a time, he had to be extra, extra cautious.

Hopefully he had a little time in the event the doctor did not check over the test immediately. But if he decided to look at it this evening, before he went to bed, Larry might have little leeway.

He rose and stretched his joints. Then, grabbing some foodstuffs and shoving them in his mouth, he moved over to the bed. Chewing on the doughy wad of protein, he pulled off his sweaty blue shirt, replacing it with a black one of the same design. He moved toward the door thinking about Napoleon.

With any luck at all she would be able to get some kind of information from Grossman-Smith. Larry remembered when she first came to him, desperate for a way out of her predicament. Having survived the battery of experiments lasting twelve years she had the unappealing choice of living with her artificial offspring or succumbing to the demands of corrupt officials for her sexual services.

It seemed that she was now a special case and almost everyone on the planet was lusting after her body. So, if she would only copulate with every known galactic creature and undergo a variety of genetic operations to salvage her insides, she could lead a life of relative comfort. The dream factories were not known for prostitution; there weren't enough women for that, but, as was said before, Napoleon was a special case.

And, as a special case, she had heard that Larry had a ship and a co-pilot's position open. He wasn't originally planning to have it filled but when he learned of her situation he made an exception. Napoleon had registered in the Galactic Pool previously, in an attempt to escape, but no Government official intended to process her application, there was too much "upstairs" pressure. But with a little red-tape cutting by Mess, she was suddenly assigned to the Black Hole.

Larry found himself outside and moving toward her abode. His concern was directing him there. Grossman-Smith was moody at best, power-mad at worst. Any personal visit, whether social or light business, was risky. No one had heavy business with Grossman-Smith. He had it with them.

Larry hopped off the transport band and moved out of the tour tunnel. The area was quiet. Unless he moved near the Spaceport it stayed quiet. The mutants that had initially roamed the countryside, created by the nuclear holocaust, had long since been destroyed by the military, the radiation, and the Natural Disaster. Now they were made by man, rendered harmless, and sold to the highest bidder. So the forests were quiet, the towns were quiet, and the cities were quiet.

Larry moved through the night acquiring, as he walked, a strange feeling of peace. An inner knowledge that he would soon leave this place and not miss it, no matter how beautiful it seemed. Because he knew. He knew that the birds singing, the crickets chirping, the flies flying, the bees buzzing, and the spiders spinning their webs were just like him.

They were made. Their offspring were "real," none questioned their existence, and their brains were not big enough to understand why the inclination to attack humans, even when threatened, never occured to them.

It was a storybook world, a never-never-land, made by men, just to keep things level and assure themselves that they

were still tops in God's eye. A world made of plastic and
chemicals, unable to feel love.

And into the fairy tale came death. Larry heard the rustle
just before a shadowy bulk fell on his shoulders. He was honestly shocked, enough so that he could not prevent his stomach from leaping and his chest muscles clenching. He
dropped heavily to the ground, the bulk falling with him.

He felt himself shouting but he clamped it off at the last
moment because he felt fur under his hand as he rolled over.
He looked down to find Napoleon lying under him, her eyes
wide and desperate. He rose and she got to her knees.

"What happened?" he whispered.

In answer she rose to her forepaws. He saw her fur matted
with a dark brown liquid. He suddenly looked at his shoulders and felt the sticky wetness coming through.

"I killed him," she mewed. "He attacked me. I couldn't
think. It all burst up inside of me, I guess. My natural heri-
tage." She grinned sickly, without humor. "I slashed and
slashed. I didn't even know I was doing it." She looked
down, breathing deeply several times. Larry sank down, sitting beside her.

"When the fog cleared I was standing up and he was
splattered on the carpet. His eyes were open. The look on his
face was like this was the biggest surprise in the universe.
Imagine, a female fighting back."

Larry knew better than to try to soothe her. Her tail was
lashing back and forth. To touch her now would probably
get him a torn hand.

"I ran," she finished. "I had no choice."

"Of course not, of course not," Larry told her. He did not
have to tell her that she was in the worst kind of trouble. To
kill on Earth meant that one less real human existed in a
world where real humans were at a premium. The guilty
party would not be put to death, that would only compound
the problem. They would be "reprogrammed," their mind
made a blank slate altered to do any menial task necessary.
In Napoleon's case that meant declawing and a lobotomy,
then going to work doing the very thing she had killed to
prevent.

And even though Grossman-Smith's real identity would be

discovered it made little difference. The Government would divvy up his empire and cover up the particulars of the crime. Other cities and worlds would be informed that the right honorable Masterdon-Barnes had been murdered in his quarters at the Providence Spaceport by a homicidal feline female. Clawed and dangerous. Be on the lookout. Wanted alive.

Naturally Larry would come under suspicion. Not by deed but by association. Then they would find his blood-stained shirt and his artificial life as a spaceship pilot would be at an end.

As they sat across from each other in the dark Earth night, bound by friendship and someone else's blood, Larry knew that when the morning came they would be on another planet. Or the morning would never come.

FOUR

Wolf-Hoover led his six men out of the Palace to where the seventh remained stationed. Just one uniformed man with the "M" in the triangle patch was enough to keep curiosity in control. On-lookers knew that behind that one man was all Earth's strength. Its military, its scientists, its labs. And unless you wanted a one-way trip to darkness you would keep out of their way.

The makeshift sentry turned when he heard Wolf-Hoover's approach. The other six moved around him as he thought. He deserved his name. His face was long and his hair was bushy and dark, streaked with white. His smile, on the rare occasions it appeared, was thin. His eyebrows almost naturally arched down, giving him a constant look of anger turned demonic when he smiled.

He was not smiling now, just the opposite, his face clouding even more so than usual. His grandiosely muscular body was tense, his hands clamped to his waist, his eyes down, as if he were studying air currents beneath his knees. His jaw muscles tightened and untightened, moving his grey sideburns in a ripple. His arm muscles clenched and unclenched, creating waves beneath his rolled up sleeves.

This one did not take much thinking, thankfully.

"She's not going back to her room, surely," he said to the sentry. "But we can't take chances. Go there, cover the place from top to bottom with psonic traps."

The man nodded in reply, saluted, and moved to the O'Neil drive vehicle to collect the array of electronic material necessary to turn a house into a paralytic net.

Wolf-Hoover in the meantime pointed to three of his men and said, "You check the Spaceport. No one goes in, no one goes out. Keep tracking that ship of theirs." The three saluted and turned.

"You three," he continued to the remainder. "You come with me." Wolf-Hoover was sure he was going to be the one to see action or else he would not be the one leading his men to the Weinstein-Hubbell labs.

The way he figured it, she was a cat. And no matter how independent, when in trouble, a cat will always try to return to its master. Armed and ready, the four moved to cover the master.

Larry ran down the hallway, sweat beading on his brow. The floor was completely deserted. All the scientists had gone to take what pleasures they could find. Larry's room on the top floor was clear and it was obvious from his closed door Dr. Weinstein-Hubbell was occupied.

With a little luck and a degree of skill they could find a warp engine or the necessary parts thereof, load it into the salvage vehicle, and send a message up to Mess to prepare the ship for immediate departure. If they could do this and if the warp drive could be adapted for the Black Hole and if it could be installed in time and if they could get to Destiny before they were blown up by Earth Ships and their allies, everything might turn out all right.

Napoleon shrieked around the corner, holding her spitter tightly. It had been changed, naturally, to fit her paw. She held a regular spitter out to Larry, which he took. It was a long-barreled weapon, made for two-hand use and called for great control if the owner was to avoid waste.

For out of the end, when the trigger was depressed, were spat small bands of high-intensity light, one after another, like a laser machine gun. They were killing devices, rarely seen on Earth, a black market item Napoleon managed to smuggle in after a supply run from one of the more populated alien planets.

Larry pushed the grip deeper into his palm and moved into the scientific services maintenance area. His pile of junk, left over from the last trip, was where Weinstein-Hubbell had left it. The two went around that and over to a long table littered with metal and glass devices.

All variety of tools lay about, as well as a variety of Earth and alien engine parts. Napoleon padded away from the table to check the cavernous area for any signs of what could be a warp drive.

"Now remember," Larry told her. "It could be any size, any shape. As far as I know it might be made of new materials."

Napoleon thanked him for his "help." Except the retort was not humorous in the situation. It had the ragged sound of hopeless despair.

Larry returned his attention to the table. A large hunk of machinery looked promising over at one end. He moved over there noticing various materials he recognized from his own ship's engine. Maybe somewhere in that hulk was a warp drive. He couldn't lug the whole thing but perhaps he could take it apart.

He did not want to make undue noise so he began to go to work manually. He grabbed a wrench and set to it. Occasionally he would look up but Napoleon was not in sight. Once he thought he saw movement atop a huge pile of boxes, but he could not be sure. He continued working.

Finally he came to a central core, a bunch of welded-together sections surrounding an item he couldn't see clearly. At no point could he find a grip or nut he could loosen, so he tried to pry open a section with his wrench. It was too thin; he couldn't get the leverage.

The longer he took, he knew, the tighter the net of their predicament closed, so he quickly looked around for something he could jam the core apart with. He found a closed section of tubing with what looked like a handle in the middle. It was a foot long, and perfect for leverage. He stuck one uniform end in and started to push down.

"Don't move, Baker," shouted a deep voice.

Larry's heart leaped up to his neck and his head rose so quickly his neck cracked. He saw Weinstein-Hubbell standing beside a group of four men, the one leading being a huge, muscular man holding a beamer aimed directly between Larry's eyes.

"What are you doing here, Baker?" asked the doctor.

"Nothing, really, doctor," said Larry as nonchalantly as he could. "Well, not nothing in the literal sense. I, I come down here often. To relax and tinker around. Uh, what's going on?"

While he spoke, the muscular character was turning about.

"Nothing you should know about," said the man, still aiming the beamer dead on target while turning. "Literally or figuratively."

Larry fought the urge to look wildly about for Napoleon. He instead stared straight ahead at Wolf-Hoover who was still checking the area. He tried not to think about the moment Napoleon would show herself or when anyone would take a good look at the table. For, behind a piece of engine lay his spitter, an off-world device, the clinching evidence in Larry's duplicity.

Weinstein-Hubbell spoke again, further closing the coffin on his fate.

"I was looking for you when these men arrived, Baker. I have some questions I would like to ask you about your test."

"Later, doctor," cut in Wolf-Hoover. "Baker! Have you seen your co-pilot recently?"

"No," Larry said quickly—too quickly, by the Earth Father! "Why?"

"You're lying," said Wolf-Hoover, his ingrained instincts taking over. An operation his father had granted permission for had made him into the finest enforcement official the Earth could create. He not only knew Larry was lying but he also knew that the feline co-pilot was nearby. If he had x-ray vision he would have seen Larry's spitter through the metal and acted faster.

"All right, men," he began, "Spread out . . ." The last word left his mouth after the hole burned through his brain.

Only after the huge Wolf-Hoover began to topple were the beams of orange-red light visible. They swung to the right and literally perforated two more military men. The third man swung to the left and brought up his beamer as Larry dove for the table.

As he moved forward he calculated the angle the gun would have to be at to hit the military man while lying flat on the table. Larry's right hand arched down, slapped the spitter, knocking the metal before it to the floor. Even before it hit, Larry's hand curled, turning the weapon and pulling the trigger.

Light tore at the military man's hip, his own weapon shooting harmlessly to the side. The injured man crashed to the floor, where another beam from above destroyed his skull. Weinstein-Hubbell stood rooted to the floor.

"You . . . you killed four men," he cried. "Real men."

Napoleon appeared atop a pile of boxes and jumped off, landing on her hind legs. "Not like Larry, right doc?" she said, brushing by him.

The doctor stammered. She moved up to Larry who stood with both hands on the table, gulping. Blood had begun to make lakes across the floor.

"Come on Larry," she said softly. He couldn't bring himself to look at the bodies. Trying not to think he gripped the spitter in his right hand and followed his co-pilot.

His numbness was shaken when he heard a sudden scuffling behind him. He turned at the same moment as Napoleon to see Dr. Weinstein-Hubbell bringing up a beamer from the arms of a dead military man. Automatically Larry's right hand raised, the spitter aimed at the doctor's torso. Their eyes met, the creator and the created. The man-God and the less-than-even-man.

Larry hesitated for a second. Enough time to see that Weinstein-Hubbell was not firing because he felt something for his creation, not because some sort of responsible emotion flickered deep in his pupils, not because he wanted Larry to have a last moment of dignity, but because he didn't know how to work the weapon.

In that moment, Larry wanted to die. He wanted to be paralyzed, then cut up, then set to work for the rest of his life, not knowing the wiser.

But as that endless period ended, a row of bright tubes spread by his left side and disappeared into Weinstein-Hubbell's chest. He fell back simply, without ceremony, dead. A human god gone on to whatever reward a higher form had destined. Be it all or nothing. Meanwhile the creation must continue.

Napoleon, lowering her weapon, took Larry's elbow and pulled. "It's not worth any thought," she said. "Come on."

Larry turned and ran. For all the drama of their first meeting with the reality of death, it was a fairly quiet affair. The noise of their weapons was low and no screams from the dying were heard. The only major clatter was the piece of metal hitting the floor when Larry had fired his weapon. In the huge warehouse the sound echoed and disappeared, heard only by the dead.

The two survivors ran and ran until they came to a door leading outside. There Larry finally stopped and thought.

"Did you find anything?" he puffed to Napoleon.

"No," she replied, the only sign of exertion being her chest and sides moving in and out, collecting more oxygen through her nostrils. "How about you?"

"No," he reported. Between gasps he said, "Our only chance now is the spaceport."

"But the military is bound to be waiting for us there," said Napoleon.

"But there's bound to be a warp drive there, too," Larry reminded her.

They both fell silent. Without a faster than light engine they couldn't hope to outrun an Earth Ship destroyer or even reach Destiny within their lifetimes. Napoleon began to work out strategy, Larry tried to understand that he would have to kill again, without question, without fail.

Was it worth it? He looked at Napoleon whose head was lowered deep in concentration. He looked around him. He decided yes, it was worth it. Or else why did he deserve to leave? If he survived, then life had meaning. If he died, he wouldn't care. It wasn't much, but it was all that was.

He nudged Napoleon. She looked up at him. He nodded. They were off.

Brown hair and blondie loved it. To them it was like a dream come true. How often had brown hair massacred Larry and others like him at the dream factories? How often had blondie raped Napoleon? Countless, countless times.

Ever since the first time the guards had met the two, the alien and the test tube man, they were obsessions to the pair of military officials. Their lives revolved around the reentry, and the destined outcome of their taunting—the pilots' destruction at the hands of the pair's goading.

Neither would admit their latent hatred or envy. Hatred that the cat was a free female and envy that the artificial warranted her company. But now, after they heard about Masterdon-Barnes' murder, they liked to think that they had contributed in some small way to the cat's act. After all, they figured, she was female, she was less than human, and a real man was only exercising his rights in taking her.

And to add to their satisfaction, she was a dangerous fugitive and her associate was under suspicion. No one kills a top Government official and gets away with it. Not in this day and age. Not if brown hair and blondie had anything to do with it. If they ever got their hands on the criminals they would teach them. And by all means, they intended to.

"She's a fugitive, right?" asked Blondie.

"Right," said Brown hair.

"So what is she going to do?"

"Run to her little freak friend?"

"No, he can't offer her protection."

"Hide somewhere?"

"Not for long. Wolf-Hoover'll hunt her down."

Brown hair laughed, thinking that was the end of the discussion.

"Naw, naw, naw," blondie continued. "She'll come back here."

"Why?" asked brown hair, getting back into it.

"Her escape pod is here, right? Her ship is in orbit, right? The only way to get away is up and out, right?"

"Right! So?"

"So, the three enforcers are in the Spaceport. But if you were a desperate fugitive, would you go through . . . or around?"

"Oh. I get you. You think she'll try to take off without preparations."

Blondie smiled broadly. "Right."

"So what do you want to do about it?"

"Why don't we take a little walk outside?" blondie suggested innocently.

"Don't mind if I do," said brown hair.

The two military men moved to the one area it seemed logical for their quarry to use. A patch of bush that lined a side of the concrete landing area. It was more than eight feet tall, grey on one side from the constant beating it took during take-offs, and kept the field and forest beyond from Spaceport sight. Blondie and brown hair considered it the only logical alternative to walking into the terminal and waving hello.

They beat around the bush heavily, commenting and laughing raucously at their own jokes. They both carried personal stun guns, weapons that sent out bright white bolts of light, usually rendering a victim unconscious with a massive shock to the nervous system. They matched the personality of their users since they offered no peace of death and caused headaches and vomiting days afterwards.

"We've got to hide somewhere," said brown hair.

"Why?" said blondie enjoying himself.

"Because if we keep making this much noise they will steer clear of this place."

"Naw, they don't have a choice. They'd be walking in full view of the visual pick-ups. The military enforcers would peg them instantly."

"Why do you think they haven't covered this place themselves, if it's such a great alternative?" asked brown hair, checking a bush for hiding space.

"There's only three of them," blondie said expansively. "They were told to cover the Spaceport, so they're covering the Spaceport. Men under Wolf-Hoover rarely get independent."

"Here, here," said brown hair, pointing to a large bunch of bush. "There's a space inside where we can sit. I can see it."

Blondie went over and circled the growth. "We can see all around. All right. Let's get in."

Brown hair moved to the other side, grabbed two handfuls of thin branch and pulled them aside. In the space opened was the head of Larry Baker.

Brown hair stared in surprise as an arm grew out of the side of the head and then a fist filled his vision. Something harder then flesh smashed into his face, he staggered back and fell. Blondie stumbled to the side to avoid his unconscious friend and grappled with his holster. The stunner came up in his hand, then fell when his hand suddenly ripped open.

Larry bound out of the bush and his arm swung again. Before blondie could shout in pain, metal crashed against his neck and he fell. After Napoleon had slashed blondie's hand she turned her attention to the cringing brown hair. She clubbed him with the butt of her stinger. He lay still.

Neither the two military men nor the three enforcers knew about the deaths of their associates at the lab. They were not taking into consideration Napoleon's and Larry's need for speed. Once the murders were discovered, all bets were off. Napoleon stopped being a pawn in a cover-up, and Larry stopped being a suspected accomplice. The two would become psychotic desperados, a condition rarely seen and never tolerated. They had to get the engine fast and get out.

Without a word Napoleon began to move.

"Wait," said Larry. "Can you fire this stunner?"

She looked at the device built for a human hand.

"Just barely. Aiming it and holding onto it would be a problem. Why?"

"I feel bad enough without having to shoot bystanders. If we have to fight, we had better use these inside," Larry said, motioning to the Spaceport.

Napoleon sniffed indifferently. "If I have to hold on to a weapon, I'd rather it be this," she said, brandishing the spitter.

"Use this holster," said Larry, pointing to the prone blondie, whose hand was still bleeding. Napoleon looked at the body in disgust, then pushed it over and started to unbuckle the leathery strap. Larry did the same to brown hair's holster.

They were soon ready. In one hand they carried the spitters. Low on their hips were slung the stunners. Napoleon's other hand hung at her side. Larry's other hand still held the piece of closed-off tubing he had used in the lab for leverage and on the back of blondie's neck. He peeked through the remaining bushes. Before him lay the landing area, and beyond that an open hangar area, reserved for repairs.

"We'll have to run using the landed craft as a cover," said Larry. "Then, once inside we find an engine and a ground vehicle to haul it. Then we get over to our pod and take off."

"Easy," said Napoleon sarcastically.

"Look, this is hard enough as it is," snapped Larry.

She moved beside him quickly and rubbed her shoulder against his arm. "Sorry, Larry. I'm just loosening my tail." She pointed toward the field beyond. "If we keep near cover, we'll be all right. Visual pick-ups and stun rays can't go through things."

Larry nodded. The sooner they got out of there the sooner they could come to grips with what they were doing. It wasn't guilt—they didn't owe the Earth anything. It was confusion. Death seemed so alien, but it came to them both so easily. Pushing all the thoughts out of his mind, Larry ran toward the nearest ship. Napoleon ran directly behind him. They repeated this maneuver five more times, weaving from carft to craft, trying to imagine where the visual pick-ups were aimed.

Their next run took them into the repair area. Night had been on their side, but not it was close to morning. A whole new shift would begin the new day. With any luck they would be programmed only for their prime functions, not to question trespassers. Three thread robots were moving on the other side of the area and Larry could see no humans, real or manufactured.

The two ran the length of the hanger, between standing vehicles and tables of equipment, looking for some sort of warp device. It would have helped, certainly, if they had known what one looked like. Larry heard Napoleon's hiss and found her behind a table on which a machine rested, looking a lot like the engine that Larry had investigated at the lab. Napoleon glanced around nervously as Larry checked it over.

"It looks like an engine," he finally whispered. "It has parts I recognize. And the core could be a warp device."

"You mean you're not sure?" Napoleon asked incredulously. After all he had built his own ship. Larry shook his head.

"Let's take it anyway and get out," said the feline, still wary of her surroundings.

"We should look around some more," said Larry. "To make sure."

"We have no time!" Napoleon whispered harshly.

"We have no choice!" Larry said back. "We won't have a second chance up there."

Napoleon did not reply. She just took off. Larry did the same in the opposite direction. The sun had begun to rise, sending yellow shadows across the area that was, until then, bathed in light blue. It didn't make their search any easier, however. Instead it hid many items in shadow and added a greater note of panic to the proceedings. The two finally found each other back at the same table.

"I still say this one," said Napoleon.

"I reluctantly agree with you," said Larry. "I found what I think we can use as transport over on the other side there. Come on."

They ran over to where a rectangular affair on six wheels lay. On either front end was a small cubicle outfitted with a seat, two levers, and two pedals, the other with what looked like exposed wiring coming out of three tubes in the floor.

"I think you're right," said Napoleon. "It can be driven by either human or machine."

"But not feline," said Larry, "Get in that end. I'll try to figure out this thing."

She had little choice. A yellow beam hit the vehicle entrance directly above her head, vibrating the metal and numbing her left paw which had gripped it to get in.

She whirled to see three enforcers racing toward them, weapons raised, trying to squeeze in a second shot. She didn't let them. Her spitter sent them leaping for cover. Larry jumped into the human control cubicle and pulled both levers. Nothing happened.

Napoleon filled the room with deadly tubes of high intensity light, drilling perfect holes in machinery and the floor. One enforcer sat to the left behind an Earth ship whose front end was beginning to look like Swiss cheese, another lay to the right behind a solid metal table, and the third stood back inside the entrance.

They all had to shift position continually or risk Napoleon getting a bead on them and dotting their hides. Larry pushed down both pedals with his feet. Nothing happened.

The third enforcer unwisely chose to try to catch Napoleon with a paralytic ray rather than run back for reinforcements and got a perfect hole in his arm for his trouble. She followed up by airing his legs on her sweepover to keep the enforcer behind the ship at bay.

"You know," she said to herself. "It is going to occur to them to use gas in a little while."

Larry moved the right lever and the left pedal. Nothing happened.

Napoleon hopped into the machine cubicle for extra cover while panning across the table, making the machinery jump by weakening the metal's structural strength. Under the weight of the spare parts, the surface began to buckle. The enforcer beneath knew he was going to have to run for it.

The enforcer behind the ship knew it too. He bravely moved slightly into the open and started laying down a blanket of stun rays to cover his partner. Napoleon moved her aim over to him. The enforcer on the right took the opportunity, not to run, but to aim a beam directly at Napoleon's midriff.

Larry pulled the left lever and pushed the right pedal. The vehicle moved.

Suddenly it began to swing to the left. The beam from the enforcer by the table hit harmlessly between the two driving cubicles, while Napoleon's deadly beams missed the enforcer behind the ship, cutting instead deeper into the machinery. Larry kept his foot on the right pedal and pulled back to the left lever. The vehicle moved straight to the left toward the table with the engine.

"I'll have to block the engine with the vehicle," Larry shouted. "I won't be able to defend myself while I collect the thing."

"Why should anything change?" said Napoleon through her teeth, still firing to keep the enforcers from following. "I'm having a great time."

Larry reached down quickly and grabbed his own spitter. A stun gun would hardly serve in this situation. As he neared the table he released the right pedal and pushed forward the two levers. The vehicle returned to its original direction and kept going.

The enforcers immediately leapt from their positions and started firing. Napoleon howled in fear and rage. Larry pulled back the left lever and pushed the left pedal. They swung to the left and stopped dead.

Napoleon spat in frustration and howled as she began firing both weapons, one in each hand. She seemed to be ignoring any difficulties with the human stun gun. The enforcers had managed in the interim to move their positions up to a wall of equipment stretching across most of the area. They could keep their location relatively secret and fire from several heights.

Larry quickly pushed down the right pedal and the vehicle moved forward. The air was filled with the stun beams. Napoleon angrily returned the fire, having to swing her weapon in wide arcs. Larry brought the vehicle in toward the table, pulling the left lever until they were at right angles to it, giving Napoleon better cover from the enforcer's beams but at the same time limiting her ability to fire.

The enforcer's location was too far to the left, behind them. They could cover the area with their beams, but the two fugitives would have to show themselves to fire back. Larry was planning to use this beam strategy. He poked his head out of his side to see that the table was even with the bed of the vehicle. Larry lifted his weight from the right pedal and pushed down the left. The truck stopped.

Immediately Larry leaped out. Immediately the air was filled with stun beams. They hit the floor, the table top, the vehicle's bed, and the roofs of the cubicles. Napoleon sprayed the air with her spitter while Larry jumped back into his cubicle.

"Let's go!" she cried.

"We need that engine!" he shouted back.

And they had to get it before they were hit by the paralytic rays, before gas could be used, and before the enforcers realized it was the engine that they should destroy. Larry looked back. The flat-bed area of the vehicle was between the wheels, low, near the ground. The rim of the four-legged table was already over the edge of the vehicle.

"Get ready," he shouted to Napoleon. "If this works or not we'll be getting out of here!" Maybe Harlan's warp drive could be fixed and adapted.

He looked at the levers. Sure enough there was space to move them to the side, then *forward*. Larry grabbed his spitter and spun around. He stuck the weapon outside the cubicle and fired, slicing across the legs of the table. The left legs splintered and broke. The table fell in that direction, dumping everything on top into the bed of the vehicle, including the engine, which slid, then rolled in.

"Hold on!" yelled Larry, dropping the spitter in the cubicle and hauling the levers to the side. Napoleon gripped the side of the cubicle with one paw and anchored her legs as Larry shoved the levers forward and jammed down the right pedal.

The vehicle rushed backwards. Larry pulled the right lever back a bit. The vehicle turned right. Suddenly the two were facing the enforcers, moving away quickly. Together they riddled the wall of equipment with rays. Somehow, somewhere, a collection of holes weakened the bottom, collapsing it in on itself. And, in a chain reaction, all the machinery began to topple.

The two pilots watched, still firing, as huge chunks of metal crashed to the floor, smashing and pieces flying off in all directions. They saw one enforcer run back to the entrance, leaping through just as a hunk of metal crashed where he had been a moment before. The other enforcer was not so lucky.

He was standing on top of the heap, hoping to get a clear shot, when it fell. He fell as well, sandwiched between two bulbous plates. Thankfully, Larry only saw him bouncing off the one below him. The second fell on top, covering Baker's view. But there was little doubt that the man was completely crushed.

Larry tore his eyes from the spectacle and looked back, trying to locate their pod. As they sped out into the sunlight he spied it near the end of the take-off area. Thankfully if he just moved the left lever a bit they could head right for it.

"Napoleon!" he yelled over to her. "The hatch! The hatch! Open the hatch!"

She looked over to see him pointing toward the pod. Dropping her spitter on the cubicle floor she jumped out, onto the paved ground, and sped on all fours toward the escape pod. Thankfully for her the flat-bed vehicle wasn't very fast and she out-distanced it, arriving at the pod flushed, tail high in the air, but several seconds before it. Rising quickly she pulled open a large hatch.

At that moment Larry slammed both feet on the left pedal. All six wheels locked, the vehicle skidded a few feet, Larry working the levers to keep it straight, and then stopped. The payload did not.

The smaller parts flew inside the pod as Napoleon spun away to avoid getting hit. The engine slid, rolled, then bounced right onto one of the pod's chairs crushing it, but hardly touching the control board.

"By CHESHIRE!" she shrieked.

Larry ran up, his arms full with his two weapons and the closed-off tube, and jumped in. He threw his stuff on the floor and hopped into the other seat.

Napoleon jumped in after him and sealed the hatch. She hardly had time to check the other two doors when Larry contacted Mess and initiated lift-off. She hurled herself to the floor before centrifugal force did it for her. The Black Hole's escape pod blasted into the sky.

At the same time Mess was automatically sending their larger salvage vehicle back to the ship from outside the late Weinstein-Hubbell's lab.

Larry grinned. He had made it. A decision he had made by necessity only a few hours ago was now an unavoidable fact of his future. Suddenly he had a destiny, a chance. Like it or not, come what may, he was free. He decided again, without haste, that the only way Earth would claim him again would be in death.

Harlan was waiting for them as they pulled themselves out of the tunnel into the passageway of the Black Hole.

"What happened? Did you get it? Do you know where my sister is?"

Larry ignored him, pulling off his shirt in triumph and shouting over his shoulder, "Mess, status!"

"In what way, status?" came the computer's retort, dampening Larry's heroic swagger. "What do you mean, status?"

"You ton of tin-plated trouble! The ship! Is it spaceworthy?"

"Of course it is. What do you think, I've been playing with myself up here?"

"The salvage craft?"

"Returned and tucked in."

"Any approaching craft?"

"None. If any do come, do I have permission to fire?" Larry could not be sure whether Mess' voice held fear or anticipation.

"Let me know if anything shows up, then ask again."

"Right," said Mess. It was anticipation.

"Did you get the engine?" Harlan pressed.

"Mess," Larry said in reply, "There's a hunk of machinery where the co-pilot's seat used to be in the pod. Get it, and everything else, moved over to the engine area."

By the time the trio reached the engineering section the floor was littered with debris. Larry retrieved his spitter and the metal tube he had used in the lab and as a club on the two military men. Admidst the pile of rubble sat the hunk of engine they had risked their lives for. Harlan faced Larry, beaming from ear to ear.

"You have it," he said. "I recognize the design."

Larry and Napoleon relaxed visibly. Up until this moment they weren't sure what they had.

"Great," said Larry, pointing over Harlan's shoulder to the hunk of machinery. "How soon can you install that thing?"

Harlan glanced around. "That? I can't install that. That's not an O'Neil drive."

"What?" Larry exploded. "Then, then what is?"

"That," said Harlan, pointing at the metal tube in Larry's hand. "*That's* a warp drive."

FIVE

The Black Hole was not a very pleasant place for the next few minutes. As Harlan settled into the engine area and began preliminary tests to ascertain whether a complete or partial transference could be made to warp drive, Napoleon paced, her tail lashing, and Larry stood against a bulkhead, breathing shallowly.

He'd take a few large breaths everytime he'd get woozy, then breath shallowly again. The whole idea that he was at the mercy of a piece of closed metal tubing that he had been using as a club was annoying. His annoyance was compounded by the possibility of imminent destruction by Earth ships of the Destroyer class just at the moment freedom was at hand. To have to die after killing was a terrible thought. Each second was too long, each minute made up of too many of those too-long seconds. Too soon, Mess interrupted.

"Ship approaching. Permission to fire."

Larry glanced at Harlan, who worked obliviously, then straightened. "Not yet. What kind of ship?"

"An Earth Ship. Warrior class."

Larry felt a little better. At least it would be a one-on-one fight. A Destroyer had the capability of an armada of Warriors.

"Followed by a Destroyer," Mess finished.

"What? What? You said ship, singular!" Larry shouted.

"It was appearing on the screen as I was talking," said Mess. "Sorry. Permission to fire."

"On a Destroyer? Are you kidding? No!"

Napoleon stopped pacing near Larry. "Should I move to the weapon area?"

"No," said Larry. "Not yet. Mess, what are they doing?"

"As near as I can tell they are stopping in the same formation. Warrior before, Destroyer behind. Permission to fire, please."

"No. Stopping? Why are they stopping?" Larry asked aloud. Napoleon remained at his side. Harlan kept working. "Mess, are they sending a message?"

"Well," Mess seemed reluctant to say. "Yes."

"Why didn't you say that?" Larry exploded.

"I knew you had a lot on your mind," said Mess.

"You knew nothing! You space-happy system of soggy sensors! You wanted to fire and run. A message would have gotten in your way."

"No, really . . ." said Mess.

"Listen to me, Mess," said Larry. "Shooting at a Destroyer is tantamount to self-destruction. You don't want to be destroyed, do you?"

"No."

"Then put through that message!"

Mess declined to reply; instead, a voice that could best be described as "civilized" filled the engine room.

"Earth Ship Black Hole, Black Hole come in please. Answer, if you will."

Larry tried to think quickly, succeeding at the act but not coming up with anything to show for it. He looked at Napoleon who shrugged.

Still working, Harlan snarled, "Stall. Stall for time. I can patch in partial use, which will give us a head start, then install the rest."

"Mess," Larry called. "Pick up and return Napoleon's voice only."

"Me?" she mewed. "What'll I say?"

"You want me to transmit that last statement?" Mess asked politely.

"No, not that. Wait until I tell you," Larry shouted, then

turned to his co-pilot. "Give him a story. Make something up. Just keep him going for a while."

"Wonderful. You're a great help," she said. Larry squeezed her arm. "All right, all right. I'll think of something."

"Now?" said Mess. Napoleon nodded at Larry.

"Now," he said.

Napoleon's usually strong voice suddenly became plaintive and panicky. Her strong shoulders hunched and Larry could see her stomach muscles bunching.

"Hello, hello," she cried in a wail. "This is the Black Hole, who is this?"

"This is the Earth Destroyer Constellation, young lady," returned the cultured voice. "We have been informed that a female feline and a Weinstein-Hubbell creation have been responsible for the deaths of seven people, five of them military, one scientific, and one Governmental. What do you know about these grave charges?" The voice seemed unconcerned with the possible pun inherent in his last words.

"He made me do it!" Napoleon yelled. "I didn't want to. He just went crazy!"

"Is this the creation you are talking about?" returned the voice.

"Yes, yes. He just started killing!"

"My dear," soothed the voice. "A creation can not go crazy."

Napoleon grimaced, but continued nevertheless. "This one did! He's different. He was given a full mind, not like the rest. It was awful, just awful." She had lowered her voice and gave just the inflection of a sob at the end.

A masterful performance, Larry decided, but then she had been giving performances all her life to lust-soaked humans.

There was a short pause from the Constellation, then the voice resumed. "Is this the Baker individual?"

"Yes, yes!"

"I have been informed that what you say has some bearing. And, unless he managed to find another young female along the way or altered his computer's voice, you would be Napoleon, the feline companion?"

"He made me, I tell you!"

"I shall assume that is an affirmative. You say he made you join him on this heinous crime?"

"Yes. Please, please help me."

Harlan continued to work feverishly, hanging below from a metal awning, but he couldn't resist smiling. The feline was doing it up perfectly.

"We shall do our level best," said the refined voice. "However, I have been advised that there may not be complete truth in what you say. According to my reports you seemed to be firing an illegal weapon quite independently. And quite well, too, I've been informed."

Nepoleon bit her lower lip in frustration before going on. "He had a spitter on me! I couldn't help it!"

"And I have one of the gentlemen you were firing at with me, and he says, and I quote, 'That is a lot of Mantas meat.' Unquote."

Napoleon turned helplessly to Larry, her arms out. Larry looked at Harlan. Harlan kept working.

"I'm afraid the evidence is against you, my dear," said the voice. "Number one, it would be hard for him to drive the spaceport vehicle and keep you captive at the same time. Two, you were seen on a video pick-up, running ahead of the vehicle. And three, Baker was known to be at the scene of the second five murders when the first was taking place. I'm sorry but I'm afraid I must deliver an ultimatum."

"Just a little while longer," Larry heard Harlan say. "Just a bit more time." Larry made a circular motion with his arm. Napoleon raised her paws, shaking her head.

"You must surrender immediately," said the voice. "Or we shall be forced to annihilate you. The Baker person can be recreated if there is any inclination, but you, my dear, are one of a kind. It would be a shame, but it would be necessary."

"I tell you I want to give up!" Napoleon screamed, her face screwed up in an expression that showed anything but capitulation. "I'm sure the authorities will understand if I explain, but I can't! He won't let me! He has all the weapons and he's completely insane. Can't you understand? I'm in fear for my life!"

"My heart goes out to you," said the voice. "But not my mind. You leave me little choice. Surrender or nothing."

Harlan pushed his hand out, once, twice, three times. Larry opened his palms up, in a "what can you do?" sort of gesture.

"All right. We surrender," said Napoleon.

"A wise decision," said the voice in a tone like he had expected it all the time. "We will dock and board within three minutes. I look forward to meeting you, my dear. I hear you are extraordinary. Earth Destroyer Constellation breaking contact."

Napoleon snarled at the air.

Larry said to Harlan, "Well?"

"We may have just enough time," he replied, not stopping for a second. "Get to the control area. Give me until the last moment before docking, then hit the engines full. If it works we might make it. If not, we'll be blasted out of space in seconds."

Larry and Napoleon looked at each other. Mess put their feelings into words.

"Terrific."

The two took off to the bridge. Larry threw one look back to see Harlan still working with incredible speed. But then the thin pilot was out of the engine area and running after the receding form of Napoleon. She had dropped to her forepaws and was moving through the cramped hallways on all fours, her tail high.

Larry pushed his legs faster, over shooting turns, sliding and careening off the walls. By the time he stumbled into the bridge the feline was engaging all the visual pick-ups.

The four screens, stretching from the pilot's to the co-pilot's area, were filled with the metallic expanse of the Warrior ship. Like four walls closing in on them. Before moving to his seat, Larry stood next to Harlan's space bullet suit and looked around. Before him spun the Earth. Behind him was the blazing sun, its possibly devastating effects on the neural centers dampened by the automatic mechanics of the ship. And on either side was the galaxy. Larry moved forward.

"Mess, approximate time of docking," he said from his console.

"What about it?" was the machine's reply.

Larry silently reprimanded himself for taking the computer for granted. Through clenched teeth he gritted, "When-will-it-occur?"

"Approximately," Mess seemed to stress. "Thirty-six point two seconds from now."

Larry ignored the sarcasm. Too much was at stake. "Start a visual countdown," he instructed. A small panel lit up beneath all four screens, the illuminated symbol for thirty-five appeared, and started regressing immediately.

Thirty-four, thirty-three, thirty-two . . .

"Have you included an area of risk?" Larry asked, eying the numbers.

"Of course," said Mess. "But wouldn't it be much easier to simply blast . . ."

"Never mind," said Larry. He watched the visual pick-ups, thinking, hoping, that the computer was just blowing off steam. Out of the portholes and on the screens all the stars were blotted out by the now-solid wall of the Warrior ship. Just beyond lay the Constellation, hanging in space like a mother hawk waiting for her offspring to bring home dinner.

But the Warrior's approach was slow, slower than usual, not the swooping triumph they had expected. Larry suddenly realized that it was because he and Napoleon had killed seven people with speed and deliberation. If he had been told of any creature doing that he would have considered the motive to be insanity. Then if he had been informed that he was to be responsible for the creature's capture, his approach would be as cautious and slow as the Warrior's.

Twenty-five, twenty-four, twenty-three, twenty-two . . .

Larry sat down and engaged his controls. The engine switch sat like a coiled snake by his left hand, waiting to strike. He wrapped his fingers around the metal viper. Ignition a second too soon would give the Destroyer time to blast them. Ignition a second too late would catch the Warrior docked. Warp speed would probably rip off a weak section of the Black Hole's hull and send them spinning into the cold vacuum of space.

Larry could almost feel the slimy scales beneath his palm. It was sweat sliding down the slick switch. His fingers tightened as the Warrior grew larger in the screens and out the portholes. He glanced from side to side. Napoleon stood by her chair watching the countdown.

"Better sit down," he said quickly. "We don't know how this drive'll work."

"*If* it works," said the co-pilot, moving quickly to the front of her chair.

Fifteen, fourteen, thirteen, twelve . . .

"You should have let me fire," chided Mess shrilly, then started verbalizing the countdown. "Ten, nine, eight . . ."

The Warrior was only feet away, moving up for the final docking.

"Seven, six, five . . ."

Harlan still worked feverishly in the engine area. Mess' voice boomed throughbout the ship.

"Four, three, two . . ."

Harlan swung up to his feet as Larry's hand started to move on the other side of the ship.

"One, zero."

Larry's arm moved back.

Harlan pushed himself forward as a blinding white light filled the area. The flash was silent but extremely powerful. Harlan was sent rolling across the floor. Even with his incredible muscle coordination he wound up in a ball against the wall.

Larry blinked and the Black Hole was somewhere else. There was no sudden thrust, no centrifugal force, no unbearable pressure, not even a queasy stomach, nary a vibration of movement. Here was no warp drive. This was beyond warping space for travel.

Napoleon did not blink and was watching the screens when it happened. One second the Warrior equipment filled their view, the next stars sped by like solid beams of white. There was no Destroyer, no Earth, and no moon before their stunned faces. They were somewhere else and still moving. Moving fast.

"Incredible. Absolutely incredible," said Napoleon.

"Mess," Larry found his voice. "Is it all right? Can you

handle it?" If the computer got overloaded they might find themselves flattened against a comet.

"Wow, this is great!" said the computer.

"Can you handle it?" Larry repeated.

"Sure," said Mess euphorically. "After so many supply runs it's an absolute rush."

"A rush?" Larry echoed quizzically, turning to Napoleon. "What's a rush?"

Napoleon grinned. "It's a drug term. I hear tell Dr. Palsy-Drake was something of a drug addict near the end of his career."

"He wasn't an addict!" shouted Mess. "He could stop at any time!"

The reverie was interrupted by Trigor who strode in, shaking his hands, his fingers sailing in the wind like loose springs nailed to a fence. The faster-than-life drive was so powerful his limbs were still buzzing.

"That was no warp drive," said Larry to him.

"By no means," said Harlan curtly. "This is hardly a quarter of its full power, and although we caught the other ships by surprise they should be able to catch up in a short time."

"How?" wailed Larry.

"Gradations," said Harlan simply. "They can accelerate. We can't. Yet."

"Mess, how soon will they catch up?" asked Napoleon.

"I have to calibrate the new speeds," said the computer. "Let's see now, follow the six, carry the two . . ."

Harlan laughed in spite of himself.

Napoleon, used to the machine's quirks, snapped, "Go ahead, laugh. But in a few minutes we'll be back in the same position as we started. Only at faster speeds."

"Seventeen minutes, twenty-six seconds, to be a bit more exact," said Mess.

"Can you connect the other seventy-five percent in time?" chimed in Larry.

"Not in time," said Harlan. "No."

Larry stared at him. What was it all for then? The killing, the escape? He couldn't stare at Trigor's passive face. He turned to stare instead at the sun. Through the tempered porthole glass it shone black with its rays giving off unnatural colors, colors that danced across a rainbow's spectrum. It was the source, the giver of life and a harbinger of death.

And its trap was snapping shut again. This star, named Sol, kept its prisoner called Earth alive. He had thought they were free, but they had only gained a temporary intermission. He was beginning to think that he would never escape the snare of the doom star.

"So there's no hope," he said to the burning mass of gas. He turned back to see Harlan looking honestly surprised.

"Certainly there's hope. I am here," he said.

"But you said that you couldn't connect the rest of the engine's power in time!" Napoleon exploded.

"It is true that I cannot unleash the rest of the device's might with the limited tools on board, but I did not mean to give the impression that I was beaten."

"You didn't mean to give that impression?" said Napoleon increduously. "What other choices do we have? Dismantle the ship for the Constellation? Put on space suits and sneak out the back?"

"We are wasting time," said Harlan, strongly. "Your suits I will not need. Only my own."

"It seems to me that you could be a little clearer," interjected Mess.

Harlan chuckled.

"He's laughing again," said Napoleon, throwing up her paws and turning away.

"You mean," said Larry. "Fighting a Destroyer in that thing?" He pointed at the hulk of space bullet.

Harlan nodded. "In a bit I will be ready. I can defeat both ships. Then I can connect the drive and we can be on our way."

"In that thing?" Larry repeated, his voice rising. Even though Harlan had arrived alive across hundred of thousands of light years in it, the reality still didn't seem possible. One man? Against two Earth Ships? "Listen, I don't know what kind of ships you're used to, but a Destroyer? They have weapons . . . why, they can . . . I mean . . ."

"I am not asking your permission," Harlan interrupted briskly. "I am requesting and will require your aid. This is the situation. I will fight, regardless, whether you are destroyed in the process is up to you!"

"Please elaborate," Mess immediately interrupted. "Quickly."

"It will take me longer to suit up than we have time for. I must test my repairs. The Warrior and Destroyer must be kept at bay until I exit."

"You don't have a chance," Napoleon began.

"*He* doesn't have a chance?" Mess piped in stridently. "*We* don't have a chance, you mean."

"It seems as if this is our *only* chance," Larry interrupted, touching the feline's arm, though still staring at Trigor's impassive face. "If you want to commit suicide, the least we can do is join you." He then turned to the computer's console. "Start a visual countdown to the time the Earth ships will be in range," he instructed.

Fifteen minutes and twenty-six seconds appeared in the boxes below the four screens. Larry faced Napoleon.

"Here we go again," then he turned to Harlan. "Well? What are *you* waiting for?"

The man with the civilized voice sat in his control chair amidst the largest array of destructive weapons he knew of. It was a very secure feeling. In his role of Commander on one of Earth's four Destroyers, he was privileged to be in one of the highest positions of the Earth hierarchy, and he looked it.

Silver hair, artificial both in color and composition, swept back across his head. Molded features, the best the land-bound scientists could chisel, sat across his visage. A supple body, as much the work of his tailor as of exercise, sat on an individually contoured seat.

The only evidence of his original nature lay in his hands. On first glance they appeared as rugged and as strong as the rest of him, but on closer examination it could be discerned that this was exterior painting, natural flesh tones highlighted to make them appear hewn.

Actually they were naturally soft and hardly lined. Hair had been added to the backs and behind the first knuckles to further the deception. Still, he never shook hands and had others do whatever manual labor that was required. Among the highest of the military it was rumored that if he were stuck in a room with two exits that had only doorknobs, he would never be seen again.

These rumors never reached his ears, however. He was, after all, the Commander of a Destroyer, capable of incredible devastation at a mention. He cared little for the prattling of others. He cared even less for the prattling that was reaching his ears at the present time.

"This is entirely unfair," said the voice in a deep whine. "It's unnecessary, foolish, and endangering the lives of true humans."

The man with the civilized voice listened, hardly believing that such a deep whine could be created. He pictured the speaker. Obese, sparse blondish hair standing out in tufts on a pale, speckled head, a roll of fat waddling over his waistband as he leaned forward in his command chair, jowls flapping back and forth as he complained, his face a bowl of sweat.

"In moments we will be in visual contact," continued the deep whine. "Then, who knows what will happen. I respectfully request again to drop back and let your own Destroyer handle the destruction procedures."

The grey-maned Commander leaned forward and spoke, his voice resonant.

"Stuck-Mark, be reasonable. You are hardly in any danger. It is a small vessel . . ."

"With two murderers on board!" the quavering bass interrupted.

"But this is our territory now," continued the man with the civilized voice. "We rule the Earth space. No other ship can match us."

"Did you see when they took off? I was in the space lock! If we docked it would have been disaster!"

"For them, only for them," continued the Destroyed Commander, gently. "My dear Stuck-Mark, did you *see* their vessle? A patchwork affair, a paltry example of inferior craftsmanship."

"But who knows what devices they had hidden on board?" quaked the fat Captain. "They have the light drive . . ."

"Stolen from an Earth lab," soothed the Commander. "Badly installed. Still, we will catch up and destroy them."

"But can't you lead? Why must we face them first? It is unnecessary, it is endangering the lives of true . . ."

"Yes, yes, I know," the Commander sighed. "Tell you what. When the other ship gets into visual contact, why don't you relinquish command to your second and come over here?" The Commander knew that Stuck-Mark's first mate was an artificial, created for robotlike navigation of the ship.

"Do you think I should? Would it be all right, do you think?"

"Of course, of course. Consider it a training device for your men. Elucidate on the importance of our mission, then drag your butt over here."

"Thank you Commander. Thank you very much," said the deep voice.

"Not at all," said the Commander, breaking the connection, then barking, "Corman-Heath!" A short, curly-haired man appeared beside the central chair.

"Yes, sir."

"Please handle Stuck-Mark's situation when we sight the Black Hole."

"Yes, sir."

"Get him to the transfer point, then tell him something's wrong with our space lock and cut communications. With any luck he'll be stuck in there while his crew does the rest."

"Yes, sir. Do you think he'll try to jettison sir?"

"He'll dare not. Even that idiotic coward would rather face possible death then certain death. If he instructs his crew to retreat, either I will blast him, or a Governmental Board will assign him to labor duties."

"Then there is a chance the killer's ship is dangerous, sir?"

"Of course. Why do you think I'm having that idiot be in the lead? The Warrior will take whatever that flying junkyard dishes out and then we'll know what we are dealing with."

"But surely that ship is not capable of harming a Warri— . . ." the ensign began.

"They have killed seven true humans!" the Commander cried. "Try to understand that, Corman-Heath. I know you are young and that murder of true humans is incredible but it has been done. *They* did it. Who knows what they are capable of?"

The curly-haired aide pondered that for a moment then spoke slowly, still uncomprehending. "Sir, if they do indeed fire upon the Warrior, what will you do?"

The Commander rubbed his soft hands across his sculptured face, letting his erect body relax into the contours of his chair.

"First we received word that the labs wanted both subjects alive for test purposes. They felt they could eradicate the violent urges in all artificials permanently. Then I get a priority call from the Government office of Linn-Bok who instructs me that the pair and their ship are to be eradicated at all costs.

"It seems that he had gotten word that their murder spree and light-drive robbery are only the surface to a much greater danger. Where he received this information and from whom, is beyond me."

The Commander fell silent and Corman-Heath concentrated on his words while the artificials around them tended to the needs of the ship. The time of reckoning was at hand. Weapons were readied. Tactics were programmed. Plans of attack were considered and prepared. Lights lit. Flashers flashed, alarms sounded, all automatically.

"Sir," Corman-Heath repeated. "What will you do if the Warrior is fired upon?"

"What I always do," said the Commander. "Exactly what I want."

"Enemy ship sighted, sir," said a voice.

"There they are!" shouted Mess.

Larry was off and running. He passed Harlan whose head stuck out of his space bullet, facing forward, facial muscles flickering as he tested his suit. Larry moved out the rear hatch, sped down the hallway, took a right, a quick left, then another right, coming to another hatch. He spun open the door and stepped into a rectangular room.

Directly before him was a small, slatted window above a small escape hatch. To his right was a six- by two-and-a-half-foot slatted window facing the front of the ship. Lying across the length of the right side of the room was a console table with no chair. Right next to the door he had entered was a large stick switch. To his left was a wall on which a space suit was attached in a standing position. Larry moved over to the console table and pulled down a tiny switch below a speaker.

"I'm here," he said. "What's the situation?"

"They're still not in firing range," replied Napoleon. "Mess has calculated the approximate time they will be. Do you get it in there?"

"No," said Larry. "This room was installed because it was available. I had no idea I would have to use it. It is only connected verbally to the bridge. You will have to keep me informed. I can only see out the port and forward sides."

"Uh," said Napoleon. "What's port?"

"Actually I'm not sure," said Larry seriously. "I meant left. I'm getting tense."

"So am I," said Napoleon. "Keep talking."

"How much time left?"

"Less than three minutes."

"How is Harlan doing?"

"Still quivering. No sign of aggressive movement."

"All right. Have Mess prepare our defenses and give him permission to fire at will, but only at the first sign of attack. Their orders may be for capture only."

"Wishful thinking," Mess' voice interjected, snorting.

"Just get prepared," warned Larry.

"I was ready half an hour ago," Mess said.

"Butt out, you blood-thirsty bunch of bulbs!"

"Hysteria in battle is not a good trait," the computer intoned as a parting shot.

"I hope your housing gets a direct hit!" Larry shouted.

"Take it easy," Napoleon cautioned.

"One thing I can say for that machine," Larry muttered. "He gets my adrenalin pumping. How much time now?"

"Two minutes, thirty seconds."

"Listen. I have only the minimum of sensing and defensive devices in here. I'll need the Warrior's coordinates on a projected course once he gets in firing range. Do you have that?"

"Not really. What do you mean?"

"You will have to tell me, once the Warrior gets in firing range, what course he's most likely to take. They have pre-planned attack directions. In order for this to work I have to shoot at where he's going to be. Once his direction is projected by Mess I'll have to lock it into my aiming machinery here. The firing switch is four feet away. I can't change the aim at a moment's notice."

"Two minutes to firing range. Do you see them?"

Larry looked out the slatted window beside him. The slats would swing down automatically in the event the room, which was stuck on the hull, was blasted off into space. Once that happened, and given that it was a "clean" hit, Larry would have less than a minute to get into his space suit and out the hatch. And since the room was so hastily installed the equipment could not be worked in a space suit.

Larry saw something move into sight for a second. It was a small dot of glistening metal. Like a shooting star with no tail. It must have been the Destroyer.

"I think I saw one of them. What's their formation?"

"Warrior ahead, Destroyer behind, the same as before."

"Start defensive maneuvering."

"One minute, forty-five seconds to firing range."

"Mess, any radio transmissions?"

"Nothing."

"Any projected course maneuvers?"

"Not yet. It's too soon."

Larry busied himself preparing the board. Everything was soon on and ready. Disuse had not worn anything away. All that was left to do was to lock in the enemy's flight coordinates.

"Larry," came Napoleon's voice. "Do you think we should send them a message?"

"Like what?" he replied, keeping an eye out for the trailless comets. "You want to do your damsel-in-distress act again?"

"No, but something, some other delaying tactic."

"Fine, but you'll have to do it. I can't get contact from in here."

"But they know my voice already."

"This is a delaying tactic, not a second date. If you want to say something, go ahead! How much time?"

"Fifty-five seconds."

"Message coming in," interrupted Mess.

"Go ahead," said Larry. "Nap, it's your move."

"Black Hole," came the civilized voice. "This is the Destroyer Constellation as you might well imagine. There is forty-five seconds before we will be in firing range of your craft. You have absolutely no hope of survival and I would very much like to talk to you personally.

"However if you persist in your escape or, indeed, try to defend yourself, you will be destroyed utterly. Please respond, Black Hole."

There was twenty-five seconds left. Larry looked again and could see the Destroyer fairly clearly in the distance. A more nebulous spot preceded it, the Warrior ship. Both were bright new ships, kept in peak condition since they had never been called on to do an offensive maneuver before.

"This is the Black Hole," Larry heard Napoleon say. "We're sorry, but this new engine went awry. We couldn't stop it. It just suddenly took effect. We couldn't control it."

"Ah, my dear, it's you again! How nice. First you accidentally murder several people under duress and now the light drive you absconded with is ruling your life. You are helpless, is that it?"

"Yes, yes, that's it," Napoloen replied, all pretense leaving her voice.

"Ah, well, it is a pity. You are now in firing range and since you can not stop to let us board you we will have to blast you out of existence."

"Wait!" howled the feline. "Um. We can always try to disconnect it."

"Yes," replied the Commander. "There is no harm in trying. You have ten seconds, then I will instruct the Warrior to move in."

Napoleon, tail lashing, broke the connection. "Larry?"

"Don't slow down. Maintain evasive manuevers. Harlan, are you ready?"

Trigor didn't reply. Napoleon turned to see the helmet section slowly lowering to cover his head.

"Almost," she said for him. "Unless he has to do more tests. He'll have to leave by the bottom hatch. There is no way he'll fit through a regular air lock." The bottom hatch housed the salvage ship.

"Permission to fire!" Mess boomed.

"Go!" shouted Larry. "Give them the works. Give me the projected coordinates as soon as possible."

"Larry," Napoleon cut in. "If we fire, won't they just destroy us?"

"I don't think so, Nap. I hope not. If they wanted to destroy us they would have already. I think they want to see just how dangerous we are. That's why the Warrior is in the lead. We fool with that and the Destroyer's around to pick up the pieces."

As he spoke, before his eyes, a corkscrew of light spun out toward the Warrior ship. Mess had been unleashed and was taking full advantage of it. The Warrior had begun to move out of Larry's sight line when the corkscrew dissipated on its left side.

"Hit!" said Napoleon. "It's still moving, though, picking up speed."

"Keep firing, lay on the fireworks. I don't care if you hit them or not. Just keep them dazzled and get me those coordinates!"

"The Destroyer is hanging back," said Napoleon. "You were right! The Warrior is turning back in our direction!"

They were both shouting at the top of their lungs. Behind the co-pilot's back the space bullet had begun to turn soundlessly. Nine by five feet of monolithic rock began floating toward the rear of the bridge.

Larry saw flashes of light reflecting off the side of his hull, his hands poised over his navigational equipment.

"What is going on? I can't see! Tell me what is happening!"

Both Napoleon's and Mess' voices filled his little room.

"Incredible! Lights are blasting all over the area, every color! . . . Warrior ship moving down, probably for a bank run! . . . I can't tell if we're hitting it, too bright! . . . It will fire under us and move back for a run on an opposite cross! . . . It's getting faster, faster! . . . No damage, no damage! . . . They're underneath, I can't see them anymore!"

Suddenly Larry was thrown backwards off his feet. As he was in mid-air, the ship was thrown in the opposite direction, so his back met the floor moving toward him. He was hurled forward, his middle smacking against the edge of the console, which was moving back as the ship righted itself.

"We're hit, we're hit!" Mess screamed.

Looking out the front Larry clearly saw the Warrior streak off to the left, banking up. It was like a "W" stuck on an upside down "V," brightly edged and marked with equipment. At the tips of the "W" were weapons, at the central crown were windows of the bridge banked by more weapons. At the tips of the upside down "V" were the engines.

"Damages!" Larry shouted above the loud complaints of his ship and computer. "Napoleon, report! Give me those Warrior flight coordinates!"

"Superficial damage to our right side. Lower observation bubble completely destroyed. Area sealed off. A little farther to the right and it would have blasted the bottom hatch. Area sealed off," said Napoleon strangely.

"The coordinates! The coordinates!" Larry repeated hysterically.

"He's coming back on the same pattern in the opposite direction," said Mess, quickly giving Larry the coordinates. His hands flew across the console. He moved dials, then stabbed buttons. Move, stab, move, stab, move, stab. As the last dial was locked into place, a countdown suddenly appeared at the top of the console. It showed eight seconds, thirty-two microseconds, and began counting down. Larry bounded over to the wall's switch.

"Don't let it hit us!" he cried. "The ship has to remain steady! Lay down cover fire!"

The sky began to crackle outside. Larry saw the spectrum of colored lights spin, streak, arc, and zig-zag toward the oncoming Warrior. It created dazzling fireworks around the gleaming ship, doing as much as a waterfall off a boulder's back.

Larry watched as the enemy ship moved down from the upper left of his slatted window toward the center. Four seconds, three seconds . . . if it opened before it got below them Larry's room would be the first to go. It would rip off the ship and shatter like glass, shards spinning out in all directions . . . two seconds, one second.

Even in eight seconds, thirty-two microseconds, Larry's mind caught the beat; he made his mind instruct his arm to move the switch down in exactly the space of a second, even making an extra millisecond for the space between the switch and his hand. At one second the switch was up; at zero seconds the switch was down.

A great vibration shook the room. Below the soles of his boots the floor rippled as if it were a gentle wave. Then, before his eyes, six wide bands of beige light reached out and cut the moving Warrior in two. The four points tore off the crown and spun away. The crown began to spin down. The bands of light seemed to slide into a slot of space and disappear. The Warrior just broke up and went away.

Larry was aware of a roaring in his ears. He still stood with his hand tightly clamped around the switch, his other hand clenched into a fist, his knuckles skeleton white. He suddenly noticed hoarse cheers coming from the console's small speaker.

"You did it, you did it," Napoleon proclaimed. "I can't believe it! Did you see that?"

"Enough," Larry found his voice. "There's still a Destroyer out there." He moved over to the hatch and moved into the hallway. He couldn't help leaning against the wall of the ship proper and taking several deep breaths. Then he began to run back to the bridge, hoping there would be one when he got there.

"Extraordinary. Unbelievable. Impossible. Incredible."

"Thank you, Corman-Heath, for your enlightening critique," said the Commander drily. "Still, it happened and our dear friend and colleague Stuck-Mark had to pay for underestimating the enemy. That brings their average up a bit."

"What, what was that weapon they employed sir?"

"It is hardly time for an armament lesson," said the Commander. "But since it is harmless to us, I shall enlighten you. It is a pirate device. Many of their ships were almost totally covered with those devices and were used as a last resort since both ships had to be stationary for it to work.

"If capture and boarding were imminent they would engage the weapon and slice up the opposing ship. Our murdering friends must have laid their bloody hands on a grid of six and adapted them for use."

"What are you going to do now?" asked Corman-Heath.

"You are becoming annoyingly echolike, Ensign. Is it necessary for me to advise you of my every thought? However, you are young and eager to learn so I will allow you to plumb my private feelings. Laboratories and lechers to the Earth Father, I say. I am going to engage this ship in battle and wipe it from the sky."

"What is the situation?" Larry asked as he ran into the bridge area.

"They are moving in. I'm sure they intend to blast us," said Mess glumly.

Larry moved over to his seat and sat before a magnification of the huge, turtle-shaped ship moving forward. The turtle's head and legs were inside its shell and no appendage holes were visible, but Larry knew that from anywhere on that seemingly smooth surface great destructive power could be unleashed.

"Mess," Larry said. "Any suggestions?"

"This is it," said the computer. "It is all over. I never thought it would come to this. I knew you two were unorthodox, even a little crazy, but I never thought I'd be facing a Destroyer. It's too much I tell you, too much!"

"Damper down," Larry spoke urgently. "Don't go to pieces."

"Pieces, pieces, that's it!" Mess spoke quietly but quickly. Vacuum-packing noises came from the computer's speakers and the machine's console slid back and a vaguely humanoid shape ran out, clanking.

It had two arms but at the end of each was a vertible potpourri of equipment, a drill, a clamp, a wrench, a hammer head. It had two legs, but at the ankle joint was a small retro-rocket. The thing had a head but instead of features there was one rectangular grid and smooth indentations where the ears should have been.

"I don't know about you, but I'm getting out of here," spoke the Mess-man. Larry spun in his chair to see a noisily retreating robot.

"Wait a minute!" he cried. "Where's Harlan?"

The space bullet was conspicuous by his absense.

"I don't know," said Napoleon, turning as well. "I didn't hear him leave . . ."

"Our visual pick-ups haven't located him," Larry continued. "He must still be in the ship. Or under it."

"He couldn't get out the back hatch. I said the only place he could get out was . . ."

Larry was up on his feet and running for the bottom hatch switch as Harlan's voice filtered up through a console speaker.

"How do you get out of here?"

"On Destiny we are shot out of tubes. All our ships are equipped with tubes for emergency circumstances. I couldn't find any here," Harlan explained as Larry opened the bottom hatch from Napoleon's console. The feline's eyes were glued on the screen as the Destroyer loomed before them silently, daring them to open fire.

"We don't have tubes," Larry said. "We have an escape hatch for our salvage craft. It should be opening now. It's in the floor and about twelve by ten feet."

Harlan's equipment registered the moving hatch and his suit moved, still erect, to the opening. It stood momentarily at the edge, then fell forward, out of sight and into space.

Exhilaration blasted Harlan's consciousness as his instincts took over. His suit shot forward beneath the Black Hole and toward the massive structure before him.

"Look!" Napoleon said, pointing at the screen. "There he is!"

Larry looked up and saw a meteorlike light rock zip by and head toward the Destroyer.

"Come around," he instructed Napoleon. "For a better look. This I want to see."

"Sir," said a voice. "They are coming around to face us and two items have left the ship. One humanoid-shaped piece of machinery is moving away and a projectile is moving toward us."

"Another secret weapon, eh?" said the Commander. "Analyze."

"Our imputs do not react to it, sir. It seems to be rock, but a rock or mixture or rocks that have not been programmed into our computers."

A sudden feeling of fear touched the Commander on the back of his neck.

"Destroy it. Immediately. Completely."

"Yes, sir. Energy bolts aimed." The helmsman pushed a button. "And fired, sir."

The Commander and Corman-Heath watched as a huge ball of fire sped toward the oncoming projectile. The distance between the two diminished rapidly until the energy bolt blotted the hunk of oncoming rock from their sight. Corman-Heath sighed but the Commander leaned forward, dread coloring his face.

Then the bolt moved on and burst. The projectile was still coming.

The realization of doom completely engulfed the Commander, and all pretense left him. He was on his feet, shouting.

"Blow that thing up! Now, our most powerful bolts!"

"We can't sir," said Corman-Heath. "It is too close."

"Do it, now!" The Commander was babbling. "If we use it we'll get damaged. If we don't use it we'll be dead. There are legends, there are legends about . . ."

The Commander never got a chance to elaborate.

From the bridge of the Black Hole it looked as if a fly went after a volcano and won. They had seen the first energy bolt simply move away from Harlan and self-destruct. The second, far larger one, left the Constellation, sped up to the space bullet, and *turned around*.

As it moved back to the Destroyer, Harlan dipped down, quickly circling back toward the Black Hole as the ball ripped open the Earth ship. Larry watched as the huge, gaping hole quivered, then sparkling pieces of iridescence, reflecting the doom star's light, and totally frozen by space, poured up and out.

Then the hole widened until the ship was almost torn in two. More spinning, self-destructing matter flew out in all directions. On the screen Larry saw a magnified man, his face four black dots, fly up, then completely disintegrate, his interior pressure pushing out in the air-free darkness.

Their view was filled with totally silent destruction until another, greater flash engulfed what was left of the Destroyer, swallowed it, and then itself disappeared. Bright, hardly bearable light filled the Black Hole bridge, followed by a great rocking. Larry turned and shielded his eyes with one arm while holding onto his seat with the other.

Then the crystalline beauty of space returned with only a few lazily drifting pieces of metal as evidence that the Destroyer Constellation had ever existed.

Napoleon stared at the screen once again and mewed softly. Larry stood up and began to walk slowly around the bridge. From time to time his arms or legs would shake. He stopped until the tremor subsided. Then he would start moving again. Finally he walked off the bridge and to the left. He stepped into the head, placed his hands on the opposite wall, looked down, opened his mouth, and threw up everything he had eaten in the last twenty-four hours.

Harlan returned with the freeze-dried Mess manifestation in tow. Napoleon closed the bottom hatch behind them and Trigor chose to unsuit there, once air had been pumped back in. Mess clanked back up ahead of him, complaining about what space did to its interior, even though he had thought he was prepared. Still muttering it entered his console and took up its position as the omnipresent kvetch. Larry sat beside Napoleon, discussing their situation with little joy.

"Do you think they'll send another ship after us?" she asked.

"I doubt it," he replied, a little color returning to his cheeks. "When they understand we destroyed a Destroyer and a Warrior they'll probably let space have us. Our price tag has already been too high. They don't have the ships or the manpower to spare."

"If this were Destiny," said Harlan appearing in the hatchway, "we would not rest until you were dead."

"Well, this is not Destiny," said Larry as Harlan entered. "Earth is no garden planet and has very little to protect. Since it is obvious we are escaping and can annihilate anything they throw at us, they will probably not bother seeking immediate revenge. But they won't forget. We still have a debt to pay but Earth won't go out of its way to collect it."

"It's a pretty big debt to collect," said Napoleon. "Seven on Earth, eight on the Warrior including the Captain, Cheshire knows how many on the Destroyer."

"Forty-four," said Mess. "Four true humans and forty artificials."

"The forty-four are on my account," said Harlan. "I have killed many more."

"Thank you all very much," said Larry wearily. "But I don't feel like making up death tallies."

"Hey, Larry," purred Napoleon. "Don't let it bother you. Why should it?"

"By the Earth Father. They were people. True humans, artificials, what does it matter? Good, bad, what's the difference? They existed the same as I do. Half-brains, whole brains, they lived. We were put in a position where it was either them or us. It was them, but it's nothing to celebrate or congratulate. The whole thing was sickening."

He sat down heavily. Napoleon looked at Harlan. Harlan looked at Napoleon. Napoleon shrugged.

"Never mind, never mind," said Larry. "Let's get out of here."

Mess refrained from telling him that there was no "here" in space. Even it had a diode of tact. But what Harlan said next broke Larry's depression.

"On one condition," he said.

Larry's head rose. "What?"

"On one condition," Harlan repeated. "I will finish installing the drive on one condition."

"What is it?" asked Napoleon, warily.

"That you tell me where my sister is."

Larry was up. "We owe you our lives. You did something

incredible. But you're asking for the impossible in return. I don't know where your sister is. I wish I did."

Harlan remained immobile. "Then I am afraid I cannot connect the drive."

Larry couldn't believe it. It was happening again. Again and again and again. The trap opens, then closes, then opens, then closes, never giving him a chance to escape completely.

"I don't know where your sister is! Why should I lie or hold back the information? I tell you I don't know!"

"Then we will stay here until you find out," said Harlan quietly.

Larry began to walk in circles, his arms chopping at the air. "I don't know, I don't know, I don't know!"

"I do," interrupted Napoleon.

Larry and Harlan looked over as one. Larry did a double-take and walked away, shaking his head.

"How embarrassing for you," Mess sympathized wickedly.

Harlan moved to stand before the sitting feline. She rose sinuously.

"Grossman-Smith told me before I . . . before he died, about a man named Bishop-Fortune. He is not on Earth. And there's really only one other place a man of his nature does really big business."

"And where is that?" asked Harlan a little too calmly.

"Jackpot," said Napoleon.

SIX

If Destiny was a jewel and Earth a stone, Jackpot was cut glass. Flashy, faceted, sharp, and transparent. From a distance it looked expensive, bright, enticing, inviting. But up close one could see the cheapness and get badly cut on the edges.

Jackpot was the vice planet. Or, if you listened to its rulers, the famed Intercouncil of Brotherhood, a world of amusements, dedicated to the creatures it served. It had the largest and most extensive spaceport in the galaxy and the biggest entertainment area as well.

All the mental and physical needs of every species known were seen to inside the walls of hundreds of establishments, all incorporating the sciences of countless planets. Drugs—liquid, powdered, gaseous, and solid. Games—for the hands, for the eyes, for the body, for the mind. Females—the most beautiful and experienced. Endless variety in the never-ending night. Action all the way, for a price.

The commercials battled for space on the pod's radio, overlapping each other, scrambling each other's signals. A message that was strong in the upper atmosphere would be pushed out by a recording controlling the lower. Once the pod neared the touchdown, the incoming messages were a jumble of music, screeches, snatches of different languages, and feedback.

Larry's space-suited hand switched it off. He turned to

Napoleon, also in a space suit, her tail wrapped around her waist. In the opaque, milky-grey atmosphere, he touched her shoulder once. She returned the signal. Now all they had to do was wait until the mechanical ground crew pulled them into the entry chamber and hooked up the spaceport's computer with their own.

After Harlan had connected the rest of the light-drive power, Larry had spent most of the three-month trip to Jackpot adapting one escape pod for this deception. It had been decided earlier that if a rescue was to be attempted they couldn't just drop down and say, "Hello, we are fugitive murderers from Earth with a disgraced traitor from Destiny here to abscond with his kidnapped sister."

So Mess had been reprogrammed, not to lie, but with a separate truth, including flight information and a pod altered to suit the requirements of a ship from Lustre, a planet with a thick atmosphere and intelligent, six-legged creatures who seemed to be, otherwise, all nose.

The Jackpot Spaceport was sectioned off, naturally enough, and if incoming landing requests were phrased in Lusterian and an incoming ship identified itself as a Lustreship, then space would automatically be prepared in the thick-atmosphere area. Larry was aided further in the subterfuge by a totally automated ground crew. Some simple restrictions had to be followed and several easy questions answered, but then the doors of Jackpot were swung open. Little wonder it was the most exciting and dangerous planet ever inhabited.

Even at that moment, Larry heard the final necessities being taken care of. The computer link was broken and a voice in Lusterian was translated by Mess through receivers in their space suits.

"Have a good stay. Momentary transferral complete. Credit has been entered to the sum of two thousand."

Napoleon had spent the trip salvaging material from the ravaged observation bubble that could be traded for credit, not much, but enough to get by. The pair didn't intend to stay long.

"Remember," Larry said. "We have about fifty feet to cross before we reach the lock. Once there it'll take some three minutes to open. Then we'll have another ten feet to the credit box, then another twenty to the outside."

They both started taking off their suits. Napoleon eyed the interior of the pod, trying to locate her pile of equipment. She caught a glimpse of metal as the murky atmosphere shifted. She pounced on it before she lost track again. On her knees she unclipped her helmet and pulled it off.

Holding her breath and keeping her eyes closed, she sought with her paws the small tank and thin tubing. Finding it she brought it up and slipped a clear mask over her mouth and nostrils, then turned a dial on the end of the tank. Air rushed back into her lungs.

She sighed with relief, eyes still closed, and resumed groping. Her paw then came up with a pair of goggles that she slipped over her eyes. Opening them, she welcomed back the world of floating grey, and sat on her haunches, starting to undo her boots.

For the next few minutes, curling on the floor, she took off the rest of her space suit, uncurled her tail, and strapped the air tank to her back. As she pulled on a slit body suit Larry nearly tripped over her legs.

Kneeling down he placed a hand on her thigh, then quickly moved it over to her shoulder. He squeezed. She reached up and accidentally pawed his ear. She lowered her arm and tapped his shoulder back. They were ready to go.

Walking through the atmosphere was like fighting condensed cream of mushroom soup. The pressure was bearable but the going was slow and exhausting. They only had fifteen minutes of air in their tanks and had already spent five of them in the pod, disrobing.

After another three they were at the hatch. Three more and the hatch was open. Another minute and they collected their credit disks from a slot in the wall. Two more minutes and they were at the door leading out. Larry pushed, then slid. The door swung open and the two stumbled out into bright light.

Larry swung the door back and it shut allowing only a few dark strands of grey atmosphere to settle slowly to the rich, brown ground and disappear. Thankfully, none stuck to their skin or clothes and they pulled off their face masks with pleasure.

Before them moved a picture straight out of their dreams. Creatures of every sort walked, rolled, slithered, oozed, floated, and flew, alone and in groups. Creatures of incredible complexity, and protoplasmic gobs with a single slit, shared space on a single walkway.

Larry was in absolute awe. He took two halting steps forward then stopped as if he were still in the Lusterian atmosphere. Napoleon stood rooted next to him. Earth was never like this. Four, maybe five, alien types interacted there. But here they seemed countless. Most were air breathers, others carrid some sort of adaptor with them.

Napoleon looked Larry up and down. He was wearing his usual grey pants and boots with the blue U-neck, but he held a small green sack in his hand, containing, she knew, a direct communication link with Mess and the Black Hole, two spitters, and their credit disks. However, his face was frozen, his eyes wide, and his mouth open. She giggled. He turned toward her, snapping out of it somewhat.

"What's the matter?" she asked innocently.

He turned back to the incredible throng, then glanced at her, grinning like a small boy.

"Nothing," he said. "Nothing at all . . ."

His reply was cut short by a loud roar coming from beside them. Surprise hunched Larry's shoulders as a three-fingered, pasty-white fist slid by his head and bashed the wall behind him, accompanied by another howling cry.

"Earth people," came the translated words from Larry's belted translator. "I hate Earth people! Ouch!"

Larry jumped to the side to face a large, bald man with a wide red mouth, eight yellow-brown teeth, two pear-shaped nostrils, and one red eye in the middle of his forehead. He was rubbing his hand. Standing beside him was a wide, short man with a wide red mouth, eight teeth, a nose, and one black eye.

Napoleon's forepaws lowered toward the ground as her back arched. Her hair stood on end as she growled. The smaller cyclops started to move forward, then a six-legged creature with four stalks undulating in the air cut him off.

The stalks clacked together in a rhythmic fashion as Larry noticed a series of eyes lining two sides of one leg facing them. The clacking stopped. The translator remained silent. The big one-eyed man growled again.

"Answer the master," said Larry's translator. "Or we will get the answer from you."

The pair stood in stunned silence as the six-legged character clacked again.

"We are strangers here," Larry attempted. "We don't know the language."

At the sound of his voice the alien skittered back and the big guy moved forward. It was obvious from his expression that he was not from the welcoming committee.

Napoleon threw her air tank forward. It hit the ground and rolled into the six legs of the stalker. The creature fell to the side. The giant's head turned and Larry quickly swung his own tank in a fast arc as Napoleon sprung into the air.

The tank landed on the side of the giant's head and the feline landed on the smaller man's chest. There was the combined sound of a clapper hitting a bell and a cat's howling attack. The giant stumbled and fell to his knees. Both Napoleon and the smaller cyclops fell, a cloud of dust rising, as her limbs slashed back and forth. Then she was off, running toward the crowd of living things that paid no attention to the scuffle whatsoever.

Larry ran by the felled giant who was shaking his head slowly and hit the six-legged alien with his green sack as it was trying to get up. It collapsed to the ground again, its legs akimbo. Larry followed the moving tail. He weaved in and out of the strange creatures who reacted to him as if he were an earthen fly, with slightly annoyed apathy.

Suddenly the tail disappeared and Larry came upon Napoleon walking as if it were a dull day on the Denver Plateau. He matched her stride.

Several seconds went by before either spoke.

"You should have seen your face," Napoleon said pleasantly.

"Before or after the attack?" he parried.

"Both," she countered back.

Larry chuckled, somewhat artificially. "I guess the mark of greeting on this planet is a punch in the nose."

Napoleon laughed. "Then I suppose the stories we've always heard about this place are true."

The two looked around as they walked. Buildings of all shapes and sizes surrounded them, each with long signs declaring the wonders to be found within, often in so many languages that the legends covered an entire wall. The stories did seem to be unexaggerated.

Stories were told halfway across the galaxy about endless vendettas undisturbed unless an innocent was hurt or killed. Then, there was some question as to the definition of "innocent" on this planet. Stories about the elite corp of Peace Containers, specially trained creatures of every race with the ability to deal out death, literally, at a mere thought, from a crystal imbedded in a corner of a forehead. Stories about fugitives and criminals who had fled here and settled, no questions asked, unless they tried to involve an "outsider" in their business.

And stories about the Intercouncil of Brotherhood, the inter-galactic team of executives controlling the world. Kill your neighbor, rape your son, lose all your credit, but don't hurt business. That was their creed. And even with all the different races, all the different backgrounds, all the different customs, it worked for them.

It made little difference that the death rate on Jackpot was high. Many people came to Jackpot to die happy, was their reply, as they raked the credit in. For behind the slogans and stories and easy joy was incredible economic brilliance. Enough intelligence and power to control world monetary markets and the fates of billions on many planets. It was an incredible place, a chillingly pitiless masterwork, cloaked by a shrill laugh and the clatter of small change.

"They're true," Larry said, almost in wonder.

It was Jackpot's version of dusk so the diversions consisted of harmless gambling and games of less-strenuous skill. Lovers of the more difficult, dangerous, and dirty pastimes waited for night to fall. And, of course, dream factories dotted the landscape. Many establishments included this as part of their services, and there were restaurants squeezed between the pleasure palaces, but no aromas wafted from their doors. With so many races shoulder to shoulder, one creature's meat could indeed be another's poison. Many deaths on the planet had been attributed to one poor soul's stumbling into another's environment.

Napoleon and Larry moved into a tiny bistro with several sections tailored for a variety of aliens. They found a little compartment with small tables and chairs near the back. It served to remind them how unimportant man was in the universe. The other sections outnumbered the humanoid area four to one.

They sat in order to get something to eat and to think. As soon as Larry's pants touched the seat the table top glowed.

"Please place your credit disk on the table," said his translator.

He raised his eyebrows in surprise then dug out one of the small, plasticlike circles from his bag.

Once the disk was placed on the surface, the translator said, "How can we serve you?"

"A menu?" Larry suggested.

The table lit up with various depictions of foodstufs, then small lists appeared facing both Larry and Napoleon. It was strictly an Earth-imported diet, dull and doughy. It was what they had been eating for the entire trip.

"Do you have an off-Earth meals," Larry asked, "not poisonous to the human system?"

"Any receipes from Mandarin?" Napoleon suddenly suggested. Larry noted her face held an unusual intensity.

"Off-world, yes," the translator replied. "I'm sorry, however, to admit we have no Mandarin dishes." Two new lists appeared, proceeded by more appetizing pictures. Napoleon looked disappointed. Larry looked famished.

"Is this real food or fabrication?" he inquired.

"Our meals are made from the finest ingredients available and under the strictest nutritional supervision," the translator replied. "In order to give you the most natural . . ."

"Real or fabricated?" Larry repeated.

"Our meals are made from the finest . . ."

"All right, that's enough. I get the message."

Larry ordered a colorful meal of soft meatlike material

covered with a thin, crunchy coating, not sweet, and drenche
in a lumpy sauce. Napoleon was served a chunky, dark mi
ture in a bowl. They both ordered beverages, hers a bieg
liquid with streams of red, his a golden concoction.

Even though it was artificial the two ate with eager aba
don since it was the first thing they could have called a
"old-fashioned" meal in months. As Larry was finishing the la
of his sauce, soaking it up in uniform pads of a doughy mi
ture, Napoloen leaned back.

"We must have stepped into the middle of a discussion,
she said.

"What?" he asked, popping a piece of the pad in h
mouth.

"The cyclops twins and their six-legged friend. They mus
have been using us as examples in an argument."

"Or they were customs," Larry proposed. "Or we wer
punching bags. Or victims. Or maybe they were questionin
us about leaving the thick atmosphere center. That six-legge
alien could have been a Lusterian detective."

"Whatever. I would imagine it hardly makes a differenc
on Jackpot," Napoleon said as Larry washed down the last o
his meal with the last of his drink.

"We hope you have enjoyed your meal," said the trans
lator. "The cost has been automatically deducted from you
credit disk. Thank you. Enjoy."

"Very neat," Larry commented, putting the disk back in hi
bag. They got up and moved around the rest of the table
which had filled up in the meantime with other excited pa
trons. No one stopped them as they were leaving and Larry
noted that they had seen no living employee, human or oth
erwise. He imagined that if any trouble started the only
pieces to be picked up would be the customers.

The two went out the door. A blinding blast of sight and
sound immediately plastered them up against the restauran
wall. Night descended quickly but not quietly on this world
And if the Earth pair thought it dreamlike before, now be
fore them moved a tornado dipped in hell.

The pure mass of undulating matter was breathtaking
The sounds were excruciatingly magnified and the color
crowded on top of one other as they assailed neural centers

It occurred to the still-comprehending part of Larry's brain as he struggled to get his senses organized that the restraurant had been completely sound-proof and windowless. Napoleon was too occupied trying not to slink away with her tail between her legs to consider such things.

This place made the pleasure palaces of Earth seem rustic. The incredible garnishness of it all was compounded by catering to the basest instincts of many races, not just humanoid lusts. It was a powerful mixture, intoxicating to the uninitiated.

In a few moments Larry's eyes were able to uncross and Napoleon was able to straighten up. They both fought the urge to run away, screaming. In this crowd there was nowhere to run to and their shrieks wouldn't even be heard. Larry took Napoleon's neck in one hand and she slid her arms around his waist. He felt her claws emerging through his shirt. He moved off to the left where he saw a barely opened yellow door. He pulled it open and jumped in, Napoleon still clinging to him.

The door slammed behind them and they grappled for some sort of support. Somehow Larry got his hands on a rod sticking from the wall where he stood gulping and waiting for the ringing to leave his ears.

When he was able to hear clearly again he picked up a diminished roar and a humor-filled voice saying, "First time, eh? It can be a little bit of a shock until you get used to it."

Larry turned to see a hairy, four-legged thing with a big snout smiling at him. In an unusual display of verbosity Larry said, "Huh?"

"A bit of a shock," the snout said. "The whole thing. I said the whole thing can be a bit of a shock."

"A *bit*," Larry snorted, trying to find his feet.

"What? I can't hear you," said the snout.

Larry turned back to the creature. "I said, not just a bit!" he shouted.

"Oh, yes, quite right," said the snout back.

Larry noted finally that although its mouth was moving normally, the volume the creature was able to achieve was on the level of a scream.

"Where is the feline I came in with?" Larry asked.

"What, eh?"

"The feline I came in with!" Larry shouted over the din.

Napoleon tapped him on the shoulder. Larry jumped.

"Right behind you," said the snout, laughing. Larry turned to see Napoleon smiling, her paws over her ears.

"Thank you," said Larry, turning back to the creature.

"What?"

"Thank you!"

"Certainly," the snout snorted. "Not to worry, not to worry. You'll get used to it. I never thought I would either, but look at me, the old pro." The snout laughed again.

Larry did indeed look at it. It had two big eyes, making half-balls near either side of his head and a long snout that ended in two nostrils above a wide, thin mouth. A mane of dark hair surrounded two upright ears, more like Napoleon's than his own, above a wide brow.

The body was neither hairy nor four-legged as Larry had originally surmised. It wore a fur covering in the shape of a sleeveless long shirt. It was now upright and leaning beside Larry, holding up a two-fingered hand toward Napoleon.

"Until it gets better you might want to try these," he said. In his dark palm were a pair of ear plugs. Napoleon put one paw out and the creature dropped them in it. "My name is Palend," he continued. "But you can call me Pal."

Napoleon had gotten both plugs in firmly and said, "Thank you, Pal."

Palend did not say anything so Larry shouted, "She said . . ."

"I can hear her fine," said Palend. "I was just appreciating her is all. She's quite a fine-looking cat."

Larry turned to see Napoleon's negative reaction. She just kept smiling. He didn't know whether she didn't want to bother correcting him over the din or didn't mind. At any rate she remained silent so Larry shouted, "My name is . . . Baker-Harlan and uh, this is . . . Trigor-Mess."

Napoleon turned to Larry, glaring at him through squinted eyelids as Palend replied, "Enjoy. Can I show you around this fine establishment?"

Larry nodded, his throat getting sore. Palend started to move down into the room proper giving Larry time to look around. The rod they had been leaning on was a bannister, leading to a ramp. Beyond was another sea of creatures dotting every few feet between islands of machinery.

Bright, flashing, boxlike machines topped with clear sheets. Wall-sized machines with seats, bright lights, eyesockets, and buttons. Cone-shaped machines with silver balls rolling in complicated cylindrical patterns leaving a trail of blue filings.

And the creatures in the room swayed with the machines. Back, forth, right, left, hands moving, bodies jerking. It was a cataclysm of passion, minute flashing of emotion, and a continual build-up of need. It was the Earth pair's first intimate experience in an intergalactic amusement center.

"This is an establishment of innocent delight," Palend was saying as a creature behind him smacked the side of the machine with a hoof. "A place for games of limited skill, constant entertainment, and limitless variation. The rewards are not for one's credit disk but for one's soul. Oh, yes, that concept does not just exist on Earth. Here we sell joy, thrills, and finally, contentment.

"You seem quite proud of this place," Larry shouted to him.

"I should," said Palend. "I own it."

The trio passed near one boxlike machine with another long-snouted creature playing it. It tapped a button at one end, sending a silver ball shooting out, leaving a trail of bright blue orbs. As the ball bounced off the rear of the machine, the initial blue began to turn green, then fade out only to be replaced with a new stream of orbs as the ball picked up speed. Like the wake from a pebble thrown in water, it created ripples that would eventually disappear.

The ball moved down the brightly lit board almost as if it would roll off the side, then the creature pressed another button and the ball spun off to the right, vibrating into noncircular shapes as if it were made of liquid. Then, hitting a small star-shaped bump, the ball burst into three, spinning off in all directions. Then the entire board changed.

A veritable roller coaster of paths appeared, all coming from a green mound in the center. The three balls took separate paths, curving, twisting, up and down and all around, seemingly making choices as to which path to take by themselves. The creature chuckled with genuine glee and started pressing his buttons wildly.

The balls were creating a blue-tinged silver ballet before Larry's eyes. Finally one, two, three balls disappeared into the green mound. The creature stopped bumping and waited, his eyes darting from one part of the board to another.

Then, as if someone had pulled a bright tablecloth off to reveal an even brighter table below, the board changed again. A maze of grooves appeared, lined with circular posts. Six balls appeared as well, falling down across the lanes, jockeying for position. The creature's eyes lit up and he started pressing the buttons again.

Balls changed lanes, swung in toward the posts, bounding off in all directions, richocheting off each other, creating a rainbow of colors. At times the board seemed to be filled with silver and blue, obscuring all else. Larry managed to tear himself away to see Palend's smile widening across the bottom of his snout.

"A delight, agreed?" he exhorted.

"Agreed," said Larry.

"What?" said Palend, moving an ear over.

Larry nodded vigorously.

"Care to try one?" invited the affable Palend.

"I'm afraid we must keep a most pressing appointment," Napoleon interrupted.

"Do not be afraid," replied the snout. "Even business on this world can be a pleasure. If I can be of any further assistance, please inquire and do not worry. I see the gleam in the human's eye. If he can, he will be back to play here."

"Perhaps you *can* help us," Larry spoke up.

"Perhaps. I have machines at many other establishments as well."

"We need to find the offices of Bishop-Fortune," said Napoleon. "Could you give us directions?"

Palend's eyes were suddenly bracketed by lids coming from both directions, above and below his bulbous pupils. It created the needed effect of his vision narrowing.

"It cannot be . . . my judgment has never been this

wrong . . ." he stammered. His cloven hand settled just above Larry's elbow. "I take my life in my hands. I must ask. You do not actually intend to patronize his establishment, do you?"

The room still raged around Larry. There was no reason to reply to the horse-headed creature. He had said himself that such a question was a terrible breach of manners between alien races, but the look on Palend's face was so intense and concerned that Larry could not help but reply.

"Not exactly," he said.

Palend turned toward Napoleon. "So lovely, so strong," Larry heard him mutter. His mouth worked some more, but no words came. He finally turned back to Larry.

"Please come with me for a moment. Do not doubt that it concerns your very lives. Please, do not fear me. Come."

Larry nodded and Palend moved the two toward a small gap between the row of wall-sized standing machines. The creature stopped in front of them, entering another as a doorway slid open automatically. Larry went in before Napoleon, noticing a vaguely humanoid individual on his right, eye glued to a hole, pressing a button repeatedly, and giggling like a child.

The room was small, bright, and sparsely furnished. The walls were a clean beige but with strips of blue, green, red, gold, and silver circling the room near the ceiling. Palend's desk was a large console with a chair on a track in the floor. He moved there, punching a button that closed the door.

The sound of the game area remained, received on speakers lining the desk top. Another button pushed and the noise disappeared. Another button pressed and a screen lit up with the entire game area pictured.

"In case of trouble," Palend explained. "Please, sit."

The other three chairs in the room were cushiony pockets close to the floor. The Earth pair shared a glance before Larry settled into the soft plush of the seat, enjoying the quiet, listening to his ears buzz. Napoleon waited a moment longer, then curled up, feline style, in another. Palend himself sat, and pushed a fourth button.

"Refreshments?" he asked.

Larry declined for the two of them.

A tube appeared between his fingers as his hand raised to his mouth. He put the opening in his mouth, squeezed and swallowed.

"It is sometimes the only meal I have all night," he expounded.

"We don't have much time," said Larry.

"Naturally, naturally," Palend said with a sigh. "I apologize deeply, with honesty. This is hard for me. I put myself in a terrible position."

You seem concerned only with our well-being," said Larry. "Please speak freely."

Palend rose and came around the console to Larry. "I thought you were experienced travelers," he said. "It became apparent quickly that you were novices here. Not just in my establishment but in the ways of this world. But you must be warned. Do you know what will happen to you if you enter Bishop-Fortune's?"

"I honestly do not," said Larry.

"You will never leave," said Palend. "You cat would disappear and you would be paid or killed, depending on your inclination to sell her."

Napoleon sat up. "Not here, too! I thought this world had enough females."

Palend turned his attentions to her. "Felines are unheard of throughout this galaxy, not just on Earth. How can it be you don't know that?"

"I was kept pretty much in the dark all my Earth life," she remarked bitterly.

Palend nodded, then continued. "I would not be surprised if you have already been scouted. Perhaps a good many pleasure palaces have already been made aware of your presence. Even now they may be making plans to acquire you."

"Then no female is safe on Jackpot?" Napoleon snarled.

"You are a feline," Palend stressed. "Creals, Moffats, Farzaks, Methsons, Lidenboks, Pankies, even human females we have, some in overabundance. But hardly a feline."

"Then there are others?" Napoleon asked excitedly.

"Earth artificials," Palend replied. "And . . . and once one sickly female child was smuggled in, but she died while being . . . cultivated for service."

Napoleon snarled. Larry climbed up to the rim of his chair.

"Why are you telling us all this?"

"I don't know," the snout said. "I'm putting myself in terrible danger as well. If the palace heads knew I interceded and could prove it to the Intercouncil . . ."

"I just cannot understand," Napoleon exploded. "Why me? What is so marvelous about me? I don't spend hours preparing my fur or my face. I don't trim my whiskers. I don't shine my claws. Am I so important to be possessed, bought, sold, and bartered, like one of your machines? Why must I be hunted?"

"If you are not aware of your own magnificence and uniqueness, it is hard for me to explain," said Palend. "You are a true female, created by nonartificial means, one of full mind and inner fire. Your very existence makes you wanted."

"What is the difference?" Napoleon persisted. "Because I was born? I might as well have been made for as much as I knew my parents. I was on Earth before I could understand, sent from lab to lab . . ."

"Nap," Larry said gently. She quieted, throwing herself deep into the pillows of the seat.

"You are in danger," Larry told her. "That much is obvious. We have to do what we came to do, then get out. We can hope that the various palaces will do nothing in these crowds."

"No, they can do anything in a mass," Palend corrected him. "She could be silenced, drugged, and spirited away before you even noticed she was missing."

"This is incredible," Larry blurted. "Palend, you have done us a great service. You have also exposed yourself to great danger. And I'm afraid I must ask you to open yourself and your good name to more."

Palend leaned back on his console, and folded his arms, a finger on each side of his elbow. "I considered that before warning you. Pray continue."

Bishop-Fortune's pleasure palace was a magnificent structure designed to fill the patron with awe while keeping him in his place. All the other establishments were built with the customer in mind, but his house was made to tend to its own ongoing good. The visitors were incidental, hardly important. Bishop-Fortune was doing them a favor by letting them enter and pay.

The cavernous insides made Larry feel small. The delicate-looking, frizz-haired girl with an ugly three-inch scar across her face greeted him haughtily and reacted to his request with twisted amusement.

"The Destiny Girl?" she sneered. "You sure about that, Earthen?"

"Yes, yes, I'm sure," Larry replied hastily. "I have credit. I can pay."

"You had better, Earthen," the girl replied wickedly. "It is still early yet; she may be able to squeeze you in."

Her face emitted three shrill barks of laughter, making her scar turn red, then white. Her face settled back into her version of superiority and her hand came up, curling.

"Let's see your credit risk."

Larry reached into the small brown pouch under his belt and took out one shiny circle. The girl snatched it and flipped it on the counter beside her. It shone yellow, then red.

"Not nearly enough, Earthen," she laughed. "Where do you think you are? We don't cost dirt here, Earthen. We're respectable females—we don't come cheap." Her raucous laughter filled the plush foyer again, where only she and Larry stood. "If you want to taste the sweetness of Destiny," she snarled sarcastically, "You'll have to cough up more."

Larry reluctantly reached back into the pouch and pulled out Napoleon's disk and laid it in the girl's hand. She flipped it onto the counter, which glowed yellow and stayed that way.

"Just made it," she announced. "You can go through, Earthen, but don't dawdle. You hardly have time to sneeze. Enjoy," she spat, turning from him as if he didn't exist.

Larry retrieved the disk and moved up a ramp toward a

glowing porthole. This was the final test. If this sensor picked up any alien material, be it a weapon, communication device, visual pick-up, or photographic material, his trip would be severely curtailed. Larry did not hesitate, he moved up and through.

Nothing, no immediate reaction. Just a sudden yellow bath, then a curtain of black. Then he was in a hallway of dark green. To his side stood a man in dark clothing. In the dimness it was almost impossible to see his features, his size, or his coloring. But it was obvious he was a man and that in the middle of his forehead shone a red jewel.

Here was a human Peace Container. Bishop-Fortune was so powerful he warranted one of each race in every section of his establishment. It was all just as Palend had said. The different entrances for different races, the insulting hostesses, the sensing porthole, the Peace Container. He could explain it all up until then. He could supply Larry with the small credit disk pouch and the fingernail communicator made of alien material that sat comfortably inside his right index finger, but he could not instruct him further or supply him with an undetectable weapon. From here on it depended on Larry's own plan and minute timing.

He moved down the hallway. Although it was lined with doors, none had opening devices, except the one facing him at the end. He approached it and touched his hand to a plate in the middle. The door swung back, both sides sweeping outward. The hall shone with soft, white light.

Before Larry was a room and a small, carpeted balcony overlooking a deep brown, wood-hued room with a high ceiling. Before him was a pillow-strewn floor and high bookcases filled with ancient volumes. Before him were tall windows interspersed with the book cases, framed with delicate curtains that ruffled from an unseen wind. Before him was an eight-foot, framed mirror reflecting his image over a fireplace filled with softly burning wood, adding a further glow.

And before him was a girl. She held a book in her hand and was leaning over a servo-robot. She wore a white gown tied, from her waist to her neck with small, thin bows of material. It rippled across her body from the wind. Her eyes were large and dark, her hair black as space, shining with the gleam of the fire.

Larry held on to the balcony's bannister to remain upright. He tried to swallow, a buzzing filling his head, one having nothing to do with the roar of Jackpot's night. She turned toward him and looked up.

"Close the door, will you?" she said in lyrical tones, pulling the book to her chest and shooing the little robot on wheels away. It was all Larry could do to keep from falling over. He felt his face flush and he nearly tripped over his own feet turning. As he pulled the door shut he found his mouth hanging open. He shut that as well. He returned to the balcony's edge to find her smiling, almost impatiently.

"Come here," she said.

Larry nearly vaulted over, but he managed to locate the stairway leading down to the right. He quickly stumbled down, at one point grabbing the wall to keep his balance. He angrily told himself to calm down.

An instruction that did no good once he had walked up to her. Before he could think further she stepped forward and kissed him. Slowly, her hands still holding the book to her chest, and softly, a flesh caress.

Larry's mind was suddenly awash in a sea of smoke. He had to close his eyes. His hands, not knowing what to do, shook. The rest of his body acted accordingly. He felt himself tipping over. Automatically his arms sought the nearest thing to right himself. It was the girl. He felt the softness of her dress. Then he was rolling beside her on the floor.

She was laughing. "A grand start," she said. "Shall we continue?" The book was thrown across the floor. The beautiful young girl was on her knees, her hands reaching for his pants.

Larry suddenly remembered who she was and what he was doing there. He realized that they didn't have much time before the planned rendezvous.

"Titu Trigor?" he said. She stiffened. Her eyes sought his, a hard edge to them.

"What . . . who are you? What do you want?"

"You are she, aren't you?" he queried from his back on the floor.

"How did you get here? What is all this about?" She was whispering roughly into his face.

"We came with your brother. We're here to rescue you," Larry said quickly, wondering how it would sound to her.

"Really," said Titu with no anticipation in her voice. "So you found me. You'll never get me out of here." She rose and began moving quickly toward the stairway, picking up her book as she went.

This was not the reaction Larry had expected to get. He wasn't sure what he was expecting, but this wasn't it. He was on his feet, ran, and grabbed her by the arm as she made the first step.

"Don't worry," he said sincerely. "We have a ship coming at any moment. We *can* get you out of here."

She looked him in the face, shifting her gaze from eye to eye. All she saw was eager integrity. She said nothing, merely swung the spine of the book in a vicious arc. The binding caught Larry on the side of the head, pushing him down to the floor.

A numbing sensation moved over him but it wasn't until he reached his knees that the pain sped like lightning to his brain. The wavy haze that had clouded his mind turned to a red and black storm roaring inside his head, flashing bright white, green, and blue.

He heard Titu's voice through the thunder crying for help. Thoughts of survival suddenly replaced his rescue operation. Even through the violent clouds he instructed his legs to get him up and away. They replied sluggishly but still got him shakily to his feet. From there he pulled himself over to a window.

The room moved in and out of focus, shifting like a holgraphic image, as he stumbled toward the opening. As the blackness beyond beckoned him and the wind ruffled his hair he heard Titu urging someone to hurry. His knees touched the edge of the window sill. But instead of pushing him forward, it turned him around. His eyes saw Titu on the balcony, by the door, standing back as the Peace Container, his face dark, strode in. The man's glowing forehead jewel was the last thing he saw before falling back.

The ceiling moved and black swept over him again, but

his eyes did not close. He thought he saw a red bolt strea
overhead before light burst around him, but he couldn't b
sure.

Suddenly his mind was clear. The pain had receded to
throb and he could think again. He knew he was on his bac
among six-foot-high pillows. He realized he had fallen throug
a set of black curtains that separated the library from the res
of the dream factory.

Larry found his feet and stuck his head above the rim c
the pillows. Around him dozens of alien creatures undulated
quivered, and shook. He had stumbled on a communal orgy
The jellylike Umwards gave off energy that other Umward
could receive. When engaged in sexual pursuits the pleasur
was heightened in company.

The floor was completely covered in the tall padding, s
running was impossible. Larry began to bounce toward a
exit on the other side of the room.

As he neared the door he saw the Peace Container dro;
through the hole he had made in the curtained ceiling. He
rolled through the opening and down a ramp, barely missin;
another Umward couple who squished in surprise.

Larry rolled as long as he could, rising to his feet only t
jump around a corner as another red lightning bolt struck th
wall behind him. He somersaulted and was on his feet, run
ning down another hallway. He pressed his right thumb t
his forefinger twice, then spoke.

"Nap! I'm in trouble."

His fingernail replied scratchily. "Where are you?"

Larry saved his breath until he leapt through a porthol
and fell down a slide meant for Moffats.

"I just left an Umward section. I'm at the bottom of a
Moffat ramp. How do I get out of here?"

The slide had been coated with a dark beige ointmen
with which Larry was now covered. He heard mumbles from
his fingernail as he sought refuge. The Peace Containe
would be there any second.

"Palend says that you should go for the Farzak section t
the far left. There'll be enough creatures there for you to be
protected until we get there," Napoleon said from his finger

nail. "But don't go to the near left. That's the Methsons' section. You wouldn't last half a minute in there."

Larry didn't need to be told twice. The human Peace Container appeared at the top of the ramp with a Umward associate. Two bolts melded into one, striking out at him as he sped around the corner, to the far left. He ran to a door at the end and hurled his body through.

He smashed up against a huge boulder and fell back onto the dusty ground, winded. When he could breathe again, a moment later, he saw that he was in an excellent recreation of an ancient village with rooms etched out of rock. It was a veritable community of caves with bones littered about and a painted wall depicting an eternal sunset.

Larry scrambled to his feet to see that the room stretched out for some length, interrupted by campfires and boulders. Before he was able to do anything more, a huge figure moved into view from a cave opening before him. As it came out into the permanently dying light he saw it was the eight-toothed, one-eyed creature, just like the one who almost crushed his skull at the Spaceport.

He didn't need a translator to tell him what it was growling now. With a bellow the cyclops ran forward, his massive right fist moving down. Larry stepped over to the left and stuck his leg out. The clumsy giant tripped and fell, roaring with anger. Immediately the cave entrances were filled with huge, hulking brutes and their mates.

The females seemed upset at the interruption but the males moved forward eagerly. Larry realized he could not move back and he could not move forward. The Peace Containers would arrive any second and he was facing a mob of angry, one-eyed monsters.

Then, one monster got too close to another while moving in. The one on the left dug an elbow into the other's ribs, urging him to move aside. The one on the left got a fist in his face for his trouble. He rocked back and delivered a resounding blow to the other's head in return. The one on the right stumbled into another beside him and received a kick in the stomach as balance. He dropped to the ground cringing.

But the one on the left wasn't going to let the third get away with that. He buried his fist in the third's face, knock-

ing him, and two others, to the ground. All three were up
and on top of the nearest to them in a flash.

Suddenly the whole group turned in on itself. Fists were
flying in every direction as dust started making a natural curtain. One Farzak closest to Larry almost had its huge,
gnarled hands around the human's throat, when another
caught him in the back with both knees. The two Farzaks
dropped to the ground, pummeling each other with great
abandon.

Larry heard the Peace Containers enter. He jumped into
the whirling cloud of gold. The red bolts could not be loosed
for fear of harming an innocent patron. But Larry was far
from safe. One errant punch would probably rearrange his
face or permanently damage an important internal organ.

He tried to keep near pairs of struggling, white-skinned
fighters. He jumped over one team of wrestling creatures,
dodged another who were bashing at each other's faces with
little effect, and ducked as another flew through the air in
the midst of a tackle. It was like moving through a particu-
larly bustling dance floor at a slaughterhouse.

Larry turned to check on the progress of the Peace Containers. He couldn't make them out through the dust of the
writhing figures. But he knew that if any Farzak tried to in-
clude them in the battle the group would stop being "innocent" and the deadly lightning would strike.

Larry turned forward just as a glaring red eye came
leaping out of the cloud preceded by two massive gripping
hands. Larry had just enough time to fall to the side before the
hurtling Farzak crashed into his shoulder. The cyclops fell on
his head and Larry went spinning atop another two kicking
fighters. His left arm was numb, a pain forgotten when one
of the two he had interrupted swatted the back of his head.

Larry actually flew forward five feet and rolled across the
rocky ground for several more yards. He desperately
struggled to regain consciousness. He thought he saw a red
jewel among the dusty haze, but he could not be sure it
wasn't a side-effect of the pain. He could detect more fighters
all around him and felt the vibrations of their violence under
him. The jarring energy didn't revitalize him.

His sight colored dark green with a curling cloud of black

moving in. He felt fingers curling around his ankle. He was being dragged into the thick of the battle. Just before losing consciousness he figured that was it. The Peace Containers would find only a mangled hunk of battered flesh.

A beam of bright orange filled his vision and he realized he was awake and alive. A howl of pain louder than the grunts and scuffling went up and suddenly, the fighting stopped. As the golden cloud began to settle Larry saw Napoleon standing beside him, a beamer in one hand, a spitter in the other. Before this vision even had time to collect in his brain, the feline fired both weapons, howling.

"Get up! Let's go!"

Larry ignored the pain that ripped at his shoulder and neck. He rose quickly to his feet and circled his co-pilot as the Farzaks ran screaming. The Peace Containers were forced to take cover behind a rock. She was moving back as Larry noticed she was wearing a holster over her slit body suit. He reached around her waist and pulled out his own beamer.

"Up," she cried, leading the way. They ran through a hidden doorway, laying down a veritable floor of fire.

"Every Peace Container will be converging on us in a moment!"

They ran up a ramp and turned right. Larry saw one of the hallway doors with a gaping hole.

"Through here," said Napoleon. They jumped through into a billowing black curtain. The feline snarled, pulling it off them. Larry was back in the library, running beside Napoleon for the stairs.

"The girl!" Was she here?" he shouted.

"Not when I showed up," she replied, streaking up to the balcony. Larry saw a rope dangling down from a hole in the ceiling.

"Go," she said, "I'll cover you."

Larry didn't argue. He pushed his beamer into his belt and scurried up the line as three Peace Containers appeared. Napoleon fired madly, keeping them from getting a clear shot with their glowing jewels.

Larry pulled himself up and over onto the roof. He swung

the rope over to where Napoleon stood and pulled out his
weapon, switching it to its widest, deadliest position.

"All right," he yelled, firing through the opening, slicing
great hunks out of the room. A tail end of one beam ripped
open the fireplace, sending burning logs rolling onto the floor.

Napoleon was outside as the rug, curtains, and pillows
caught fire. Across the roof Larry saw their escape pod and
ran for it. The noise of the Jackpot night roared them on,
covering the chaos within Bishop-Fortune's establishment.

As the two jumped into the vehicle red bolts started ripping through the ceiling toward them. Larry initiated lift-off
just as two bolts arced by each other, creating a blood-red
"X" streaking off on opposite sides of the pod as it leaped
into the sky.

SEVEN

"I don't believe it!" Harlan roared.

"I don't care!" Larry yelled back. "If you hadn't refused to part company with that precious suit of yours for a while, you would have seen. She tried to kill me at the thought of rescue."

"It is impossible," Harlan contended. "She was ripped from her home, our parents viciously murdered, she is marketed like food, subject to the slavery of the vilest man in the galaxy, and you tell me she wants to stay?"

"I'm telling you she hit me on the head and called a Peace Container to do me in," Larry explained. "Whether she wants to stay or not is a moot point."

"Maybe she didn't trust you," Harlan mused. "Thought it was a trap . . ."

"I used her name!" Larry cried. "I told her about you. What more could she want?"

"I still don't see . . ." Harlan began.

"All right, all right," Napoleon interrupted. "This isn't getting us anywhere. What do we do now? is the question."

They all stood on the bridge of the Black Hole as it sat behind a speeding asteroid. The space rock moved in such a way, that, before it rocketed back into outer space, it stayed along the Black Hole's orbital path around Jackpot, shielding the Earth Ship from discovery. A pocket of safety but only for a limited time.

"Do what you wish," Harlan answered her question. "I am not leaving this planet without her."

"Well, that's that," said Napoleon easily.

"No, wait a minute," interrupted Mess. "Maybe something can be arranged along those lines . . ."

"Damper," Napoleon warned the machine before continuing to Harlan, "How do you propose to get her out?"

"I will simply go and collect her myself," said Harlan. "In my suit. It was what I should have done initially."

"I see," said Napoleon. "Do you also propose to have her suffocate and burn up in the atmosphere or do you think the Peace Containers will give her time to dress up in a space suit after you bash through a wall?"

"I don't feel that that is any . . ." Harlan blustered.

"Do you even know where she is?" Napoleon pressed. "The Bishop-Fortune Pleasure Palace is in a shambles thanks to us. They will have moved her and everyone else to different headquarters until they can find, and deal with, us. Do you intend to blast every place you suspect?"

"I can't say how . . ." Harlan attempted.

"Last time it was a surprise," Napoleon rolled over him. "This time they'll be ready for an attack. They won't expect it, but they'll be ready for it. They won't wait while you land and search."

"They can not harm my suit, no matter what they do," Harlan said forcefully.

"No, but they can harm your sister with no trouble at all," Napoleon reminded him.

"All right, you have made your points," Harlan conceded. "I am sorry, but this is my sister. You have described a person I do not know." Harlan's normally calm, rock-hard face had become misty, confused, and sad.

"It has been more than a year, her time," Napoleon said gently. "A lot has happened to her body and mind, none of it good. Jackpot has a way of making you give up hope sooner than you might anywhere else."

"All right, all right, all right," Harlan said quickly, straightening up and waving his hands. "What can we do?"

"Palend is following through with his duplicity," Larry took up the dialogue. "He supplies Bishop-Fortune with machines for both the personal use of both him and his patrons, and, fortunately, hates the man's guts. It is incidental that if the dream factory suffers a loss he stands to recoup his losses twelvefold."

"How's that?" Harlan inquired.

"He wouldn't explain completely," Napoleon said. "But we think there's some kind of political rivalry going on. Palend has been too small a concern to do any real bad damage up until now. But he sees us as a powerful and profitable wedge. He'll arrange suitable camouflaged transport, both to there and back."

"But they know you two," Harlan complained. "They have your descriptions. How can you hope to infiltrate?"

"Your sister was alone in the library when I found her," said Larry. "Except for one small thing. A servo-robot. A machine that serves her, like a maid or a butler."

"A servo-robot?" Harlan repeated. "Where are we going to get a . . ."

He stopped and the three heads turned as one toward Mess' console.

"What did you stop squabbling for?" asked the machine. "It's fun to watch."

"Mess?" Larry said sweetly. "You know those spare parts of yours?"

"I'm sorry sir," Mess replied. "I don't understand."

"Mess," said Napoleon. "Your manifestations."

"I'm sorry it does not compute."

"You want to be disconnected and I'll put it together myself?" Larry asked.

"I'll blast you!" Mess suddenly replied.

"Not without my permission," said Larry. "Mess. . . ?"

"No, I won't do it! It's too dangerous! I might get fried! No, no, NO, I won't! You can't make me!"

A table on wheels buzzed around the small ship's bridge as the ship streaked toward Jackpot. All around its circular middle bore the legend—Palend: For The Thrill of Your Lifetime . . . At Your Fingertips—in dozens of languages. From the bottom of the craft, two converging tubes bore the engines' power. Four small nozzles at the front were its only

weaponry and two triangular windows were its only portholes. But it was fast and capable of great agility. It was perfect for their needs.

Larry sat in one chair, Napoleon in another. Behind them
Mess moved about before a bed outfitted with straps. Above
its four wheels was a solid square of machinery—his brain,
speech, and hearing console. One flashing light on three sides
gave it three-hundred-and-sixty-degree sensors, while one side
bore six more sensors, a row of switches interspaced with
dials and a speaker grid.

Above the block was a rimmed table with plate and cup
holders. Mess spun to and fro, testing its new ability, occasionally squealing, "Whee, whee!"

"As usual, we don't have much time," Larry was saying
above the machine's playground noises. "The Black Hole
pocket will only stay viable for a few more hours. Then the
ship will be open to attack. Harlan will be outside in his suit
to cover our return in case of a chase. As long as we get back
in time and the ship stays beside the asteroid we'll be all
right."

"Not to worry, not to worry," said the moving table. "I left
enough of me back there to take care of the ship."

"We're coming in," said Napoleon. "Get ready."

The ship swept down over the main city of Jackpot,
automatically taking care of the pressure and coordination
situation. Without assistance it hovered above Palend's establishment, then slowly lowered into the plaza. The plaza
roof covered them and the console lights turned off. The door
opened and Palend entered quickly, his snout smiling, but
both lids nearly covering his eyes.

"My friends, my friends," he intoned, arms out. "You take
great risks and do me great service."

"And you us," said Larry, rising. Palend took him by the
shoulders, at which Larry winced. The creature immediately
released him.

"I am sorry. I had forgotten about your recent wounds."

"I wish my body would forget," said Larry.

"It will, it will," said Palend. "If you would wait a moment
my land vehicle will come alongside and we can get on our
way. The fewer who see you the better."

"Agreed," said Napoleon, strapping on her weapons.

The table moved over to where the three stood. "You sure this is going to work?" it asked.

Palend turned. "This must be Mess, then."

"You told it my name!" Mess cried accusingly. "Why did you tell it my name? It knows too much! Permission to fire!"

Palend moved back quickly as Larry moved forward.

"Don't worry," he soothed the snout-faced creature. "He gets a little overwrought in times of crisis." He kneeled down next to the shaking machine. "Mess, we're not on board ship now. You can't blast this fellow. He is our friend."

"Not when they start sticking needles in him!" Mess said. "Permission to fire."

"No, now damper down."

"The vehicle is here," said Palend, tentatively. "We had better get on board." He quickly moved out, keeping away from Mess' front.

The Earth pair followed him, guiding a reluctant Mess. The land rover was a boxlike affair, large enough to hold six or eight of Palend's floor machines but still thin enough to maneuver through the narrow roadways of Jackpot.

The piloting cubicle was connected to the rear storage area by a band that allowed both parts to be ninety degrees to each other on tight turns. There were openings on all four sides that made for easy loading and unloading. There were no wheels. The bottom of the vehicle was several inches off the ground and humming. It could be directed both by manual or transport-band control.

Napoleon and Larry hopped in. Mess needed a ramp set up. In seconds they were ready. The interior was windowless and held only four rectangular machines, used in front of each entrance. The rest of the area was empty except for one chair, sealed to the floor and outfitted with straps on the legs, arms, and back. They all knew what it, and the bed-in-the-air vehicle, might be used for.

As the vehicle began to move forward, Palend pointed to two small piles of black clothing on the floor.

"Better put these on," he suggested. Larry and Napoleon took up the one-piece coveralls and began to pull them over their legs. With the movement of travel to contend with, they wound up on the floor. As Larry got both his legs in, Mess moved up to him.

"In . . . in case anything . . . you know . . . happens," said the machine. "I just wanted to say that my consciousness is on a little red plate. I made sure all the other parts weren't red, so . . . in case I get . . . I get . . . well, you know . . . scattered . . . you'll know which piece is important."

Larry smiled. "Don't worry, Mess. I won't let them scatter you."

"Thank you," said Mess. "Do I really have to do this?"

"I'm afraid so," Larry replied. "Our demise would be certain if we didn't."

"Wouldn't it be easier just to blast Harlan and go?"

"We need someplace to go," Larry explained. "Right now Destiny is the only place we'll be safe."

"I won't argue the point," Mess sighed. "Just don't forget about the red plate, will you?"

"I won't," promised Larry.

Napoleon had pulled the black garment all the way on. It effectively covered her from the chin to her feet, obscuring her size. Even though her weapons were on the inside, the black sheath had no tell-tale bumps.

"How does it feel?" Palend asked.

"I can move, but just barely," the feline answered. "How do you expect me to fight?"

"I hope that will not be necessary," said Palend. "But if you need mobility just squeeze the shiny area by your left wrist. The outfit will peel off around you."

Larry pulled his head through the neck opening and rose, clasping the chest opening together. "How long before we get there?"

"My informants tell me that this Destiny woman has been placed apart from the others in a Bishop-Fortune habitat by the edge of the main city. She can keep her schedule of appointments in even greater splendor than before, I'm told.

"Naturally her security has been magnified. However, with the delay, many patrons had to be rescheduled, creating a waiting period. My machines were ordered to keep the customers happy during the delay."

"Very interesting," said Larry. "But how long until we arrive?"

"Oh, I'm sorry," the creature sputtered. "I suppose I must be nervous. In several minutes. We are taking the fastest transport band."

"Let's go over the plan one more time," Larry suggested.

"Fine," said Palend. "We enter the establishment from the back and beneath."

"While you keep the guards busy, we start unloading the machinery and Mess moves upstairs," Larry continued.

"We give it a few minutes to do what is necessary," Napoleon took up the narrative. "Then deal with the guards and get the girl."

"My ship, meanwhile, automatically comes over and lands."

"We take off and you set up the cover story," Larry finished.

"Cover story?" Mess said. "What cover story?"

"Leave that to me," said Palend. "It will look as if I, too, was a victim of an off-world attack. They may be suspicious but they will be unable to prove anything."

The vehicle began to slow. "It is changing bands," Palend said. "We must be drawing near."

The four waited nervously as the vehicle slowed even more. "Quick. Put on your masks," Palend instructed.

Beneath the chair sat two large, solid head pieces, flat white except for two opaque eye slits. With a press on the side, each popped open. Larry and Napoleon fit them on their heads and sealed them closed. With the coveralls and helmets they looked almost like robots. Their black boots and gloves completed the effect. There could be almost any humanoid form encased within.

"It is going to be hard for me to take this," Larry heard Napoleon say in her mask's receiver. When he turned toward her all he saw was the white mask and grey eye slits.

"Try to hold on," he said. "But if you feel like mewing, go ahead. Only I can hear you."

"We are inside," the two heard Palend report. "We're moving down a long tunnel, down into their receiving area. Get ready."

The truck stopped and the doors moved open. Four guards

stuck their heads inside. Then they were gone and Palend hopped out.

"Wait until he instructs us to move," Larry said. Mess remained motionless, his lights out. Larry waited, looking out the left door.

They were hovering in what appeared to be an ancient, high-ceilinged dining room. A long table lay before an empty, closed-off fireplace. The walls were pasty-white while the furniture was dark brown. One couldn't see a Farzak in there unless he smiled.

"Start unloading," came Palend's voice from somewhere outside the vehicle.

"That's it," said Larry. "Let's go, Nap. Once we get the ramp set up, Mess, you get upstairs. You'll have three minutes. All right?"

Mess remained motionless. "Mess?" Larry repeated.

"Couldn't I just blast her and say she got caught in a crossfire?" Came the machine's strident voice inside Larry's helmet.

"No! Come on, Mess, get ready."

Napoleon had hopped out, pulling the installed ramp from the edge of the vehicle rim.

"We can tell Harlan that she was executed for treachery," Mess suggested.

"No."

"That she wandered into the line of fire."

"No."

"That she fell down a flight of stairs."

"No!"

"That she asked me to put her out of her misery."

"No, by the Earth Father! Mess, you nervous network of cowardly circuits! Get moving!"

"Will you keep it down?" came Napoleon's voice in a harsh whisper. "The guards might hear you, even outside the helmets. They're not reinforced steel, you know." She had the ramp in place.

"Mess, move it or we're all as good as dead. There'll be no one to pick up your red plate then. You'll never get back to the ship," Larry said cruelly.

Mess' lights turned on and it sped down the ramp. To his

left was another ramp, leading up with a bronze-colored band lying in the center of the incline. Mess silently rolled up to it, and, as soon as its two front wheels were on either side, it shot up as if pulled.

Larry stuck his masked head out of the truck to see Palend talking animatedly to the guards. All their backs were toward the vehicle. They had not seen or heard Mess' exit. Larry started counting the seconds as he pulled the machines out of the truck.

Less than two minutes later the large rectangular games were on the floor. They had been outfitted with a system of bearing that made for easy movement. As soon as the unloading was complete, the four guards accompanied Palend back into the room proper. Larry and Napoleon retreated back into the vehicle.

"These are new, eh?" said one of the guards.

"Only my best, which is *the* best anywhere, for the Bishop," said Palend. "Specifically built for this fine establishment."

The guard who spoke moved over to the four machines. All he saw was sloping, shiny smooth rectangles of blue metal.

"They look like sculptures. How do they work? Where is the power supply?"

"Where is the power supply for anything?" Palend said easily. "Can you find the energy for our countless restaurants, transport bands, and houses? They are everywhere and nowhere. But you shall go forward and touch the machine."

That was what the guard was waiting for. He moved even closer to the nearest cuboid and placed his hands on its rounded rim. Suddenly the seemingly solid surface became clear and a vast panorama appeared depicting a forest as seen from the sky. The guard actually gasped.

"I designed this to give the customer a taste of Destiny," Palend explained. "Based on its mythical legends the player becomes a God. The object: control the weather. If you run the planet smoothly you keep playing, visualizing countless wonders, experiencing the greatest power ever known—creation.

"If not, you witness great disaster, floods, earthquakes, storms, untold devastation, and tragedy."

The guard was smiling broadly. The other three's expressions were of rapt attention. One of the trio said, "But if one isn't a good player isn't the game very short?"

"Nature's fury isn't spent in seconds," Palend smiled. "Even if the player is the dullest of men the game will automatically continue for three minutes, come what may."

The words, "three minutes," was the signal. Napoleon pulled off her gloves. She neared the open door to the left.

Palend suddenly cried, "What is this? Oh no, don't!"

The four guards whirled to where Palend was looking, turning their backs on the vehicle. Napoleon pointed a gold-covered claw. A bright yellow field of energy blanketed the room. All four guards and Palend toppled over. Only the vehicle was untouched. According to the snout-faced creature, all that he and the guards will have seen was a yellow flash obscuring all else. They would then *be* unconscious for more than an hour.

Larry and Napoleon leaped out and ran toward the bronze-banded ramp. The feline pounced upon it with all fours. She streaked up and away. Larry jumped on in a hunched position, knees bent. He, too, shot up. They moved around corners and spun up and up until each had counted three floors.

Then they both stepped to the right. Without any discomfort or dizziness they were standing before a black curtain. Without hesitation, Larry pressed his left sleeve and moved through the curtain, Napoleon right behind him. Their masks sprung open and dissolved before they hit the floor. Their black outfits ripped off and spun into nothingness like they had been sucked into a cosmic hole.

Napoleon's paws pulled out her spitter. Larry's hand had settled on his beamer in its holster as his other hand whirled the curtain aside.

Before the two stood Titu Trigor dantily undoing her gown, standing before a figure lying with his back to them, propped up with pillows, sipping a drink. Beside them was a blinking Mess.

Her dark eyes moved up and locked on Larry's light ones. Then confusion. Napoleon was flying through the air toward the girl. The man on the floor was turning as Larry pulled out his beamer while running forward.

Larry saw Napoleon's spitter drop soundlessly to a pillow and her paws hit Titu's stomach as she opened her mouth to scream. He fired his weapon as the two females fell back, the human's cry turning to a gasp of escaping air. The beamer's ray bathed the man in yellow and his head dropped, his eyes closed.

Larry didn't stop, however. He also dropped his weapon onto a pillow and leaped toward the mass of flesh and fur on the floor. He fell on top of them, and, for a moment, the three scrambled, half on the rich carpeting, half on a slick, shiny, tilelike covering. Larry's hand fell across Titu's mouth just as she was getting up wind for another scream.

Napoleon wiggled out from under them. Larry pulled the girl back, arching her body. He slammed her head against his own chest as he sat on the floor, trying to keep her disoriented. His other hand sought one of her arms. He failed on both accounts. Her head did more damage to his chest than vice versa and her breath had returned so she was twisting her limb away from his further grasp.

Larry pressed his hand against her mouth, tightening his grip, still searching along the cloth-covered body for her arms. She bit his hand. He clamped back his own yell and pulled his arm up under her chin to keep her mouth shut. Her own hands finally appeared, fingernails digging into his forearm.

Larry pushed his body down to the floor, keeping hers underneath. Her arms automatically went out to protect her fall. He grabbed one with his free hand and wrenched it up her back. Her muffled cries turned into a gasp of pain. He released it a bit and she started to buck. He pushed it higher again and applied as much body pressure as he could. She arched and spat under him. Napoleon grabbed her spitter, surveying the room.

"Do something," Larry whispered through clenched teeth.

"I can't," Napoleon whispered back. "My beamer would knock you out, too."

"Then use the device Palend gave you."

"That blankets the entire area."

"Mess, Mess," Larry continued whispering. "What happened?"

The table moved over to where the girl struggled beneath Larry.

"I couldn't do it," it said quietly. "You didn't tell me about the customer. I couldn't deal with the customer, too."

"I didn't know about a customer," seethed Larry.

"You do now," complained the machine. "I couldn't do it. If you hadn't arrived they would have known I did it and destroyed me."

"We're here now," Larry spat. "Do it!"

"I can't, I can't. We'll never escape. They'll disconnect me!"

"Mess," said Napoleon. "Do it, or I'll destroy you now."

"You wouldn't," whispered the machine.

"My hand is slipping," said Larry. "Do it, Nap."

Titu's face was red and sweating, her long black hair a pool on the floor. A small part of her upper lip could been seen above Larry's clasped hand and her complaints were getting increasingly loud.

Suddenly a cloud of smoke wafted over from Mess' speaker. Larry held his breath. Titu must have gasped when it happened because she immediately went limp. Napoleon moved in and held a beamer against her temple, just in case. Larry rolled off. His hand was a mass of wet mucous and blood. Another wound to add to his collection. He wiped it unceremoniously against his pants leg.

"You cross me again, machine," he directed at Mess, "And I'll wipe your brain. Understand?"

"I'm sorry. Really, really, really."

"How do we stand?" he whispered to Napoleon, who kneeled by Titu, still aiming her beamer.

"We've lost time. There's no room for error now."

"Let's go, then," said Larry, moving to Titu's side. Her hair spread around her face like the rays of a black sun. The muscles of her face were relaxed but not lax. Her mouth was open but not drooping. She lay against the floor like it was a dear friend. Larry couldn't help but appreciate her for a moment before turning her over.

Her unconscious face appeared angelic. There were no

forced looks of lasciviousness. No knowing quirks of the lip. No winks or arched eyebrows. No amount of makeup could hide her innate innocence. As Larry pulled her onto her back her legs peeked out from the slit evening gown, creamy white, long, and unblemished. Her round, high breasts moved freely beneath the gauzy, clinging white.

Larry pushed his arms under her shoulders and legs. He pulled her to him and rose slowly. She was light but solid and warm against his torso. One arm was across her lap, the other hanging down. Napoleon moved over and placed it atop her waist. She nodded quizzically at Larry. He breathed deeply and nodded back. They began to leave the room, Mess rolling along behind.

The ramp was still clear since the patron Titu had been seeing to had a few more minutes left. They moved down without incident but when they returned to the original level they began to hear weapon fire from outside. The trio froze.

"What is that?" Larry asked.

"Our doom, our doom," Mess crackled.

"Don't get excited," he reprimanded. "It could be another vendetta, or a fight between customers."

"It's the ship!" Napoleon said with certainty. "Palend said the security had been tightened. We were delayed so now they're shooting at our escape ship!"

"I knew it," Mess continued. "We are doomed."

"Damper down, we don't have time for this," Larry instructed, the girl still in his arms. "Get inside the vehicle. With this alarm, guards will be streaming into all areas of the building. Mess, you try to close three of these doors with electronic signals. Nap, you cover the fourth. I'll strap the girl in."

The three ran up the ramp into the cargo area of the transport. Larry lowered Titu into the chair as Mess started blinking furiously. Napoleon stood by the door, tense, waiting. Larry held the beautiful girl's shoulder as he strapped a belt across her waist to hold her in the chair.

The band pulled her dress even closer to her waist, accenting her chest and hips. Larry began to breath deeply to control his feelings. Ever since he had first seen her he had been excited even by the thought of her. The feel of her in his arms, even writhing below him on the floor, had made him aware of instincts he had only heard or read about.

He attached the waist strap, but he couldn't leave her like that, she would fall forward. He pulled another belt around that encircled her body just below her breasts. The constriction there did amazing things to his mind. He was getting angry with himself. Years with a naked feline had done nothing physically to him but a few moments with this Destiny woman in a torn frock and he was about to bang his head against the nearest wall.

The chest strap held her upright, her head lolling down. Larry's hand was reaching for her chin when he heard Napoleon's sharp hiss.

"Here they come."

Larry turned to see two men turning the far corner holding large, riflelike weapons. They were both humanoid and extremely ugly. All four doors of the transport vehicle were still open and Mess looked ready to explode.

A hysterically quick series of lights switched in different combinations across its board, trying to find the correct electrical signal. As soon as it saw the guards, though, every light on its console went on in surprise. Three of the doors closed with a resounding clang.

At the same moment Napoleon tore the men down with her spitter. Mess spun around.

"I was going to try all of them last," it said happily.

"Can you drive this thing?" Larry asked.

"Find me the motor," Mess replied.

"Cover me," Larry said to Napoleon, hopping out the door. As she pulled off the golden hand-covering Palend had supplied, and pulled up her spitter again, Larry ducked his head under the bottom rim.

"This place is going to be a death trap soon," said Napoleon, listening to the sounds of battle outside. "As soon as they find the girl gone, they'll put two and two together and get the Peace Containers."

Larry didn't reply, just hopped back into the cargo area, walked over to a spot near the back, pulled his beamer out, and fired at the floor. A gaping rip appeared. Beside it hung a thin slice of machinery.

"There," he said to the animate table. "Hurry."

Mess rolled over to the hole for a moment, then a few of its lights blinked. The vehicle vibrated and jerked to the side. Napoleon fell out the door and Larry hit the wall, his beamer clattering on the floor.

"Sorry," said Mess.

Just then three more guards appeared at the ramp. Napoleon had dropped her spitter in order to land on all fours, and Larry's weapon still spun on the ground. The feline looked up in shock, and Larry grappled with his spitter in its holster as the three men started raising their weapons to annihilate the furry female on the floor.

Mess ran them over with the vehicle. Their bodies were crushed against the wall and were made sausages beneath the turning bulk of machinery, Napoleon grabbed her spitter and ran to the moving doorway. She leaped inside as the sounds of powdered bones, ripped limbs, and burst skin died out. The men didn't even have time to scream.

"Where to?" asked Mess merrily.

"Out the way we came," said Larry numbly, grabbing his own fallen weapon, trying to ignore what had just happened. Mess had been able to destroy the three without direct permission since Larry had already instructed it to drive the vehicle. It was a manuever that had saved their lives but that was still disquieting. What else was the machine capable of doing beyond its programming? What other tricks did it have up its circuits?

The vehicle moved quickly through a sloping grey tunnel, the wall zipping past the one opening. Larry turned and saw Titu's arms shaking by her side from the vibrations as well as some quivering movement beneath the dress. He quickly averted his gaze. He had other things to worry about.

Napoleon's tail was lashing to and fro, and Larry realized that it would be extremely difficult for both of them to shoot from the same opening.

"Mess, can you open the door on the other side?"

"Mess, can you drive?" the machine mimicked. "Can you open doors? Can you gas people? Can you shine the ship? Must I do everything?"

"Quit complaining, you violent volume of volts, just answer the question. Can you?"

"I can try."

Larry held on to the wall as the vehicle slowed slightly and a variety of lights winked in groups across Mess' console. Suddenly an opening appeared in front of the truck. For a moment Larry saw a group of armed guards, Peace Containers, and others of all alien types, bunched before the end of the ramp to the outside. Most were facing the opposite direction, but the ones who weren't saw a hurtling vehicle with a human, feline, and bound woman inside.

"Wrong door, Mess!" cried Larry. "Close it! The other one, open the side one!"

The guards' weapons were firing as the front sealed off. There was a searing crackle, red light appearing between the wall and the side opening, then the trio saw the grey wall turn black in a spot as they sped by. The initial blast was followed by others.

The Bishop-Fortune group were now fully aware of their approach and were trying to destroy them as they raced for freedom. Thankfully, Palend has outfitted both the truck and the ship with protective force shields or else they would already have been ash.

The area across from Napoleon opened up. Larry moved over to it, expecting the vehicle to speed up again. Instead it slowed even more.

"Mess, what's the matter?" he shouted. "Why are we slowing down still?"

"Not now," said the table. "I'm busy."

Its lights flared momentarily and the truck picked up speed.

Larry turned toward Napoleon. "As soon as we hit daylight, fire everything you've got and keep firing. Mess, you go right for the ship, no matter what condition it's in. As soon as we're close, seal off these doors and open the front one, facing the ship, so we can make a fast transfer."

The front wall was being bombarded even more heavily. The vehicle began to buck and vibrate from the force of the onslaught.

"We're getting closer," said Larry.

"They're getting stronger," said Napoleon.

"And it's getting harder to control this thing," said Mess.

Sparks and bolts reflected off its metal surface from the gash in the floor. Suddenly the whole front wall bent in. Both Larry and Napoleon jumped to the back. Mess shut down in fear for a second, all its lights winking off. The vehicle started to slow again.

Mess blasted back on, stunning Larry with the brightness of its lights, but it was too late. The floor began to peel back. The wall began to bubble and boil from the top. The vehicle rolled to a stop.

The wall separated from the roof and the floor completely then fell off. Before the stunned trio and unconscious captive was a line of Peace Containers stretched across the tunnel, each of a different alien type, but all with brightly glowing jewels of destruction. They had banded together to create a bolt even stronger than the protective force shield.

Behind them lay the entrance to the outside and the scorched escape vehicle beyond. Very close, but it might as well have been infinity. A black Mantas, whose deep red jewel still glowed with power, moved forward.

"I am Isenraid," it hissed. "Throw down your weapons before you. Stay exactly where you are."

Larry and Napoleon saw no recourse. Mess had no weaponry to ask permission to fire with. Titu Trigor was still beyond caring. Larry and Napoleon unclipped their belts after throwing down their hand weapons. They didn't even consider trying to make a break. Behind the Peace Containers were armed guards. All in all, it was a veritable army.

They knew that even if they tried to use the Destiny girl as cover the red bolts would slice off anything in sight. The holsters dropped upon the weapons. Isenraid and three others looked at the pile. Four bolts shot out of their foreheads, then disappeared. The hunk of metal and material crumbled into a puddle of burning hot liquid and flaking ash.

"Undo the Destiny child and bring her forward," bid Isenraid.

The two did as they were told. Napoleon pulled out a ramp as Larry undid the straps, pulling Titu onto her feet. Napoleon moved back and took one arm. Larry held the other. They got under her shoulders and carried her to the floor of the tunnel. Mess was motionless back in the vehicle, all its lights out. If it could convince the massed enforcers that it was a harmless machine, it would, waiting until they left to escape. But by then it would be too late for Napoleon and Larry.

"Lay her down," said Isenraid. "Carefully."

Larry lowered her himself, on bended knee. She looked none the worse for wear, still completely unconscious and at peace stretched across the floor.

"Move over to the wall," Isenraid instructed. Larry's heart sunk. If they were to be detained for questioning, they would have been taken away. It was shaping up to be an immediate execution. The pair stood by the wall. The line of Peace Containers began to move over.

Napoleon's left leg began to quiver. "I will not die standing still," she hissed.

"Do what you want," Larry whispered back, his mind dull. "It will hardly make a difference."

She looked at him with fire in her eyes. The catlike pupils said that he could not be more wrong. To her it made *all* the difference. If she had wanted to stand still for death she would have remained on Earth.

But Larry thought it meaningless. To attack, to fight, to kill when death was inevitable seemed futile. He had tried his best; they had had incredible luck and they had succeeded. Up until now.

The Peace Containers stood before them. Mantas, human, Farzak, glop, tentacled, and stalked. Each faced them and the jewels glowed even brighter. Larry felt Napoleon's muscles bunching for the final attack. His own adrenalin started pumping through his body in a rush. His eyes found Titu lying before a kneeling guard whose hand moved toward her chest.

That opened Larry's mind up again. He realized that death was *always* inevitable and not to fight for life when there was the slimmest chance was a waste of your whole life. He was set to join Napoleon when it happened.

The opposite wall, ten feet down from them, exploded.

Napoleon and Larry hurtled forward as great chunks of

stone and metal flew in a wide half-circle, a huge cloud of dust and dirt covering the area. The force of the concussion cut a swath through the guards. A rock the size of a fist bashed into the kneeling guard's head. His hand never reached its lush target.

Titu, herself, rolled over to the wall. The Peace Containers dropped like dominos except for the two Larry and Napoleon collided with. The feline tore at the human while Larry smashed the Farzak in the eye. The falling debris forced both to roll off their executioners and scurry under the vehicle for protection. They watched as from out of the gaping hole in the wall came a huge, nine by five foot rock.

Through the grey haze a bunch of multicolored lights blinked on in the cargo area of the vehicle.

"What an entrance!" whistled Mess.

The space bullet was different this time. Its limbs were detached from the main body proper, hanging from the shoulder area like two arms.

Before their amazed eyes one arm rose. Not slowly, not quickly, but faster than the eye could see. One moment it was a crooked hunk hanging from the shoulder area, the next it was straight, aimed at scurrying guards and stunned Peace Containers. The next second four stone fingers were discernible and from those fingers came a wash of green.

The moving bodies contorted and fell. The globs of matter rippled and spread. The stalks curled and collapsed. The tentacles quivered and drooped. And most incredible of all the jewels of the Peace Containers nearest the ray turned opaque.

Mess rolled out of the vehicle to call out to its associates.

"He was talking to me!" it cried. "Get the girl and get inside the craft. He'll take care of things here."

They didn't have to be told twice. Larry crawled out and ran to the prone Titu. Napoleon scurried after a rolling Mess, bouncing over the rocky terrain. Without ceremony Larry pulled the girl up and dropped her onto his back. He trotted as quickly as possible by the space bullet.

Harlan's sensors picked up one guard and one Mantas moving back into the house. No one was outside. But he did note that there were two guards in upper stories, waiting to pick off the feline and humans as they entered the craft. That would not do.

Larry stumbled outside, seeing Napoleon nearing the escape vehicle. Mess was already putting the automatic entrance into effect. Larry got ten yards farther when a section of the house was sliced off and fell in on itself.

He fell forward from the force, Titu rolling over him. Napoleon ran up as Larry looked behind. A cloud of smoke was clearing, leaving the inside of the house exposed. Patrons were running in all directions, electrical wiring was cracking and spitting sparks. Water, wine, and excrement was shooting off in all directions. The ramp leading to the tunnel below was all but obliterated, but from beneath came another sound.

Suddenly a hole burst open and the space bullet shot out into the sky.

"Come on," Larry heard Mess' voice. "He says he'll meet us. Hurry!"

Larry turned back to see Napoleon dragging Titu by her arms toward the ship. He found his legs and ran to help her. They pulled the unconscious girl inside. Larry dropped her on the bed and had just enough time to strap her legs and chest to the couch before it was his turn to hit the floor. Napoleon had hopped into the pilot's seat and initiated lift-off.

Outside, the space bullet matched its ascent for several seconds before peeling off and heading downward. Napoleon looked closely out the small porthole. As the land receded she couldn't spot Harlan anywhere. But as she was watching, Bishop-Fortune's establishment exploded, great gobs of yellow-orange-red fire billowing up and out.

By the time the ship left Jackpot's atmosphere the house of vice was a hulk of flame, a black plume of smoke reaching for the sky.

EIGHT

"Let's burn them out of space!" yelled Bishop-Fortune.

"Hardly necessary," replied Isenraid. "Besides, you saw what the Destiny soldier did to your establishment. You should guess what I know. Killing a space bullet is no easy matter."

The two stood in a white room decorated in bright silver. Bishop-Fortune had a thing about bright silver. His hair was bright silver, he dressed in bright silver, many of his women were given silver eyes, all of his women wore silver, most of his credit was in silver, most of his star fleet were bright silver craft.

He sat in a chair built of bright silver slabs and cushioned with maroon pillows before a console of glinting silver switches—the control room of his personal space corps. He wore a vaguely military uniform but it was dotted with bright silver spots.

"I don't care," he complained. They deserve to be destroyed."

"And they will be," said Isenraid. "In good time."

The Mantas stood, a blue outfit draped across his body, several beige bandages lining his upper appendage, arms and legs.

"I have much to pay them back for, the same as you," the Mantas continued. "But I'm willing to wait to collect the ultimate amount of violence. The complete vengeance."

"You are talking in riddles again," said Bishop-Fortune. "These weren't your establishments, these weren't your men, they were mine! I have been insulted by their escape. Twice!"

"And we have been insulted twice besides that," the Mantas replied smoothly. "Once, when the space bullet escaped from Destiny, and once when the Earth pair escaped from their own planet. We had all the evidence to assume they had come into contact with Trigor but we did not act. We allowed others to deal with them. We were not sure."

"You are sure now!" Bishop-Fortune exploded. "Did you *see* what they did to my places? My two best places. I say destroy them, utterly, now."

"And I say that you should trust us as you have until now," Isenraid returned. "We have a deal, as I am sure you will recall."

"It's hard, believe me," Bishop-Fortune reminded him. "It's been more than a year."

"You have not suffered," said the Mantas. "The Destiny girl has given you pleasure, and your customers, even more. You have reveled in her beauty, you have celebrated inside her, and you have honored the credit she has brought in. That alone is worth more than both the destroyed establishments."

"Yeah," said Bishop-Fortune, remembering. "Yeah. She fought like a tigress the first few months. But I could tell she was enjoying it. They always do. The way she writhed. It was something. Strongest I ever had. I gave her to the people or else she would have gotten too sure of herself. Yeah, like a tigress. A real tigress."

"If you destroy the ship now," Isenraid interjected. "You will lose both your child of Destiny and an actual tigress."

"The cat!" Bishop-Fortune exclaimed. "That's right. That Mandarin female. Now there's a prize. With those two I'd be the biggest attraction in the galaxy, bar none. Destiny wouldn't try to find Trigor. They think she's dead. And Earth wouldn't care about an escaped murderess. They'd let me have her with blessings, figuring it was what she deserved. What an incredible conquest."

"If you destroy the ship with your fleet," Isenraid repeated. You lose both."

Bishop-Fortune sat pulling at some loose skin on his lip. "All right," he finally said. "What do you want me to do?"

"Nothing," said Isenraid. "We shall handle all the problems."

"That's what you said last year," muttered Bishop-Fortune.

"But now our space bird is coming home to roost," said Isenraid. "I have been . . . in contact . . . with Ministic on Destiny. She feels that there is no reason why our postponed plan cannot take effect. The Trigor parents are still dead and disgraced, the children are still missing. The questions are still being asked. Their loyalty is still in serious doubt. There is no reason why Harlan cannot still kill the Queen."

"And then?"

"And then Ministic takes temporary control and dispatches the space bullets to find their treacherous brother. Ministic heroically manages to flush out and destroy an Earth accomplice. By then the weapon will be finished and the space bullets will be helpless."

"And then?" Bishop-Fortune was smiling.

"The planet will be defenseless," said Isenraid. "Your fleet will move in and take control, having all the advantage and reaping all the profit."

"Ah, yes, the profit," Bishop-Fortune mused.

"Yes, mineral, and physical wealth. Ongoing supplies of food and clothing. The most beautiful females of the humanoid species. And the child of Destiny and the feline."

"Excellent," said the Jackpot denizen, rising. "Excellent. You sound assured of the plan's success."

"Of course," said Isenraid.

Bishop-Fortune moved toward the door. Before he reached it, he turned.

"Tell me something. You're not like the other Mantases. You are not so . . . fanatical, let's say. What are you doing this for? What's in it for you? A permanent home? Shared wealth? What?"

Isenraid stared impassively at the man, but he was not put off.

"What happens afterwards?" he pressed. "What will you do then?"

Isenraid moved up to where Bishop-Fortune stood.

"We will do as we always do," he said. "Advise those in power. We are rarely wrong. People listen to us. All the races listen to us. For instance, after the first attempt to take the Destiny child, did you listen to me when I advised implanting a device inside her?"

"Sure, it was a good idea. We know where she is now without having to follow her. We can pinpoint the Earth ship at any time."

"It will make the final destruction simple," Isenraid nodded. "And did you listen when I told you who the Earthen's associate on this planet was?"

"Of course. It had to be Palend. Why else would he outfit his vehicle with force shields?"

"And did you listen when I suggested the best way to achieve both your ends just now?"

"Yes. It sounds good. We not only get rid of the space bullet and the Baker guy but I get Destiny's riches and the feline as well."

"Good, good," said Isenraid. "It is as it is on almost every planet. Now you tell me, Bishop-Fortune. Who is really in charge here?"

With that Isenraid left the room with Bishop-Fortune speechless. Then he began to laugh.

DESTINY

NINE

The Black Hole was no stage for a scene of happy reunion. There were no cries of delight, no tears of joy, no solid hugs of welcome, not even comfortable relaxation.

As soon as Titu awoke and was unstrapped she ran right for her brother and tried to scratch his eyes out. When Harlan could not get her to stop he slugged her across the face.

Larry brought her to a cabin where, when she awoke, she sobbed for a few days. When the swelling of her jaw went down she cried for two weeks.

At first Harlan thought he could talk her out of it only to get screamed at. Occasionally she would attack him. That was always followed by her being hurled back onto her bed or another slap, followed by more crying.

Later, the only times Harlan would see her was when she was asleep. He would stand outside her cabin, tears collecting in his beard, sometimes for as long as eight hours.

Larry gave her her meals. The first few days she usually threw them back at him, followed by more crying. After almost a week she began to eat, but would constantly throw up and occasionally would beat at Larry as he tried to attend to the disorder.

Later she would be able to eat the full meal but would tell Larry what terrible things Bishop-Fortune would do to him, which almost always ended with her delivering a nonstop string of obscenities.

By the third week she ate in silence, but tried to make serving and cleaning up as difficult as possible. Larry would walk around depressed and Harlan remained despondent.

By the end of the first month in light drive she appeared on the bridge. She still wore her white gown, ripped and dirty and flecked with sickness. She stood at the back and said nothing. She moved away as Harlan attempted to approach her. That evening Larry asked him what size clothes she wore. He put a shirt, pants, and boots he had altered outside her door.

The next day he found them strewn across the passageway. He refolded them and put them by her door. He repeated this for a little more than two weeks when he found them thrown, kicked, or torn. When they were ripped, he sewed them up. When food was dropped on them, he'd clean them.

By the end of the second month in their three-month journey she was visiting the bridge every day, wearing the boots, shirt, and pants. Larry thought they looked very good on her. He said nothing, however. By then Harlan and Titu were actively avoiding each other. Shortly thereafter Mess spoke up.

"She's in the cargo area trying to sabotage the ship. Can I blast her?"

"No," said Larry, miserably. "Is she doing any damage?"

"No."

"Then leave her alone."

"I think I should blast her."

Larry did not reply. Napoleon agreed with the machine but had more understanding and sense to say so.

In the days that followed Mess kept them abreast on her movements and her attempts to do them all in. Then her emphasis began to change. Her endeavors leaned more to self-destruction than mass destruction.

She would sit in an escape pod trying to jettison it, for hours. Then she would try to jam open the escape hatch. Finally she would wander around the engine area trying to find an exposed area of power. Mess made sure nothing worked for her, under Larry's orders.

The ship sank into space like black depression. The passing

planets and speeding stars held no more wonder. Space became cavernous and uncomfortable to Larry who, up until then, always thought of the Black Hole as home. He couldn't understand his feelings. There were times when he just sat and stared at nothing for hours. He didn't talk to Napoleon or yell at Mess anymore, no matter how much they tried to reach him. The prospect of Destiny became an obsession.

Titu began to wear her disintegrating gown again. She would stare out the portholes, radiating beauty and hate. She was pale, her hair was matted and unwashed, she had gotten thinner, but her inner pain made her even more lovely to Larry. Her skin had become chapped, her pupils red and watery, her fingernails chipped, but she was still beautiful.

One day Destiny came into view. At first it was a speck. Later it grew into a dot. Soon it was a marble, a green-streaked marble. Then it was a jeweled ball, a sparkling space weight.

On that day Titu ran onto the bridge screaming. Larry sat in the pilot's chair looking at his thumb. Napoleon was tinkering near Mess' console trying to piece together a new weapon for herself. Harlan was wandering around the ship.

The Trigor girl ran to the port facing Destiny and looked. She then ran to Larry and started beating him in the face, her arms two thrashing windmills.

The first fist hit him on the bridge of the nose, the second in the eye. The pain was shocking enough to keep him stunned and helpless. Her small, hard fists continued to pummel him.

"Where are we going?" she screamed. "Where are we going?"

Napoleon was up and behind the girl. She wrapped her arms around her waist and pulled Titu off the pilot. Titu's legs kicked, shapely flashes of flesh streaking out under her torn dress. Her hands tried to push away the furry arms holding her. All she felt were tightly bunched muscles. When she got her feet on the ground she leaned forward and spat.

"I'm not going back! I can't! I'll die first!"

Then she continued screaming. Long, wrenching cries of "No," drawn out and finished with wracking gasps. Harlan ran in and tried to take his sister in his arms, his face twisted in despair. She pulled away from both Napoleon and her brother, spitting at them. Then she ran out the hatch.

Harlan and Larry were on their feet to follow her. Napoleon cut them off and raised her paws.

"Neither of you move. You understand? I should have done this months ago." She turned to move out. Harlan took a step after her. She turned back. "I mean it," she assured him. "Follow me and I will claw you. Either of you." Her claws were out and her tail beat at the air.

Larry moved forward and put a hand on Harlan's arm. He stopped. Larry nodded at Napoleon. She turned and ran out on all fours.

She caught up with Titu by the girl's cabin. She had tripped on her gown and was getting up, tearing at the cloth, screaming and crying. Napoleon spun her around and hit her hard three times across the face. She then pushed the girl into her cabin. Napoleon entered and closed the door.

She turned to face the shocked Destinian.

"I am as beautiful as you. I am wanted as much, if not more, than you. I have been used worse than you. I have suffered more than you. Yet I do not try to destroy myself or the ones close to me. It means nothing and it accomplishes nothing. You will stop it. Now."

"You, you do not understand," sputtered the girl. "He'll kill me."

"He has no more control over you," said Napoleon. "I thought you would have realized that by now."

"He has ships. A fleet. He can destroy us anytime."

"Then you have nothing to fear. You will be free."

"No! No! He'll kill you all and take me back. He'll use me."

Napoleon moved in and took Titu firmly by the shoulders.

"He can not take you back if you do not wish it."

"He has strength," the girl pleaded. "He has ropes and straps and drugs . . ."

"He cannot take you back. He would not take you back without trying to take me. I will not be taken because I am not afraid."

"You don't . . . you don't understand! You don't know how I feel! You're, you're not human."

Napoleon hit the quaking girl once more across the face. The tears and sobs were cut off.

"I am female. I feel the same things you do. Must I show you? I am a woman. I am not afraid of it."

The Destinian would still not meet her eyes.

"You are not afraid of him," Napoleon said with certainty. "You are afraid of *yourself*."

"I . . . I . . . am afraid . . ."

"Of yourself. You are a woman. You are a female. You were born to be used. You cannot ram into them. They can only ram into you. You are afraid of accepting that. You are afraid of liking that."

"I . . . I do not like that . . ."

"What can you do when a male you hate takes you? There is pain, but there are the other senses too. Hate is the only thing left you. But after months and months even hate is dulled. You have no choice. You live with the pain and the hate. It becomes your reality. But how can this be, you ask yourself? How can this hell be my life? How can I accept this?

"You tell yourself you cannot. But you have. You *have*."

Titu started to cry again. But they were not tears of shame or of horror, or of hate. They were tears of release.

"Then you have a choice," Napoleon continued. "You can hate yourself and your sex for this acceptance. Or you can become what they want you to become. A thing. You can shape yourself in their image."

Napoleon waited until Titu's eyes found her own. They were two different kinds of eyes, one deep and dark and tearful, the other bright, slitted, and aware. But they were all living eyes. They were all eyes that attached to aware brains. They were the same.

"Or you can understand that you exist. That you are a woman. That this is your reality and you can be the best or worst woman you want to be."

Titu shook her head.

"No," said Napoleon. "Don't do that. You must accept yourself. You are yourself. You have been used. There is

nothing wrong about not being able to fight that. There is
nothing wrong about not dying or killing yourself. There is
nothing about being helpless. You were, and now it's over.
You are still you. You have changed. That is all right, too.
You have been hurt. It is over now. Over. Understand that it
is finished."

Titu rubbed her eyes with the palms of her hands. She
stared at Napoleon, not seeing the fur or the whiskers or the
eyes. She saw another woman. She nodded.

"I'll try," said Titu.

"You will," corrected Napoleon.

Titu looked away. She saw herself reflected in a porthole.
Her dress was ripped, exposing most of her chest. Her face
was streaked and dirty. Her eyes were puffy and bloodshot.
But she could see the woman beneath, superimposed on the
green planet of Destiny. She turned back to Napoleon.

"I will," she said.

The four sat on the bridge in a semicircle. Mess was kind
enough to supply two more chairs. Destiny loomed large in
all the windows, bathing the area in brightness tinged with
color. Titu was once again dressed in the black tunic, grey
pants, and boots. She had washed, as well, making her look
as fresh as a new morning. Her appearance and subsequent
explanations had brightened the ship more than Destiny and
its sun combined. Larry was smiling and Harlan was nodding
his head, seriously but not gravely.

"One male after another," Titu was saying. "One operation
after another. If I fought I would be starved or put in a tiny
room, bound, blindfolded, and gagged. Hung up in the waiting area so anyone could play with me. It was never-ending,
awful degradation."

Larry wasn't smiling anymore.

"It came down to Bishop-Fortune being my only savior after awhile. You didn't come," she said to Harlan. "And he
would tell me all these stories about what happened to you.
That you were killed and your suit was a coffin in space
. . . that you had tried to assassinate the Queen and were
executed. That you went crazy and killed our parents.

"Then he would drug me and later tell me all the things I

had done under the influence. I had to listen and respond to him. The one time I tried to think for myself he put me on the open market. That was where you found me," she told Larry. "When you first told me the truth I thought it was another trick. To degrade me even more. Then I couldn't face that truth. I could never escape. He'd always find me."

"You have escaped," Larry reassured her.

"Classic brainwashing technique," explained Napoleon. "The starvation causes an imbalance in the brain fluids, where the subject is open to a far greater range of suggestion. Normally things you would never accept become all too possible since you can't think straight."

"Incredible," said Harlan. "What kind of people are these? You mean you did not want to return to Destiny because you were different?"

"I can't explain it exactly," said Titu slowly. "I wasn't fit. I wasn't worthy or something like that. I just couldn't think and I was so used to not thinking I couldn't break it. You see, it's easier not to think. It's easier to be what they want you to be. It's easier not to look at yourself. It's easier to look at yourself through others."

Following the silences, Titu asked uncomfortably, "So what now?"

"I have to tell you what happened, really," said Harlan. "It is not much better than what you were told."

Titu looked from Napoleon to Larry. "I'm ready," she said to her brother, risig. Harlan got up and walked with his sister out of the bridge.

"Really incredible," said Larry, leaning back and sighing.

"And how are you feeling, pilot?" asked Napoleon grinning.

"Better." He leaned forward and cocked an eye at his copilot, who sat back regally. "You know things like the back of your hand, don't you?"

"Paw, Larry, paw," the feline retorted. "I've spent a lot of time in Earth labs and in the observation of the way humans work."

"Then explain it to me, will you? I'm confused."

"You're in love," Napoleon corrected. "Or 'in like,' or 'infatuated.' You've experienced your first full woman and your poor, undernourished psyche can hardly handle it."

"Are you making fun of me?"

"Hardly. Most of the dried-up fossils back on Earth only feel lust. Their feelings for the opposite sex are put on a level of craving. Like an appetite for food. They think they can live without love, as if that made them 'real men.' You're more real than any of them. It was no mistake they didn't make more like you. A man who honestly feels is dangerous to the way things are going."

Larry shook his head, smiling. "This is too much. I'm no different from anyone else."

"Don't sell yourself short. What are you feeling for that girl? Passion? Desire? Not much, I'll warrant. You have strong feelings but more like tenderness, regard, and affection. Attraction. You need her, you want her, but you don't *have* to have her. You know what I mean."

"Yeah, I think I do," said Larry, rising. He walked around the bridge, looking out at Destiny when it came into view. "How about us, though? We've been together a long time. We feel things for each other."

"Must we define them?" Napoleon asked, with a tinge of exasperation.

"You already have in your own mind," Larry replied. "It's harder for me. My experience is limited."

"Point taken and understood," Napoleon went on. "I suppose this kind of thing is all you can do on a three-month space trip without busy work."

"Well?"

"We have everything," said the feline, rising and approaching him. "Affection, respect, attachment, friendship. Everything but one. Attraction. For some reason we just don't excite each other. Thank Cheshire."

"What's so great about that?"

"Ah, love is a funny emotion, Larry. Could you imagine what it would have been like all these years if we *were* attracted? We'd have been eliminated long ago."

"I suppose so."

"On Earth? With every dream factory wanting me? With

every scientist waiting for you to make a wrong move? You *know* so."

They stood side by side in front of the port, Destiny making a spotlight around them.

"I know so," said Larry.

"We're talking like old friends about to die," said Napoleon glumly.

"An interesting point," said Mess.

At the sound of its voice they both jumped.

"Does anyone know what we're going to do when we reach Destiny orbit?" the machine demanded.

"That's right!" cried Larry. "We're not in the clear yet."

"We're wanted by the Earth Government, the Jackpot Intercouncil, and the mightiest vicelord in the galaxy; we're flying into an alien-spawned conspiracy and he says we're not in the clear yet," whined Mess. "We won't be in the clear, *ever.*"

"Damper, you gross conglomerated mechanism. Why didn't you speak up before?"

"You people are so much fun to watch."

"Never mind. What's our situation now?"

"Mentally or physically?"

"Both."

"Mentally you've just deciphered your place in the universe. Physically we're a few hours from orbit and in a lot of trouble."

"What's the matter?"

"We've been tracked the last ten minutes. No radio message, no verbal transmission of any kind. No overt defensive actions. Just tracking."

"Are you sure?"

"Of course I'm sure," Mess said defensively. "It took me a while to be sure that's what it was, but when I speak up you can be sure I'm sure."

"That's odd," Larry said to Napoleon. "I'd imagine we're unlike any ship they've ever encountered, yet they don't contact us."

"According to Harlan, Destiny shoots first," Napoleon reminded him. "Perhaps we had better do the signaling."

"Mess, call Harlan in here," Larry instructed, moving over

to his console. "We've been so wrapped up in ourselves we haven't thought out our approach at all."

"Slim," said Mess. "Very slim reasoning."

"I said damper down!" Larry shouted.

"Well, we're feeling much better now, aren't we?" Mess replied in a huff.

"Did you call Harlan?" Napoleon interrupted.

"Naturally. *I* haven't been wrapped up in myself."

"What is going on?" asked Harlan, moving quickly into the room, followed by Titu.

They all huddled around Larry's chair.

"Destiny has been tracking us for awhile. They haven't done anything yet. We want to know what they're likely to do," Larry said from his seat.

"They can see we are not part of a fleet," Harlan mused. "They should have contacted us."

"We should have contacted them," reminded Napoleon fretfully. "We have no markings; Larry took them off on our way to Jackpot. They might be unsure as to how to handle us."

"What do you mean Larry took them off?" Mess complained. "Larry told me to take them off. And Earth and Jackpot could have described our ship to Destiny."

"Destiny is not interested in outsiders' problems," said Titu.

"But we do monitor transmissions in case they prove any danger to our security," said Harlan.

"Some decision has to be made," Larry chipped in. "Harlan, what do you advise?"

"Contact them. Tell them the story of our escape from Earth. Leave me and Titu out. They still think we're traitors probably."

"Mess," Larry instructed. "Get in touch with the planet. Say we're the Black Hole escaped from Earth in need of assistance."

The group waited a few seconds while Mess tried a wide range of transmission frequencies.

"Mess?"

"I've sent the message out every way possible. No reply. Not even evidence that they're receiving."

"Try again."

"I have already. Twice. Nothing. We had better turn back."

"We can't," Larry said. "Harlan, what now?"

The Destinian stood with his hands joined before his face. Slowly they rocked back and forth. Suddenly he brought them down and spoke decisively.

"There's little choice. Keep sending your message. Give them the whole story if necessary, without mentioning us, with or without reply. And don't try to run their orbit or land. We have the best defense of any planet in the galaxy." He turned and walked toward the rear hatch.

"Where are you going?" asked Napoleon.

Harlan stopped by the exit. "I'm getting into my suit. Just in case. I advice you to do the same." Then he was out and gone.

"Mess, go ahead," said Larry. "Stick to the basic facts. Napoleon and I were being used. We escaped to Destiny. We come in peace with information vital to their safety and all that. Just keep repeating that and don't get strident. Tell me of any change in tracking." He turned to the two females on either side of his chair. "We had better suit up."

The hours moved by without incident. Mess kept sending the message. No reply. The tracking never ceased. They found a space suit that could fit Titu and all three donned suits as Destiny began to take up three-fifths of their horizon. They returned to the bridge, clumping in their "grav" boots.

"Any change?" Larry radioed to Mess.

"None," the computer replied.

The three moved around the area like deflated balloons. The suits were grey and blue. Larry's had a grey top and bottom with blue gloves, belt, and boots, while Napoleon's was the opposite. Titu got a mixture of the two to fit her better, made of spare parts. A grey top, a blue bottom, a grey belt, grey gloves, blue boots.

The helmets were tubes that ended in a rounded top. A clear screen stretched across their visages, ending behind their ears, giving them a better than one-hundred-and-eighty-degree view. The clear screen had the same attributes as the ship's port windows. They would gradate depending on the amount of light as well as protect the wearer from cosmic radiation. The bulbous belt was not only an oxygen holder, but a mixer of it as well.

"How much longer until final orbit?" Larry inquired.

"Four minutes, twelve seconds," Mess said tensely.

"Harlan, can you hear us?" Titu shouted into her suit.

Larry and Napoleon winced as her voice boomed through their receivers.

"No need to shout," said Napoleon. "The microphone and speakers are part of the screen. Even a whisper can be heard."

"I hear you all very well," came Harlan's voice. "As well as the computer with whom I've established a long-term communication. Now be prepared for anything. Absolutely anything. I do not like this feeling. Never in my experience have they waited this long to take action. This denotes no good. Look out for a collection of flashes from the following locations."

Harlan then rattled off sixteen coordinates before Mess interrupted him.

"But how about . . ." it too gave a different coordinate.

"That is another," Harlan said in surprise. "How did you know?"

"Because that's where the flash just came from," Mess said hysterically. "Unidentified craft sighted. Permission to fire!"

"Space bullets!" came Harlan's voice. "They're attacking. Quickly, get in in your escape pod."

"Permission to fire, permission to fire!" Mess cried.

"Harlan," Larry shouted over the confusion. "Can't we stall them? Talk to them?"

"You can't," Harlan replied, at which point Larry waved at Napoleon and Titu to get going. "But *I* can. Get in an escape vehicle and take off. I will cover you."

Larry moved as the head of the fleet of one hundred space bullets appeared on his screen. Napoleon and Titu were already out of the bridge area. He stopped by a rear panel and pulled out his beamer rifle.

"Hey, what about me?" cried Mess.

"Open the bottom hatch for Harlan, then come on!" shouted Larry as he moved out the rear. Sounds of frenzied vacuum packing assailed Larry's ears as he trotted toward the escape pod area. Then the whole hallway rocked from side to side. The space bullets had begun their attack.

"Get out!" shouted Harlan's voice. "I deflected that shot or else it would have destroyed your ship. Get going!"

Larry galloped into the escape hallway to see Napoleon and Titu huddled before a hatch.

"Too many of us for one pod. We've got to use the cargo ship, the salvage ship. Hurry!" They had left Palend's vehicle in Jackpot orbit to aid in the cover story.

The ship started bouncing in rapid movements. The three bounced about the small tube like candy in a box. The jumps subsided to a vibration and the trio found their feet again.

"Mess," said Larry. "Close the bottom hatch and prepare the salvage ship. We have to take that."

There was no reply. The three began to run toward the bottom of the ship.

"Mess, Mess where are you? Mess!"

The ship lurched to the right. The three hit the left wall. Napoleon howled in frustration as her suit diminished her natural balance and freedom of movement. Larry pulled himself erect and kept going, collecting a hunched over Titu in the process.

The ship shook back and forth but the trio kept going. They made it to the bottom hatch to find it closed and the salvage ship atop it, its doors open.

"Mess did it," said Larry. "Get in quickly."

The three pulled themselves in, Larry shutting the door after him. As soon as they were sealed in Larry saw the console lights flash. The bottom hatch opened again and they were streaking through space.

All three floated to the roof of the bullet-shaped ship. Through the small porthole in front Larry saw an incredible display of light and galactic fire. Rocks spun at each other with unbelievable agility and in amazing patterns. Weaponry of all kinds burnt, bristled, curved, and arced out of the shooting stones.

Larry pulled himself away and started to maneuver himself to one of the four seats near the tip of the craft.

"Strap yourselves in," he instructed the others. "We'll be hitting the atmosphere soon."

In one of the seats was a flat-topped metal tube lined with clear semicircles atop a smaller-necked tube atop a sloping cone that branched out into another thicker chest tube that ended in four quadruple-jointed metal legs; two ending in wheels, two ending in small, boxlike treads.

"In fifteen seconds to be exact," said the metal creature. Larry ignored Mess' latest manifestation, pulling Titu into a seat and straping her in, instead. Napoleon had manuevered into her own. Larry pulled himself back to the seat beside Mess as Harlan's voice assailed them.

"They've got your ship; I couldn't cover it all. I'm pacing your escape craft now. I'm trying to keep them off all sides but there are many of them. They've spotted me and your vehicle. How much time to reentry? How much time left?"

Before Mess or Larry could answer the escape ship spun as if struck by a giant palm. Incredible pressure pushed against Larry's head and body until the light went out.

TEN

"Ohhh. I feel terrible," said the voice.

Larry awoke to find himself under a blanket of green beneath a sheet of brown.

"What an awful feeling," said the voice.

The first thing Larry heard was a loud bonging, as if something were hitting a large bell with a soft mallet. Beyond that was a constant rustling.

"Careful. Careful, now," said the voice. "Ah, oh."

Against his face Larry felt moisture of two kinds. One was cool and the other was warm, dried in places. Beside him, against his torso was another type of warmth. Soft, pliant, comfortable.

"Wow, that's better," said the voice. "A little more."

Beneath his head was soft ground. He called on his muscles to raise him up. Complaining, they complied. Needles of ice attacked his neck, his shoulder, and his hand as he rose. All his old wounds were back to plague him. His vision clouded, but he managed to get up in a sitting position. He stayed there, looking down into his lap until he could see again.

"He's awake," said the voice.

Larry saw Mess' manifestation standing on its legs, the treads in back, the wheels in front with Napoleon in front of them, banging its chest area with a rock. The chest area was bent in several places and the feline was trying to right it.

179

She, herself, looked none the worse for wear. She turned to him.

"Welcome to Destiny," she said flatly and went back to Mess' chest.

Larry sat in a daze for a moment, then turned his head, ignoring the renewed pain. Lying beside him was Titu. She seemed to be sleeping comfortably. Her breathing was regular and full and there were no signs of external injuries. He suddenly remembered he had strapped her in but neglected to do the same completely for himself. No wonder he felt so bad.

In a pile behind them were the space suits. Beyond that was the salvage craft, now salvage material itself. Its sides were crumbled and its nose was pushed in against a thick tree trunk. It was bent in half and sitting on a large rock.

"Mess kept aware the entire trip down," Napoleon filled him in. "We were damaged and floundering but he managed to find a break in the trees and put us down with the least possible danger." Napoleon had moved over and knelt down next to Larry, the rock still in her hand. "Or so he says."

"It wasn't easy," complained Mess. "At great physical damage to myself I piloted the ship down and saved all your lives. Suffering great personal torture I might add."

Its chest area was somewhat level again, though bumpy still. It maneuvered over to where the trio of living creatures huddled.

"Where are we exactly?" asked Larry, the top of his mouth feeling like the inside of his nose.

"Don't I even get a 'thank you'?" asked Mess.

"Thank you," said Larry, swallowing with difficulty. "Where are we exactly?"

"I don't know," said Mess. "When we were hit the navigational equipment was damaged."

"That always seems to be the first to go," interjected Napoleon.

"I brought us down on my own imput with great anxiety and daring," the machine added proudly.

"All right, you vain vessel of verbosity, we said thank you," Larry retorted.

"He's feeling better," Napoleon told the machine as she rose.

Larry took a moment to look around. The blanket of green was leaves. The sheet of brown was tree trunks. They were at the base of a very high forest. But where, exactly? Destiny was covered in forests.

Titu sucked in a deep breath beside him, making a snoring sound. Her body curled and her eyes opened. All heads turned to her. Mess didn't have to, since its sensors covered its crown all the way around. The raven-haired girl sat up quickly.

"Destiny," she said. "The forest of Destiny. We're here."

"Yes, we're here," said Larry. "But where here? Which forest?"

Titu pulled her legs around, making two crooked "v's" beneath her torso. "I'm sorry. I was confused. Until I noticed you I thought I had awakened from a nightmare. As if I had never left."

The group fell silent, remembering what they had been through. And thinking about what might come.

Titu scrambled to her feet and looked about. "We must get out of here. All forests are the same on Destiny. Wild beasts roam freely. We hunt them from our automatic stone factories."

"Automatically?" Mess echoed. "You mean involuntarily?"

"No, we have factories that line our cities," Titu explained. That hunt down the forest creatures for food and clothing. The beasts are too dangerous and too numerous to be hunted by our people. They are pinpointed by sensors and killed by beams from a distance. We collect them later."

Larry and Napoleon looked quickly around, viewing the seemingly calm forest in a different light.

"But if they sense the creatures, they must know we're different from them," said Larry. "Maybe their equipment can't detect us at all."

"No," said Titu. "They must know we're here. We crashed the ship on the planet. No other attack has managed to do the same. I'm sure they're trying to locate us at this very second."

"How long have we been here?" Larry asked hurriedly.

"A few minutes," said Napoleon. "I haven't been counting."

"I have," said Mess. "Fourteen minutes, forty-two seconds."

Titu gasped.

"Let's go, let's get out of here," Larry declared. He saw that everyone had on his or her shipboard clothing, he and Titu the shirt, pants, and boots, and Napoleon wore sandals on her rear paws, special palm protectors on her forepaws, and a leotard with lacing up the front. The beamer rifle was strapped on her back.

"Anything else in the ship we need?"

"Nothing," said Napoleon. "No food, no water, no other weapons. Nothing."

"Come on, then," said Larry. He took Titu's hand without thinking and started walking away from the ship. Napoleon reached down and picked up a thick wooden staff as tall as herself that she had fashioned just after taking the suits off her companions and just before tending to Mess.

As she began to rise and Larry reached the top of a small knoll with Titu, a strong buzzing was heard in the distance, getting louder.

"Get down!" Titu cried.

She fell to the ground pulling a surprised Larry down with her. Napoleon stretched her arms and legs out immediately, spread-eagled even before she hit the leafy surface. Mess pushed its own legs out until they were parallel to the ground. Then, turning one wheel to the side, it pushed itself over.

The buzzing filled the air now. Through the trees Larry saw flickering sparks. Suddenly loose chips of bark were flying all around him. Leaves started swirling from the forest floor. Titu cried out in fear. Larry wrapped his arms around her protectively. Napoleon gritted her teeth and screwed her eyes shut.

It was as if their own section of forest was caught in the eye of a minute inferno. Everyone's hair stood on end and crackled. Heat singed their skin and small shocks touched every nerve. Even through closed eyelids, patterns of electrical force appeared. Then just as quickly as it had come, it disappeared.

The buzzing receded and the wood was silent again. Larry

was afraid that when he looked up his friends would be smoking carcasses, but when he raised his head he saw Titu and Napoleon doing the same. Mess was blinking on its side. They all looked around from their prone positions to see if they were all in one piece. It was discovered that they were. Suddenly all heads turned to the escape ship.

It was totally unrecognizable. The top half had melted down, covering the bottom with gobs of pulpy metal. The bottom area was lined with ragged tears and holes. It was half the height and twice the width it used to be. Smoke was curling from the holes as the remnants of electrical circuitry and furniture burned. It was a frightening example of devastation that wasn't lost on any of them.

Napoleon jumped to her feet and ran over to where Titu and Larry stood. Mess pushed itself erect with difficulty and rolled by the three, not stopping, blinking erratically. The flesh and blood followed without a word.

They ran for quite a distance without stopping, until their hearts thudded heavily in their chests and their legs felt like sacks of sand. The actual distance was not that far. Although they all were in fine physical shape they had been in space too long. Larry stumbled before anyone else. Titu knelt down next to him.

Napoleon knocked on Mess' back with her staff to get him to stop. None of them had spoken as yet. The fear of omnipresent death had settled on them all. The thought that the buzzing could return and single out any or all of them created an undiluted paranoia. They each looked at the horizon differently.

The spaces between the trees held danger. Somewhere out there could be a crosshair or beam of energy that would transmit their image to the eyes of the hunter. Even Mess was not immune. Its own situation was especially acute. Without the protection of the Black Hole to call on, it felt extremely vulnerable. Even as the group rested, their eyes and ears were wary. And with good reason.

The buzzing started again. Napoleon was the first to hear it.

"Look out," she howled and ran in the other direction. Titu

and Larry followed only to stumble to a halt as the way before them disintegrated into rubble. A wall made of flaming wind faced them, hurling up dirt, bark, leaves, and rocks.

They all turned and ran in the other direction, terror being their spur. They ran farther this time, ignoring their various aches and wounds. Each area they entered changed subtly but it all looked the same to them. Trees, leaves, trees, leaves. Unending green and brown. Unending shadows and shade. The united hands of the foliage above kept the sun from their view. When next they stopped they unconsciously chose an area of light.

"This is useless," Napoleon gasped, sitting atop a rock, breathing deeply. Larry and Titu, bringing up the rear, sank to their knees as they neared her. Mess just kept right on rolling.

"We don't know where we are or where we're going," the feline continued. "These hunters, whoever they are, seem to love noise but they aren't the best shots I've ever seen."

"It is surprising," admitted Titu, breathlessly. "They have a great reputation."

The buzzing started once more.

"Here it comes again!" Napoleon cried, leaping up.

Larry and Titu fell forward. The feline hopped over three large rocks and leaped between two huge trees as the crackling storm smashed down. The rocks she jumped over exploded and the trees she threw herself between were sliced halfway through. Hunks of stone thunked into tree trunks hundreds of feet around. Leaves rustled madly as other rocks rushed past them. Their dust settled atop great strips of bark ripped from the cut trees.

Larry pushed himself to his feet and ran unsteadily to the sagging opening the torn trees had made.

"Nap? Are you all right?" he yelled hoarsely. "Nap!"

In answer, the tree to his right began to crack above its wound. The huge arm of the forest began to topple. In its path lay Titu. The Trigor girl had risen to her knees with her back to him, her ears buzzing still, making her unaware of the situation. Larry ran to her as the falling tree picked up speed. The uncut trunk had begun to rip open, spitting wood and bark chips. Larry grabbed the girl under her arms and lifted her, still running. His shoulders popped and his head filled with pain. Titu flopped into his arms like a rag doll, her feet flying back into his.

His freedom of movement was cut, but not his momentum. As he felt himself falling he threw his weight to the side. The two hit the ground, which thankfully sloped downward, and rolled. Branches cracked under their weight and stones punched their moving bodies but nothing stopped them. As Larry spun, a huge, brown beam flew through his vision. The ground disappeared leaving them floating in mid-air. Then a great, hollow thump smashed into their ears.

The ground came back like a fist, slapping their entire bodies, jarring their teeth. The two skidded to a stop. Not three feet away was a brown trunk as thick as Titu was tall.

Larry held on to the girl until she started hitting him with the flat of one hand. He let go then and rolled the other way. His head was aching with a steady throb and his shoulders felt as if they had been cooked over an open fire. His legs felt as if they were made of knife cuts and his neck felt braided. Napoleon had to call him five times before he heard through the pain.

He turned to see the cat standing on the fallen tree trunk, pointing off in the direction she had run originally. Larry tried to listen but his ears were roaring. He tried to get to his feet but he could only reach his knees. Titu came over and helped him to his feet.

"Thank you," he said, not hearing her reply, as he began to move slowly around the base of the fallen tree. He walked out into sunlight. The forest had stopped momentarily to make way for the base of a mountain. Napoleon and Mess stood in the light as Titu and Larry approached.

"We were being guided," said Napoleon. "The whole thing doesn't make sense otherwise. Why should they destroy our craft completely then miss us twice? Someone is leading us somewhere."

"Must have a great sense of humor, by the Earth Father," said Larry, pushing his thumb back toward the tree.

"You'll have to come up with a new curse," said Napoleon lightly. "We're not on Earth anymore."

"By the Destiny Father?" Larry suggested, squinting at her.

"The Destiny Mother," Titu corrected, looking up at the mountain.

While the three bantered, their spirits started to rise. They weren't just targets anymore waiting for execution. They still had a chance. Maybe. They surveyed the incline. A band of rocks curved off into the distance in either direction topped by a row of trees leveling off before another bank of rocks stretched in both directions. That covered their sight lines, what was beyond would have to wait until they mastered that.

"It's one of the string of mountains protecting the central city," Titu said excitedly. "I'm sure of it."

"That's incredible luck," said Larry. "What do you think? Were we guided to this particular area of forest, too?"

"There is always that possibility," said Mess. "I was working diligently but quickly from any incoming information my sensors could gather. It might have come from Harlan or the cities below."

"You're beginning to sound more and more like a regular computer all the time," Larry said.

"Extraordinary situations call for extraordinary measures," said Mess.

"More like the electronic storms have addled your brain," said Napoleon. "Can you make it?" she finished, gesturing to the mountain.

"I built myself to handle just such an eventuality. I can manuever up to sixty degrees."

"Larry?" Napoleon next said. He had leaned forward against a rock and not moved.

"What?" he replied, still not moving.

"How are you?"

"If I'm not dead, I'm fine."

He pulled himself onto the incline, followed by the others.

They had made it three-quarters of the way up the initial rock face when the first spear hit. It was a crudely shaped projectile made from a branch and given a point by a diagonal break, but it was hurled with such force that it shattered when it struck.

Shards slapped against Titu's body. The pieces of wood stung and the attack surprised her but she held on. Her hair was plastered against her neck and hung in damp beads across her back and her face was bathed in sweat.

"Larry," she cried. "The forest creatures!"

Larry looked up to see several vaguely humanoid beasts by the next band of forest, shaking sticks and screaming through wide, brittle-toothed mouths. He was expecting four-footed animals with fur and fangs, so the sight stunned him. Their skins were dark brown, enabling them to blend in with the trees, and they had no necks. Their heads sloped into their shoulders and arms.

Their eyes were small and their noses, with two nostrils, were pushed up. Their hands, with no thumbs that Larry could see, were filled with rocks and branches, the things that they had started to rain down on the climbing party.

Titu and Larry ducked behind some boulders while Napoleon and Mess anchored themselves in the open. The feline swung the beamer off her shoulder and aimed. Before Larry could call out she fired. The orange beam sliced through the air and disappeared into the ground below the dancing creatures.

Suddenly the outcropping beneath their feet gave way and they tumbled down over the rocks, spinning and smashing as they went. Spurts of blood shot out as they fell, glinting red in the sunlight.

"They're warm-blooded," Larry spoke in a hush.

"So?" said Napoleon, her feline hearing picking up his whisper. "We've seen enough of that red stuff on this trip."

Their conversation was cut short by the appearance of many more creatures, all appearing along the lip of the upper forest, all dancing and screaming. They, too, began to hurl down pieces of stone and wood. Napoleon started her beam from the left and cut across, dumping some down onto the rocks and slicing others into pieces.

"Stun them," Larry shouted. "Switch to stun. We just can't kill them all!"

"We can't just let them kill us either," Napoleon howled. "Now or later."

"Nap, they're warm-blooded," Larry pleaded. "They're using tools. They're not just dumb beasts."

"Larry, they're warm for *our* blood," Napoleon screamed back. "And they're using their tools on us." She continued firing as the line of creatures replenished itself. "We have one weapon. Who's going to cover me while I switch it to stun? I'm not interested in fairness. I'm interested in survival."

Two more beasts toppled over, their limbs spinning off their bodies as they crashed into the stone wall below them. The remaning survivors ran back into the wood. No one in the human party sustained injury. Mess moved upward without comment. Napoleon swung the beamer onto her back and continued climbing as well. Larry scrambled over to where Titu was hunched. Her face turned to his, pale and damp.

"I thought I had seen everything on Jackpot . . ." she started.

"Those were the forest creatures?" he asked.

"Yes."

"But those weren't animals. I was expecting some sort of savage beast, like, I don't know . . ."

"I . . . have eaten their meat and . . . worn their skin all my life." Titu swallowed. "I never saw one killed before."

"You said they were dangerous."

"They are. We were taught that they were ferocious and filled the forests. I . . ." Titu grew even paler.

"Kneel down. Put your head between your legs."

"Larry," Napoleon called. "Titu! Come on."

"Are you all right?" Larry asked the girl.

"Yes," she replied, head still down.

"We had better get going," he told her gently.

She got up without incident and the two began to climb again.

The four reconnoitered at the top of the rocks. They stood among the first level of trees. The two humans were sweating profusely; Titu's shirt was torn at the side and Larry had tied his around his waist. Napoleon was wary, eying the forest. Across the lip of the rocks, the alien beasts lay dead.

"There are more of them," the feline was saying. "That much is certain. From here on up we have to be even more careful."

Larry had not argued but he had taken a moment to look over a fallen forest creature. Although his initial guess had been correct, they had no thumbs, he noticed that there was a small stub where the human thumb usually was. Were they developing or regressing?

Larry raised a rough-hewn eyelid. The eyes were smaller than what was considered normal, but with human parts, just the same. Pupil, iris, cornea. The body was covered with hair but Larry could see that they had sexual organs. The feet had five toes each, but, like their fingers, they were longer, much longer, than what could be considered normal on Earth.

He returned to the group and they moved back into the darkness of the thick wood. Napoleon led the way, handing her staff to Titu behind her, unslinging the beamer. Mess rolled its treaded way alongside Larry.

"Where do you think these creatures came from, Mess?" Larry asked quietly.

"From a sperm and an egg probably," said the computer.

"Thanks for your assistance," Larry muttered sarcastically.

"Well, if you think I'm getting into a long-winded discussion on the possibility of a higher force just to past the time, forget it," Mess said testily.

"I don't care about a higher force. These creatures could be the original inhabitants of the planet, who evolved into these tree dwellers. Or they could even be the Destinian's human descendants, arriving eons before the O'Neils."

"Quiet," urged the computerized robot. "I think I sense something."

They were moving deeper into the wood now and the darkness was coming on fast. A green-brown dusk settled over the party as they pulled their tired bodies across the steep forest floor. The wood stayed quiet except for the rustle of the wind and the party's footsteps. When Mess failed to discern anything tangible, Titu slowed down so Larry could catch up with her.

"What happens when we reach the central city?" she asked.

"*If* we reach wherever whoever is guiding us wants us to go, we'll see when we get there," said Napoleon:

"We're at your planet's mercy," Larry elaborated. "I haven't really understood anything that's happened since we picked up your brother."

No one had to say that Harlan was now gone and that no one knew where he was or that they were now complete pawns in a situation that went way beyond their control. Each knew that they had changed but no one knew where they now fit in.

"All right," said Napoleon. "I can see the light ahead. We're almost through the wood."

As the last word left her mouth she heard a rushing above her. Before she could react, a large hunk of wood fell across her face, landing on the crook of her arms. She howled in pain and fell back, the beamer spinning off in front of her. The rest of the group stopped in shock as rushing wind assailed them.

From out of the trees dropped dozens of forest creatures who bounced on the ground, rolled, and leaped upon the party. Two dark feet banged against Mess' head in the blind spot of its circle of sensors. As it began to topple over its forward wheels it said, "I knew I should have put one on top."

It moved its wheels forward and kept erect but was now low enough to the ground for five more creatures to swarm over it, pulled it down. Its wheels spun frantically as they pounded it with sticks.

Napoleon somersaulted backwards to land on her hind legs, holding her wounded forepaws close to her chest. As she dove forward to recover the fallen beamer a large branch swung from behind a tree and caught her in the stomach.

She slid backwards on her knees until another branch, wielded by another creature, smacked into the back of her head. She fell forward as if she were pulled. She lay on the forest floor, still.

Two creatures leaped on Titu, wrapping their arms around her, spinning her to the ground. The stick she held dropped away from her. Its tip bounded it over in the air and it fell at Larry's feet.

One creature was on top of Titu moving in an unmistakably sexual rhythm. Larry dropped to his knees and grabbed the branch. Two feet planted themselves before him. He looked up to see a screaming creature bringing its own stick down toward Larry's skull.

Without thinking, Larry brought his staff around in a fast arc near the ground. The creature missed by a good six inches as the wood connected with its ankles, toppling him over backwards.

Larry jumped to his feet, hearing movement behind him. He turned, swinging the branch at the same time. It felled a charging tree creature in mid-leap. Larry spun again to see the creature he had tripped trying to rise on shattered leg bones and the creature still moving atop Titu, beyond.

Larry ran forward, slammed the tip of his pole into the rising creature's chest and vaulted over to Titu, landing on top of the creature pinning her. They rolled off the girl, Larry losing his grip on the stick, but the creature was taken by surprise as well.

Larry was the first to his feet, noticing a third creature swinging a stick at his head from the side. As the creature who had been atop Titu rose, Larry fell on his back, the stick whistled above him and was stopped by the rising creature's face. Larry kicked the attacking creature in the crouch and grabbed its weapon.

Another creature moved toward Titu and Larry batted it in the head. Another came at Larry from behind. He swung the stick back, catching the creature in the throat with its tip. Another moved in from the side. Larry swung the stick back again, at waist level, knocking the creature rolling.

He stood above Titu, whirling the stick like a man deranged, ignoring his pain and exhaustion. He willed his muscles to move and they moved. The laboratory-created human being discovered his physical self. It was almost like handling a mathematical problem. Employing the proper muscles of eyes, legs, arms, and head, you could solve the problem. The stick whirled like three, weaving in and out, catching creatures on their heads, stomachs, and legs.

The creatures stopped charging. They began to circle the pair, thrusting their sticks at them, but not trying to connect. More and more joined the circle until the prone Mess and Napoleon were obscured from sight. A solid wall of brown-skinned creatures with sparkling eyes faced them.

Larry kept his stick raised, slowly circling himself. Titu rose to her knees eying the veritable platoon of tree creatures in fear.

"What are they going to do?" she whispered while rising.

"How should I know?" Larry said helplessly.

Suddenly a part of the circle began to separate. As Larry and Titu watched, a tree creature appeared through his fellows, holding the beamer rifle like a club. It walked over to where Larry stood and grunted, brandishing the weapon. Larry watched unmoving. The creature turned and motioned to the others, growling again. The circle moved back, leaving a large area clear.

Through the shuffling brown legs Titu could see a battered Mess and an unconscious Napoleon. The creature with the beamer turned back to Larry again, once more brandishing the weapon, and grunting through a large twisted grin.

Larry remained watchful. The creature repeated his action. Larry watched. The creature frowned and moved back. He growled at the crowd. They began to move forward. Larry tensed and raised his stick. The crowd seemed to sigh collectively and moved back again.

At this, the first creature actually smiled. He put the beamer between his legs and rubbed his hands. Two other creatures ran forward suddenly and seized Titu. Larry spun as she was dragged away but a loud growl from the first creature forced him to turn back. The creature had its hands at its sides. It slowly took the beamer by the barrel and brandished it like a club.

Larry suddenly knew what was going on. He was being challenged. He had shown ability, so now he was being challenged by the tree creature's leader. Four other creatures were standing on each side of Titu, separated by the length of their sticks held at waist level before them, effectively making a cage. It was obvious she was the victor's prize. To the loser, defeat or death?

Larry had little choice but to find out. He slowly undid his shirt from his waist. The creature facing him was thin, but tall and well muscled. His ability at fighting and climbing must have been excellent and well developed. Larry figured the only way to get out of this in one piece was to play on the creature's supposed lack of subtle intelligence and human experience. Although they were rulers of the forest, according to what Titu said they had yet been unable to deal with advanced technology.

Larry took off his shirt and hurled it in the air. All eyes followed the garment and an audible gasp went up as it unbunched and the sleeves rippled in the air.

Larry lifted his staff and swung. It seemed destined to become part of the creature's skull but at the last second the beamer stock moved up and blocked. The creature stepped back out of the way of the twisting weapons and spun the beamer out from under Larry's stick and swung it backhand at Larry's head.

Luckily it was used to the longer sticks so the butt of the weapon breezed by Larry's forehead, ruffling his eyebrows. Both fighters thought their strategy sure, so both were surprised at the subsequent failure.

Larry then had an opening, but not enough leverage. He managed to poke the creature before it batted away his stick with the beamer skipping to the left. Larry moved to the right as the creature pivoted. The beamer sped down to cleave Larry's skull. The stick came whistling across and knocked it out of the way.

But the strike was telling. The stick stung his hand with tight vibrations and solid bands of pain moved up both arms. The beamer came right back, speeding in from where Larry had deflected it. He wasn't able to get his stick back up in time, and the butt hit his left shoulder and sent him stumbling. Titu's white face passing through his view.

He sliced his stick back and forth through the air to keep the creature away while he tried to think straight. The creature began pivoting again. Left to right, right to left, left to right, right to left. His dark skin began to blend in with the cover of dead leaves on the ground.

The pain in Larry's arms began to throb. The creature's edges were beginning to blur. Larry held his staff up, his eyes moving with the creature's movements. The creature ran in semicircles, pivoting back and forth, turning, twisting, moving in and out. Larry just stood and moved his body, trying to face him at all times.

The creature began chattering in a sing-song voice. He kept moving, right to left, left to right, right to left, the song coming in from one side, when the creature was on another. Larry felt the energy rising in the crowd. He knew that the creature was going to attack any moment and it would have to be just luck to guess which direction the blow would be coming in.

The movement intensified, the sing-song got louder and louder. It reached for its crescendo. The creature's left foot didn't pivot, it rooted itself. Larry swung left. The creature swung right. The weapons met in mid-air.

A sharp cracked filled the clearing and echoed through the wood. Larry felt his arms shake in their sockets. His back was stung with a slicing pain, but his feet held. His staff didn't. It shattered with the force of the speeding beamer. He felt the slice move under his hands and separate.

The end of the stick was dust, the middle was a forest of broken edges, the grip was a split piece. The creature's back was to him for a split-second as it followed through, but there was nothing for Larry to attack with. The creature spun toward him with beamer intact.

The creature smiled and moved in. Larry kept his eye on the beamer. He knew this creature was not going to congratulate him for a fine fight and invite him over to the tree for refreshments. He would split his skull and use Titu in any way he saw fit. They may have been more intelligent than they were given credit for but they weren't civilized by any means. It was time to use that advanced technology against them.

The beamer began to curl in and out. The hard butt moved in semicircles. The creature came closer and closer. Larry stood his ground. The creature swung; Larry jumped. The beamer hit him in the solar plexus as his arms sought a hold. Larry's feet kicked out, catching the creature under the knee. Larry hit the ground on his back, holding onto the butt of the weapon.

The creature stood holding onto the barrel. It took a step in to wrench the beamer out of Larry's grip but fell from the wounded knee. Larry pushed his finger past the metal guard and depressed the trigger.

A beam of orange moved up the creature's arm and pounded him in the chest. He flew back, releasing the barrel and landed on top of his shoulders. He tumbled over onto his side and lay still.

Larry gripped the weapon tightly. He noticed the barrel had been turned to the stun position during the fight. Then Titu was tenderly touching the myriad scratches across his trunk.

"Are you all right?" they asked each other at the same time.

Titu couldn't help but smile. And even after all he had been through, Larry felt his face flush. He turned to see a group of creatures prodding their prone fighter.

The rest of the group had accepted their leader's defeat but they weren't happy about it. They broke the circle, growling and grumbling at each other. Two took the unconscious creature by the arms and pulled him away. The others moved as well, occasionally howling and leaping.

"I can't believe it," said Titu. "They're leaving us alone."

"Well, I won, didn't I?" said Larry. He got to his feet, beamer in hand. "They have rules. They have weapons. They have organization. They're not just animals."

He trotted over to where Napoleon lay, Titu at his side. A nasty bump appeared on the back of her head, blood already clotted and flaking. Larry shook her gently, ready to jump back if she tried to scratch him while asleep.

She mewed, then growled deep in the back of her throat, her eyelids fluttering open. "Ouch," she said, touching the back of her head. "Ouch, ouch, ouch. By Cheshire, that hurts. What happened?"

Larry quickly explained while the huge mass of tree creatures receded into the forest. The cover of the wood seemed to open for them, their bodies mysteriously fading as they walked.

"All right, so you passed the test, and you're an honorary tree creature," she growled. "What now?"

Titu was about to reprimand the feline for her lack of feeling and Larry was about to explain that she was always testy after waking, but the forest roof ripped open answering her question.

The trees above them tore, spilling branches everywhere, leaves a flutter. Lightning bolts of many colors reached down, plucking tree creatures up and hurling them away. Still other rays burnt them where they stood. Animal howls were drowned out by an incredible burst of wind and noise.

Napoleon grabbed a tree, her claws ripping grooves in the bark as she was pushed back by the force. Larry and Titu grabbed each other and went rolling off along the swirling ground. The beamer rifle flew into the wood.

Through the trees broke a space ship. Shaped like a great pair of frowning lips it ripped open a landing space and settled down into it. As Larry and Titu stopped rolling they felt something hard poke their heads and bodies. They were weapons held by men in space suits.

As Napoleon opened her eyes after the wind had died down she saw a semicircle of weapons pointing at her. Other space-suited men collected the carcasses of the dead tree creatures, dumping them on a large mesh tarp which they laid out. She heard one of them say, "Destiny will eat well tonight!"

Larry and Titu were herded back to where Napoleon stood. Her skull injury was bleeding again and her fur was dirty, coarse, and tufted in bunches. Larry's hair was matted as was Titu's, with his shoulders and neck a livid red and his arms and torso dotted with cuts. Titu's shirt was ripped along the sides and front, exposing her dirt-streaked frame. They all faced the bright silver ship, waiting to see what would happen next.

From out of the top of the ship a man in a bright silver space suit beckoned. When he was sure all eyes were on him, his arms reached up and removed his bright silver opaque helmet. When he spoke his words were meant only for Titu.

"My dear," said Bishop-Fortune. "What a pleasure it is seeing you again."

ELEVEN

Titu's face began to collapse into fragments of pain and defeat, until she felt Larry's hand at her elbow and heard Napoleon snarl. These two had existed up until now as slaves. Slaves of ignorance, of bigotry, of preconceptions. Their world had stuck them in neat classifications. They had fought their way out, declared themselves as free individuals capable of deep emotion and incredible physical feats in the face of ridiculous odds.

She was luckier. She was a slave for a little more than a year. A year that meant nothing. A year that could not be forgotten but could be used to make her own freedom all the more precious and her self-awareness all the more powerful.

Her face stopped its fall and, before all their eyes, put itself back together into the same look of defiance that glowed on Larry's and Napoleon's faces. Bishop-Fortune, his loose outfit swirling, looked disappointed.

"Most of my girls drop to their knees when I claim them or at least burst into tears."

"I'm not one of your girls," Titu said evenly, the words almost catching in her throat.

"You are. You shall see when I return you to Jackpot," Bishop-Fortune assured her. "Whether you know it or not, you are. As is the cat beside you."

"Little chance spawn of Earth feces," called Napoleon clearly. "I've faced the likes of you before."

198

Bishop-Fortune blanched visibly. No creature this side of the universe had ever said anything like that to his face.

"I shall be prepared, cat," he boomed, finding his voice. "You shall be declawed before you are brought before me."

"When I ripped Crossman-Smith to shreds," said Napoleon, grinning, "my claws were *sheathed.*"

Bishop-Fortune tried to deliver a withering stare but even astride his great steel ship and draped in sparkling silver, Napoleon defeated him. His concentration broke and he turned, beckoning downward.

"Little matters, small, inconsequential matters," he said, turning back to them. "When I get you back to my establishment you will pay dearly for your actions. You are helpless, totally alone."

"If I'm alone then I'm never totally helpless," Titu heard the feline say clearly. Bishop-Fortune went on regardless.

"The coup is complete. Five of you, Harlan, Titu, Baker, Napoleon, and Palend." He ticked them off on a hand. "No more effective than a gust of wind." He dealt with each finger one by one. "Harlan is certainly destroyed. Titu is my prize again. Baker is as good as dead, his head destined for a pike in the central city square. Napoleon is another of my prizes and Palend has paid for his interference without the assistance of the Intercouncil." His hands curled into a fist.

A figure began to rise up beside him. It took shape slowly, growing from the ship-top entrance. The first thing Larry could discern clearly was the red jewel in the middle of its forehead.

"Isenraid," he breathed.

"Indeed," shouted Bishop-Fortune. "You pitiful creatures. You have no idea what you have been involved in. The control of a paradise planet. A world of incredible wealth. You entered the story after years of ground breaking. You only stumbled into the final phase."

"Explain!" Larry shouted. "You've known where we were all along. You circumvented Destiny security. How? How?"

"The Mantas race has been adding to the Universe's might for centuries," hissed Isenraid, now standing atop the ship alongside the vicelord. "We lust for order. A common order, unfettered by race or boundaries. When none exists, we create it. Destiny was not part of the universal order. Steps were taken eons ago to correct that."

"Then you were not born here?" asked Titu. "You were not spawn of this planet?"

"No, my child," said the Mantas. "We were seeded. My race travels through the galaxy pinpointing worlds outside the Universal Rule. We strive to unite each under The Rule, the only true Rule. Once we establish ourselves on a world we aide others until we acquire positions of power. Then we help the planet adjust."

"We made a deal," Bishop-Fortune translated. "I would supply the physical might while the Mantases infiltrated and paved the way for me. But I needed an assurance af their cooperation and good intentions. You," he pointed to Titu, "were that guarantee."

"Her?" Larry exploded. "A person? You gave a human being in payment?"

"It was what he required," the Mantas said simply. "It was for the best. Her family had been chosen to take the blame for our actions."

"But when your brother got away," continued Bishop-Fortune. "Ceratain precautions had to be taken."

"We watched and waited," said the Mantas. "Knowing he would rescue her and return here."

"So we planted a homing device inside her one night. We've known where she's been every moment."

Titu looked in shock at Larry. If she were expecting disgust or accusation in his look back she was disappointed. He looked to her in shared pain with rage and a growing shrewdness. He touched her arm, shrugging like it wasn't important.

Bishop-Fortune was now openly disappointed. He thought such a revelation would make at least one of them sick with remorse.

"Others have been seeing that all is in readiness," continued Isenraid. "The Queen has 'taken ill,' Ministic has closed down the factories, and sent the space bullets to destroy your ship and the traitor Harlan Trigor."

"My fleet is on the other side of the planet," Bishop-Fortune gloated. "When the Queen is dead, we will attack."

"No!" screamed Titu, moving forward and pleading. "How can you? You have lived with us all these years," she cried to Isenraid. "Your children have grown side by side with ours. You know the love our people feel for your race. Have we been meaningless ciphers to you all these years?"

"Order must be maintained," hissed Isenraid coldly. "The Rule must be obeyed."

"Don't you realize what you are doing?" Larry spoke out, holding Titu back. "Have the years in this place not touched you? Good can not be taken to an extreme. Your wish for order will destroy this planet! You've settled your pact with scum."

"We will see that this world is used to its best advantage," spoke the Mantas. "One world's wealth is the solar system's wealth."

"Well, it has been fun," said Bishop-Fortune. "But I have a world to see to," He signalled and the line of space-suited guards began to move in.

"The space bullets will stop you!" Titu screamed.

"No, they won't," said Isenraid with certainty.

The line of guards continued to circle them.

"Prepare to sleep," said Bishop-Fortune. "When you awake Titu and Napoleon will be back where they belong. Baker will join Palend. Your luck has been incredible. Absolutely. The five of you have been incredibly lucky. But now your luck has finally run out."

"Six," came a voice. It boomed out of the forest and echoed against the mountain. So grand was it that everyone stopped for a moment.

"Six," the voice repeated. Bishop-Fortune looked around wildly, shouting instructions to his men that they couldn't hear over the reverberation.

"The six of us have been incredibly lucky," continued the voice. Isenraid spotted the shaking branches and pointed off beyond. The guards lined up away from the human trio and the two atop the ship waited as the leaves parted.

And out rolled Mess. His wheels were bent and wobbling. One of his treads was broken and the leg attached was twisted out of shape. His torso area was rutted and sliced in places. Three of his six sensors were cracked and dark. And he moved unsteadily, in fits and starts.

Around Larry and Napoleon the guards looked in absolute wonder. Bishop-Fortune began to laugh. Titu placed her hands on Larry's shoulders for support, frowning.

"Another trick?" came Bishop-Fortune's voice. "Another secret weapon? Destroy that machine immediately," he instructed his guards, his voice dripping with mocking scorn.

Larry's brain was awhirl. What had the machine done this for? To overcome its programmed rule for self-preservation in order to buy them time was unbelievable. It was a machine; it wasn't capable of feeling or sacrifice.

Bishop-Fortune and Isenraid stood imperiously on the ship. A group of guards pulled their spinners over to aim at Mess. It made a ludicrous target. The machine stopped rolling before their weapons. Its remaining sensors blinked red and its head popped off its body.

Larry grabbed Titu and Napoleon and jumped to the side. The guards immediately opened fire. Larry rolled and watched helplessly as the spiraling projectiles bore into Mess' body. The head moved over, hovering eight feet in the air to avoid the fire. As Bishop-Fortune shouted and pointed at the head, Mess' wheels moved forward. The body arched down, the open neck pointing at the huge, silver ship.

The spinners tore into the body as the machine fired. A huge flame was emitted from the neck hole, pointing up. The force of the weapon rocked the guards. The next second Bishop-Fortune disintegrated. The ashes of his body flew off in all directions, a cloud of atomized red and silver. He looked like a tiny sun glistening in the forest before his remains dotted the top of the ship and surrounding trees.

Isenraid was hurled off the top of the spacecraft by the concussion. He lay dazed, one leg broken, his head waving from side to side. Then his eyes and jewel cleared; he turned toward Mess and a red bolt struck out from his head. It connected with the center of Mess' "chest." The machine exploded with a force that killed several guards nearby. Metal parts reached high into the trees, then fell, spun, and floated down. Mess' sensors went dark and his hovering head dropped to the leaves.

Larry picked up a dropped spinner and drilled a hole in the middle of Isenraid's face as Napoleon leaped onto a tree. As the Mantas' face ripped back onto the silver ship, covering the area with a terrible stench, her claws dug deep into the wood and she scrambled up to a large branch overhanging the ship.

From there the feline leaped onto the silver craft and disappeared inside, howling with bloodthirsty glee. Titu, in the meantime, had also relieved a guard of his weapon by hurling a rock through his face plate. She and Larry stood back to back blasting away at the stumbling guards.

"We've got to get under cover," Larry shouted to her without turning his head. "Start moving behind those trees."

The pair started over to the right but not before a guard got a bead on Titu. He was depressing his trigger when the side of his head was crushed.

Suddenly the air was filled with tree creatures, falling upon the space-suited guards with undisguised cheer. Larry and Titu stopped firing for fear of hitting the celebrating creatures as they beat at Bishop-Fortune's army.

Larry saw one guard felled from behind. As the dying man collapsed forward Larry got a look at the assailant and his weapon. It was the tree creature Larry had defeated in the challenge of minutes before. It brought the beamer rifle down once again into the guard's head. The butt bit deep and came out of the helmet red. The creature looked up right into Larry's eyes. There was understanding there. Not a salute, not a wink, but understanding, nevertheless. They were now equals, worthy of mutual respect. The creature smiled and waved the rifle. Larry brought his own weapon up, brandishing it with a joy he thought he'd never feel.

The area was awash with carnage. The trees were shaking with the screams of tree creatures and the rattles of dying men. Out of this massacre appeared a walkway, seemingly materialized from the top of the ship to the forest floor. Napoleon appeared at the crown, Bishop-Fortune's weapon in paw.

"Come on!" she yelled to Larry. "I'll cover you."

The two began to run for the stairway when Larry stopped. Titu stopped automatically as well.

"You go ahead," Larry told her. "I'll be right there."

She didn't argue, cutting down a guard who was trying to shoot them instead. She then ran for the ship, knocking stumbling guards out of the way.

Larry ran in a wide semicircle, the center of which was the scorched piece of dirt where Mess had been destroyed. He found what he was looking for at the base of a thick tree fifty feet beyond. Larry reached down and put the red plate filled with micro-circuitry in the waist of his pants. Then he turned and ran for the ship.

"This is a friend of mine," said Napoleon as she picked her way among the four slashed and cut corpses on the floor of the bridge. She motioned toward a pale, brown-haired youth standing by a console fitted with six screens and advanced technological equipment.

"Hello," he said uncertainly.

"Do you know how to run this thing?" Larry asked.

"He's alive, isn't he?" said Napoleon out of the side of her mouth.

"Sure, sure, only don't kill me, please?" The boy looked incredibly frightened, his freckles becoming more apparent on his sallowing face.

"I told you kid," said Napoleon. "Just do as we say and you won't get hurt."

Larry looked at Napoleon with angry disbelief. She shrugged. He returned his attentions to the boy. "Take off," he instructed.

"But . . . but I thought you wanted me to fly the ship?" the boy stuttered.

"I mean lift-off, get going, let's get out of here!"

The boy nodded vigorously and hopped into the pilot's chair.

"You remind me of my computer," mumbled Larry, as the boy switched on the console. The machine had denied its two primary programs in order to save their lives. One, its safety and two, its permission to fire. It seemed like the old coot Palsy-Drake had managed to shove feeling into his creation. He had succeeded in getting Mess to think for itself, acting on the basis of emotion, opting for a noble sacrifice instead of continued existence.

The ship rose slowly and moved into the bright Destiny sky. The interior was far smaller than the ship was made to look from the outside. There were eight seats before a small hallway leading to four small cabins and a combination bunk room and eating area. The chairs were in two rows of three with two seats by the piloting console.

At present the floor was slick with blood and the screens were full of death as the battle between Bishop-Fortune's men and the tree creatures turned into a rout. Larry looked closer and saw some creatures actually firing the spinners at their victims. The leader of the group was waving the beamer rifle by the butt as the image receded.

Napoleon stood beside the young pilot, her hand on her weapon while Titu sat behind Larry, her face averted from the ripped corpses behind. Larry plopped down in the seat beside the boy.

"How did the guards get to us?" he asked.

"They have a loading area below," Napoleon replied. "They dropped them out on the other side of the trees."

Larry surveyed the mass of forest on the screen, his face grim. He could have asked the boy's name. He could have asked how he got involved with Bishop-Fortune. He could have asked him where he got his flying training. He didn't. He did not feel like it.

"Do you have a communication system?" he finally inquired.

"S-sure," answered the boy, pointing to a boxlike compartment on the console near Larry.

"What does this use?" Larry asked, eying the group of buttons. "Voice or code?"

"Code. It's a standard Jackpot issue code."

"I know that," exclaimed Titu, rising out of her seat.

"Get on it then," said Larry. "Try to raise Harlan. Tell him about the fleet on the other side of the planet."

"But," Titu's voice quaked. "But Bishop-Fortune said he was destroyed."

"What does Bishop-Fortune know?" Larry said. "Bishop-Fortune is dead. I'm betting Harlan isn't. I'm betting his skill

that he was always bragging about has kept him alive this
long. I'm betting we can still do something to save this planet
from a bunch of fanatical do-gooders."

Larry turned to the pilot as a shocked Titu hunched over
the communication device.

"What was your next stop?"

"The Mile Long Palace, sir," the boy replied quickly. "In
the central city."

"Take us there, then," said Larry with certainty.

"But, but, sir," the boy sputtered. "Without the rest of the
fleet it'll be a death trap there. They'll . . . they'll kill us."

Larry felt like crying. Such waste, such absurdity. All in
the name of greed and conformity. But he didn't. His face
showed only confidence.

"Take us there," he repeated quietly. "Win or lose, we're
playing this game out to the end."

Harlan sped up, then around to the right. In his wake
silent thunder rolled, accompanied by multicolored lightning. The vacuum of space was filled with the soundless buzzing of dozens of space bullets, all moving with stunning
speed in complicated geometric patterns. And all were trying
to destroy.

All but one. Their target. Their target had little interest in
fighting back. He was flying a defensive pattern, the finest of
his career, the finest of Destiny's history. Brilliant maneuvers
based on mathematic theories concerning a space bullet's
shortcomings. No matter if they faced him in number or one
on one, he would arrange that their killing blasts would take
in their fellows. And if they employed weapons not powerful
enough to hurt their kind, then they couldn't hurt him.

So they tried to wear him down. For hours they sought to
tire him, to make him careless. By the time Harlan received
the coded signal, the tactic was working in reverse. Two
other space bullets had collided and had to be towed by two
more. Before he received his sister's transmission Harlan had
thought of it as "four down—ninety-six to go."

But now, with infinite care, finesse, and cunning, Harlan
Trigor began to lead his brothers to the other side of the
planet.

TWELVE

"One hundred space bullets," said Ministic, by the throne. "One hundred space bullets I sent into the sky to kill your brother." She took a moment to stab one metal-tipped arm at Titu as she paced back and forth on the upraised section of the royal room. "And they all failed. Harlan Trigor kept them at bay for a half a day. Half a day!"

Larry, Napoleon, and Titu stood among a throng of Mantases in the Mile Long Throne Room, a stone-and-wood-mesh palace now awash with the quivering blue, black, and grey of the entire Destiny insectlike population.

Upon landing in a small area reserved for the royal craft, the Mantases had swarmed onto the ship, disarming the trio, killing the young pilot, and taking the three remaining to face the Queen and Queen's aide. But at great cost. The Mantases had died in great waves at the hands of the three survivors. When the guns had been ripped from their grasp they had used their hands, tearing at the mass of aliens until they were borne away before Ministic.

She stood there, her royal robes a kaleidoscope of swirling colors, billowing off in every direction as they curled around her body. The aide's pendant reflected the sun's light as it streamed in from the row of windows set high in the walls, stretching out of sight from the center of the throne room.

The Queen, herself, was still, dressed in a royal dressing gown. She was strewn in her chair, eyes closed, mouth hanging open. She breathed shallowly, her rich red hair piled clumsily atop her head, strands curtaining her face. But through the makeshift bangs the humans could see a dark bruise on her temple.

Ministic stopped pacing before the throne, standing to glower at her prisoners.

"Do you want to know why I had you brought here?" she asked with intensity. "Do you want to know why I did not allow my brothers and sisters to rip you apart like the youngster? Because I wanted you to see our final victory. It is important that you know that my race, my rule, even in the face of defeat, even unallied, is stronger than anything you know."

Ministic shook uncontrollably as she talked, vibrating as if she were wracked with fever. Beside her two other Mantases worked on a square block of machinery about three feet by three feet.

"Why go on?" asked Titu. "It is finished. My people will know of your treachery."

"No!" Ministic screamed. All around them the Mantases chattered waving their arms, the deadly mandibles slicing the air. Ministic's were totally covered by metal gauntlets, reaching from her first arm joint to the tip, leaving her with one thick steel finger on each appendage. "It is not over. With or without your people, Destiny will know The Rule. Where there is one Mantas there are all Mantases!"

The room reverberated with the cries of the aliens. All arms were up, all eyes aglow. All one with some shared inner fire.

"The space bullets have destroyed Bishop-Fortune's fleet," Titu pressed. "Harlan has led them to it. Even now they are returning. You have nothing to gain. Surrender!"

"We do not surrender," Ministic said quietly, calmly. "We plan ahead. As soon as Isenraid informed me of Bishop-Fortune's demise at your hands, seconds before his own death, we altered our strategy. This eventuality, yes, even this, had been considered. We were aware of this possibility. Even before your brother escaped, even before you were taken, the situation had been analyzed.

"As we had considered that your brother might escape. As

we had considered that he might acquire allies. As we had considered our moves to fit all eventualities, even if the allies were one million in number! This is one of millions we calculated. All the variables, all the variables were considered."

The Mantas' voice had risen to a shriek then slowed to a deep crawl, its body hunched, the tone gentle. Suddenly it reared to its full height again, its arms up, metal glinting in the illumination.

"Oh creation! Why do you always leave us? We long to be with you!"

All the Mantases looked in the same erect position. Larry and Napoleon exchanged glances. Here were the worst sort of conquerers, the sort who would commit mass suicide to achieve their ends. When they had no respect for their own kind in life, they had none for any other living race. Titu huddled by Larry's side, almost overcome with awed fear.

Then the spell was broken. The huge mass of creatures began to disperse.

"Go!" cried Ministic. "Prepare!"

The trio watched incredulously as the room emptied except for Ministic and the two Mantases by the cube. The Queen's aide pointed a metal-tipped arm at the trio. "I have been chosen as the assassin. I will kill the Queen. The space bullets will be destroyed by their own weapons. My people will turn on the residents of Destiny. They, as yet, know nothing of what has transpired. They will soon be dead or helpless. We will put out a message to the other worlds. Then it will only be a matter of time before the first Ruler arrives."

"It is a waste," Larry said passionately. "You're wasting all your lives. You're killing for the wrong reason."

Napoleon stared at Ministic, the former's voice a savage ripping sound in the cavernous hall. "There are no wrong reasons in murder. There are only different ones. Death is death. Life goes on for the killer. For the dead it is over. We, out of all in the universe, should know that."

Larry turned to his friend. "We killed for a reason, yes. The Mantases are killing for no . . ."

Napoleon leaped in the air before Larry's sentence was finished. But the ploy did not work completely. Ministic was taken by surprise but not soon enough. Her arm swung and a white bolt struck out from her metal point, catching the feline in the side, spinning her around and hurling her back onto the floor. She fell in a slack pile, her limbs smashing sickeningly against the stone and wood, her fur smoking.

"Nap!" Larry cried, pulling her prone body into his arms. Her eyes were closed and he could not see whether she was breathing.

He laid her down softly and checked her heart. It did not beat. Larry's torso rose, his fist spinning toward the ceiling. With a terrible scream he brought it down to her chest. Then again, and again, and again, each time screaming with all the power he could push through his vocal chords and his muscles.

Then he sobbed, his head sinking to Napoleon's prone figure. His tear-streaked eyes sunk into the fur of her chest. When he rose, his face held a terrible smile. He turned to face Ministic.

"A weapon, as you have observed," said the Mantas as if Napoleon had never attacked. "A poor one versus the one we have prepared here," she motioned to the Mantas-tended block. "But effective for our purposes. You will be killed, as will the Queen, but only when we are ready. You shall see. The Rule will be served."

As she finished speaking the wall a half-mile down blew inwards. The explosion sounded like a clap followed by rainfall at such a distance, but Larry could see clearly the group of space bullets in formation speeding down the high-ceilinged room, tearing the ornaments from the walls and ripping the rugs from the floor. Ministic did not move as this occurred. She stood, still facing Larry, Titu, and the fallen feline, the metal tip pointing.

"Prepared?" she asked of the pair beside her.

"Yes," answered one.

"When I say," said Ministic.

"Agreed," said the other.

The room began to throb with the power of the space bullets. Dust, long since wedged in uncleanable cracks, flew up and swirled in the wake of the stone army. Larry saw them growing larger and larger in number in the hall, more and more screaming in from the hole beyond. They roared forward with no sign of slowing.

"Now," Ministic spoke.

The Mantas pressed a button. All the roar suddenly ceased. A moment later it was replaced by the whistling of the bullets losing all power and altitude. Then the noise of destruction boomed as the nine-foot rocks crashed to the ground.

Their momentum was such that they sped down, hit the floor at high speed, and, either sunk, bounced, or rolled. Wood chips flew everywhere. Floors and walls smashed open as the rocks collided with them. Human boulders bounced end over end until they slowed and crashed heavily down.

Some spun in the air like rotor blades, dropping to the floor and spinning. Most just hit the floor and stopped jarringly as the wood and earth surrounded them, some sinking as far as eight feet. The castle shook as if in the hands of a large earthquake. The raised platform gave with the rolling shocks. Ministic remained standing and the two other Mantases gripped the block of machinery.

In the space of seconds the room was littered with dozens of stone monoliths. Larry and Titu rose slowly from the floor. The shaking was so intense that the thought of escape was impossible.

"They are now entombed," said Ministic. "They cannot sense or move. The power of their suits has been nullified. Here they will starve, die, and decompose. Their ashes will remain in their suits forever. Some may suffocate. Some may go insane. Some may experience unbelievable hallucinations before death. Some may even be preserved, mummified, held in eternal night."

Titu stood by Larry, her arms at her sides. She wanted to do something, but what could she do? All during the space bullets' defeat Ministic had not turned, not even glanced away as a falling rock missed her by inches. If Napoleon with all her speed and agility could do nothing, what could Titu do? But she had come too far to die. She had to do *something*.

Larry stood, facing the Mantas with the same odd smile. Inside he felt doom clawing at his heart. His fingers tapped each other nervously, the thumb rubbing the forefinger, then tapping, rubbing, then tapping.

"Now I must kill the Queen," said Ministic. "Then I signal my people. Then I send the message to the stars. But I cannot do this and keep you captive. So . . . now you must die."

Titu couldn't bring herself to charge or even run. She felt the energy of Ministic's emotion. She felt the end coming near. She felt as if she had but a moment left to give her death meaning. Her arms reached out and encircled Larry's waist. His arms encircled hers without his even turning. It was natural, not subservient, not desperate, but natural, easy. Necessary.

Ministic paused. "You will never know The Rule," she said sadly, as if it were the worst fate imaginable.

"We know ourselves," said Larry. It was a long, hard road, but he could die now. Given several more moments he would not want to, but at this moment he could. He wouldn't really mind. Now, do it now!

Ministic's weapon emitted its bright beam. Even though it traveled, it moved at such high speed that its emission seemed to materialize in the shape of its path. The beam made a giant "L" when it should have made an "I." The top moved from Ministic to Larry, then the bottom moved away from Larry.

All three were stunned. Even as the beam destroyed part of a wall, Ministic fired again. The same thing happened. The beam arced away from the humans and buried itself in the floor. Larry didn't know how it happened but he wasn't going to stand around figuring it out. He leaped up the steps toward the Mantas.

Ministic managed to back up one step and fire twice more before the human was upon her. The beams sped away from Larry with a crackle as if they were frightened of him. With a push, Ministic was hurtled off the raised platform. She crashed onto the wooden floor, breaking an antenna. Larry turned and charged the remaining Mantases.

"The machine," he yelled to Titu. "Destroy the machine!"

Titu ran up the steps after him. The pair moved in to grapple with the remaining creatures.

"Watch out for the mandibles," said Larry. "They're poisonous."

Then he jumped into the air and kicked out with both feet, the way Harlan taught him on the way to Jackpot, catching one creature on the shoulder, knocking it away. It toppled down the steps, as Larry fell heavily on his back.

The other Mantas swung an arm down to pin him with its mandible when Titu hit it on the side of the head. The alien's blow was deflected enough to miss Larry and it lost its balance. Larry kicked up between the mantas' arms and slammed it backwards off the platform. It crashed down on its back.

Larry jumped up and gripped the block of machinery. He pushed and pulled but it wouldn't budge. He pressed every button he could find but nothing happened. He heard a noise and, looking up, saw Ministic on her feet, her arm pointing at them.

"Look out," he warned, pushing Titu down as the beam moved. Again it turned away with a crackle. Suddenly the answer occurred to Larry. The weapon was not crackling, he was. It was the communication device under his fingernail, the one with which Palend supplied him. He had inadvertently switched it on while he was waiting for death, and now, somehow, it was counteracting the weapon's electrical current, like two magnets repelling each other.

"Larry," Titu shouted. "The Queen!"

He broke out of his thought, to see Ministic moving around the platform to get a clear shot at the unconscious monarch. Without thinking Larry ran two steps and leaped, his hand outstretched. The beam shot out and arced away as Larry's hurtling body crashed into the throne.

Ministic turned her aim to Titu as the chair rocked and Larry fell.

"Down!" he yelled from the platform floor. "Get down behind the machine!"

Titu ducked and the beam shot harmlessly over her head. Ministic dare not try another for fear of destroying the weapon that kept the space bullets in check.

But Larry had jarred the throne when he fell against it, shaking the Queen from her position. Before Titu's horrified eyes, she slipped from the seat and tumbled down the stairs rolling to Ministic's feet.

The Mantas looked up in triumph. Her arm lowered. Larry stumbled up, knowing he could never reach them in time His hands gripped the throne and Titu looked in horror as behind Ministic, Napoleon rose.

Her chest was singed, the fur black, streaked with long red cuts. But her wound had nothing on her face. She looked totally alien as she stepped soundlessly up behind the Mantas. Her eyes were thin strips of black on a red background. Her claws were out and curled at her sides. Her mouth was open wide in a devilish smile, her teeth sharp and dripping saliva.

With a screech she was on Ministic's back, tearing. The Mantas' beam cracked into the floor between the Queen's outstretched arm and curving hip. The Mantas' face showed shock before a paw ripped across it, opening the head up in four long cuts. The feline's feet moved up and down along the insectlike body. Napoleon's head rose over Ministic's shoulder and sank her teeth in the creature's neck.

Larry watched, his fingers clenching and his shoulders hunching as the Mantas stumbled back. The veins in Larry's neck stood out as he sent the heavy wooden throne sliding across the platform. Titu dove out of the way as the solid chair crashed into the three-by-three-foot metal block.

Napoleon's head snapped up as the two items slipped from the platform and fell toward the floor. She leaped off the Mantas, scurrying away on all fours. Ministic tripped forward, her body flapping like the remains of her gown. Inner liquid drooled out darkening the rainbow colors. She managed one alien scream before the block of machinery shattered on the floor.

Her arms jerked up in surprise as fourteen space bullet beams immediately converged on her body. With an otherwordly ripping sound her top half spun away, born on the prismatic hues of her dress. Her legs fell over lazily afterwards.

Somewhere on the planet one hundred and one space bullets began to rise.

EPILOGUE

Larry found her sitting on a rock by a rolling stream of water. She was unclothed, a red body suit lying beside her, crumpled on the ground. A shaft of sunlight spotlighted her head and torso, the heat feeling good against her healed chest wound. Yellow-orange hair had begun to grow there again, but it created a dish effect on her, as the new fur tried to catch up with the unaffected coat. Her eyes were closed, her face at peace, but she was not smiling.

He sat down on a tree trunk that had fallen across the small river and let his legs hang down over the clear and dazzling rushing water, which seemed to be covered with cut diamonds. He wore a Destinian outfit made from material spun by tree worms on the other side of the forest. It was rare and expensive but he couldn't bring himself to wear the hide of the tree creatures, not after what he had been through.

Napoleon opened her eyes and looked at him, the sun creating a halo effect around her face. She stretched her arms and legs, the muscles tightening with attractive curves. She mewed with pleasure, then turned out of the sun.

"Hello," she said.

"Hello," he replied.

"How did it go?"

"Well," he said, bouncing slightly on his wooden seat. "It went well. The Queen voiced her appreciation yet again,

then filled the air with all the difficulties there would be i
changing their system and dealing with the tree creatures—
they still haven't given them a name yet—and how the plane
couldn't afford any further strife at this time.

"I reminded her, tactfully of course, about the fact tha
not only had the tree creatures proven to us that they wer
intelligent, but they had Bishop-Fortune's weapons and wer
learning how to use them. I humbly recommended that Des
tiny had better make peace with them before they decided t
make pieces of Destiny."

"She must have loved that."

"Not at first, naturally. She reminded me that the tre
creature's meat constituted a great deal of their diet. I in
quired as to whether they had showed any signs of cannibal
ism. They had not so I proposed that the tree creatures mus
eat something too. It would behoove Destiny to find ou
what.

"It's amazing, you know, how a planet can rationalize a
less than moral existence. They had learned from Earth's mis
takes, all right, but when it came to a choice between moral
ity and expediency, the people chose meat.

"I further advised that the human population on Destiny
was still small enough to make certain changes in their life
styles without crippling everybody."

"It's not like they haven't had to go through some hard
changes already," Napoleon interjected.

"Yes," agreed Larry. "Every Mantas wiped out. Total
search and annihilation. As soon as Ministic died they tried to
scatter but it seems that the space bullets were faster. Except
for Harlan, of course."

"Has anyone seen him recently?"

"No, he just stays inside his old home. Everytime Titu
comes out, she says he's thinking."

Larry looked beyond the feline into the wood. "That was
their basic mistake, you know, the Mantases. They had lived
as Destinians too long. They hadn't considered the tree creatures in their plans. They thought the same of them as the
humans did, so when Bishop-Fortune jumped the gun and
tried to collect us before Harlan was actually killed, Isenraid
allowed him to play his forest game."

He fell silent and returned his gaze to the water. Napoleon scratched the healed patch of skin, feeling the peach fuzz of her regrown fur.

"So that was it, then?" she inquired.

"Basically," he replied. "I've been inducted as an aide to handle the tree-creature situation since I've already proven myself . . ." His voice faded away. Napoleon knew already that he had accepted the position.

They sat, on the rock and the tree trunk, for a while, drinking in the leafy surroundings, feeling the warm air on their skin. Then Napoleon rubbed her thighs, stood up, and walked over to Larry's side.

"We started as strangers," she told him. "I don't want us to end that way."

He turned to look into her face, his hands in his lap, his legs still hanging down. He stared into her eyes for a moment before speaking.

"What do you say, Nap?" he asked with pain in his voice. "Have a good trip? Nice to have known you? Stop by if you ever come this way again?" His vocal chords constricted and his vision misted, making his eyes sparkle in the sunlight. He looked back at the water, ashamed of himself.

Napoleon walked into the water, it rising up just above her ankles. She placed her paws on Larry's knees, looking up at him.

"I don't know," she said tenderly. "I don't know what you can say. But I can say thank you. Thank you for saving my life and for being my friend. You have a good life here. You have a home and challenges and a partner that are worthy of you. You're an extraordinary person, you'll be happy here."

Larry looked down at her, tears forming in his eyes, his voice breaking. "But you were always my partner, Nap. I don't want to lose you."

His head bent and the sobs came, unashamedly.

"You'll never lose me, Larry. You'll always be with me," she said. "But this is not my place. I don't know if I'll ever find it, but I have to go and look. I would never be happy here."

"I know," he said, looking beyond her again, letting the tears drop onto his shirt. He wiped his eyes with the back of his hands, but couldn't keep from crying again. Before the torrent came he managed to say, "I'll miss you, Nap."

Then they were in each other's arms, standing in the little river. Napoleon held him, feeling the pain she hadn't felt since the last of her sisters died so many years ago. But now, as then, she didn't cry. Her face was twisted in love and loss, but she didn't cry.

She took his head in her hands and kissed him on the cheek. He took her into his arms again and rubbed her back slowly, her paws on his chest. Then they took one last long look at each other, his hands on her shoulders, hers on his waist. They walked out of the water and headed back toward the central city.

The ship was ready. The citizens of Destiny had built a new intergalactic vehicle for Napoleon out of gratitude. It was outfitted with an O'Neil light drive and a dazzling array of weaponry and sensors. She originally did not want it to be so spacious but the Queen had insisted, giving the feline enough room to really move about. Larry had built the computer personally and it was rumored that Harlan had calibrated the engines.

The citizens had gathered for her departure. The Queen, Titu, and Larry stood before the crowd, decked out in rich, royal finery. Napoleon, herself, wore a leotard Titu had made for her of a deep rust color, a brown and green patch on the left breast signifying Destiny. Words below it spelled out in the ancient space traveler's language, "Seek long enough and you will always find your Destiny."

Larry moved up to her at the last minute, reaching under his tunic. He pulled out a red plate covered with microcircuitry. He gave it to the feline, telling her to push it in the slot he had left in the computer console. Then he had to avert his gaze, his eyes misting again.

Napoleon smiled at him warmly as he returned to the crowd. She had already said her good-byes. So, with a final wave, she entered her ship, the door closing behind her automatically. She felt sorry Harlan had not come to see her off, but everyone knew he wasn't the same since the Mantas massacre.

She walked to her pilot's console not really noticing the particulars of the ship. She already knew it inside and out, having designed and helped build it. She sat in the custom-fitted seat and turned on the screens. She saw Larry and Titu laughing and crying in each other's arms. Before she broke down she initiated lift-off.

The screens were off. The red plate lay uninstalled on the computer console. The Universe rushed around the ship, the computer handling the navigational chores, even without a personality.

Napoleon's figure lay hunched over her controls, her head in her arms. Two channels of black wetness had appeared beneath her eyes. The mark of feline sorrow. She cried and cried. She had felt the tears growing as the last of Destiny's lush greenness gave way to the black space beyond.

For the first time she felt totally alone. No more friends, no future, no God. She, too, had thought she could live without love not truly knowing until she had left it behind. She wished she could have told him before she had said good-bye. Her body wracked with unknown emotions.

Then it jerked up as the clear voice boomed over the communication speaker.

From the womb we are born,
It is what we must be;
We're divers for glory,
And the sky is our sea.

"Harlan," she cried. "Harlan, is that you?"

"Yes," said the voice, echoing her emotion.

"What? What are you doing?" she laughed through her sorrow, choking on the words. "Why are you here?"

"I couldn't stay," he said in anguish. "My parents are dead. My sister has her own life now. My planet betrayed my trust. I had to leave. But I could not move inside our galaxy. We both have too many enemies. I followed you. You are the only other person I know who has shared my pain, who has lost as much as I have."

His voice turned hesitant, hoping.

"Can I join you . . . for a little while?"

"Yes," she said happily, blinking with the tears. "Yes. For a little while."

The feline and the space bullet sped into the unknown, side by side.

ABOUT THE AUTHOR

RICHARD S. MEYERS began his long time affection for science fiction when a friend steered him toward a copy of THE PUPPET MASTERS by Robert Heinlein. Since then he has managed to become the assistant director on an award winning student science fiction film, assistant editor on the short lived MOVIE MONSTERS magazine, author of two fantasy action/adventure books (under pseudonym). He is also an active member of the Science Fiction Writers of America, and the author of an ongoing Space Colony dramatization in *FUTURE* Magazine. Besides cartooning, film-making, and acting, his major interests have led to three non-fiction books on television and two on movies. His feet are firmly planted in southern Connecticut but his head's in the stars.

A FRIGHTENING NEW NOVEL BY

BRIAN McNAUGHTON